"Indeed, we look to God for everything. He has been proven faithful and steadfast. We put ourselves and our work in His almighty hands. The Lord has been most gracious to me, unworthy as I am, allowing me to teach the dear Yamacraw children the Good News of our Lord Jesus—our most Precious Treasure. Although I leave this place most reluctantly, I trust Him fully and will follow Him down this untrod path to Bethlehem. I put my work and myself in His hands. My eyes fill with tears and my heart overflows with joy, for I hear the whisper of heaven's bells ringing out across this land."

—JOHANNA HUS
IRENE, GEORGIA COLONY
SEPTEMBER 12, 1737

Savannah Secrets

The Hidden Gate
A Fallen Petal
Double Trouble
Whispering Bells

Savannah Secrets

Whispering Bells

Shirley Raye Redmond

Guideposts

Danbury, Connecticut

Whispering Bells

Chapter One

"ANOTHER CREEPY OLD HOUSE." JULIA Foley shuddered.

Meredith Bellefontaine ignored the comment as she parked her SUV behind Pastor Ed Markham's minivan. Stepping out of the vehicle, she paused on the gravel of the circular driveway in front of the rambling, three-story historic mansion. Faded green shutters framed the tall, yawning windows. One of the five chimneys jutting from the roof appeared to have crumbled to nothing but rubble.

"Creepy," Julia insisted as she emerged from the passenger side of the vehicle. She glanced at the flat roof, the white fluted columns, and sprawling veranda. Spanish moss, hanging from a large oak tree, draped itself across one edge of the roof like a veil. "But certainly not as decrepit as the old Besset estate the historical society is renovating. I don't think it's as old as the Besset place either," she added, referring to the historic home at the center of the first case she and Meredith had solved together.

Meredith nodded. "River View was constructed at the beginning of the Civil War."

Julia guessed that her business partner knew exactly how old this mansion was. As the former president of the local historical society, Meredith knew pretty much everything there was to know about Savannah and the city's historic homes. This grand old house, with its elegant proportions, must have been a sight to behold in its heyday. Now, neglected and rather forlorn, it appeared to droop in the heat of the August morning.

"I wonder why your pastor wanted us to meet him out here," Meredith said.

"I can't even begin to guess." Julia slung the strap of her chestnut-brown Jenny N. tote bag over her shoulder. "According to Carmen, he called asking that we join him here as soon as possible. It's fortunate that we were both free. Ed said it was important."

Actually, what their wisecracking receptionist had said was that Pastor Markham sounded a little *loco* and they'd better get out to the old River View place *muy rapido*—very quickly.

"It looks haunted, but I'm willing to take on any ghosts we encounter to get a clipping from that." Julia pointed to a late-blooming purple clematis vine clinging to a tall ornate trellis on the side of the house. "Miss Dicey used to tell me stories about her house, but I've never actually been here before. Have you?"

Meredith chuckled as she crunched over the path of ground shells toward the mansion. "Of course. Miss Laodicea Oglethorpe used to entertain in grand style many years ago. When I was just a girl, Mama always held up Miss Dicey, with her air of daintiness and refinement, as a model for all the young ladies to aspire to. She's always ready to tell anyone who'll listen that she's a direct descendent of General James Oglethorpe, who brought the first settlers here in 1733. Her favorite line is, 'He established three rules for the new settlement of Savannah: no slavery, no liquor, and no lawyers.'"

Julia came to a halt on the path. Grinning, she said, "I never heard her say that. Is it true?"

"Yes indeed." Meredith grinned back as she pushed against the old gate. It yielded with a reluctant groan. "General Oglethorpe considered lawyers to be 'the scourge of mankind.' And that's a direct quote in writing by the general's own hand."

Shaking her head admiringly, Julia said, "Of course, you would know." She followed Meredith through the gate and up the long path to the veranda.

"I once asked Daddy why Miss Dicey never married," Meredith said. "He said it was because she was too proud of the Oglethorpe name to give it up."

"Do you think she's at home?" Julia asked. "Perhaps Ed has come to visit her?"

"Miss Dicey is definitely not here," Meredith replied. Julia's shoulders slumped with disappointment. "The old dear is a hundred years old, if she's a day, and now lives in a nursing home."

Julia cast a sidelong glance in the direction of the lush vine with its deep purple blooms.

"Do you think Miss Dicey would mind very much if I took just a snip or two of her clematis? I'd like to transplant a sprig on the side of our house." She loved her rambling home with its spacious green lawn. When her hubby, Beau, wasn't cutting the grass on his riding mower, he spent his retirement years fishing and golfing. She had taken up gardening—when she wasn't assisting Meredith with Magnolia Investigations, of course.

She and Meredith had been college roommates once upon a time at Georgia Southern University. They'd kept in touch with Christmas cards and the occasional birthday phone call. When Julia moved back to Savannah fifteen years ago, the two friends had met by accident at the Sentient Bean. Julia had been thrilled. She and Beau enjoyed Ron and Meredith's company, and the couples had become close friends. After Ron's death, when Meredith considered reopening his detective agency, it seemed only natural that Julia, with her background in criminal law and her experience as a judge, should join her. So far, the Lord had blessed their endeavors.

"Miss Dicey wouldn't mind if you took a snip or two, I'm sure," Meredith told her as they mounted the front steps. "She loved her garden and was always happy to share iris bulbs or cuttings from a particularly lovely rose or flowering vine."

The front door swung open then. Ed Markham stood on the threshold to greet them. The pastor's face glistened with perspiration, and his blue broadcloth shirt was damp with sweat. There were sweat patches under his arms too. "I've been keeping my eyes peeled, looking out for y'all. Thank you for coming on such short notice." He grinned. "I've got a bit of a conundrum, ladies, and I need your expert advice. C'mon in. We're going to the music room." His brown eyes sparkled with good humor. He didn't appear worried or troubled.

Julia felt puzzled. She'd known Ed for years. She and Beau worshipped regularly at the New Beginnings Church. They had quickly come to respect Ed's sound theological sermons and lively preaching style. His wife, Naomi, was a sweetheart who did everything from leading the choir to teaching Sunday school with grace and good humor.

"So, what's up, Ed? Our receptionist said it was urgent." Julia wiped the perspiration from her upper lip. It was hot enough to melt butter in here. She guessed the place was overly warm and stuffy from being closed up for so long. "Has there been a break-in?"

She glanced around as they passed from one spacious room to the next. She took in the cobwebs in the corners near the ceiling and the furniture protected by cotton dust covers. Meredith was right—Miss Dicey hadn't lived here in years. Was it possible that trespassers had been tempted to steal some of the valuable antiques? She paused to admire an elegant staircase and portraits of long-dead Oglethorpes mounted in gilded frames upon the walls. "Oh my," she muttered with awe. "Miss Dicey certainly lived high on the hog."

"I've always loved this old historic home," Meredith told her with a sigh. "It was one of the finest in its day."

Glancing down at the faded rug and the specks of chipped paint along the baseboards, Julia felt a twinge of sadness. It seemed a shame that a place so beautiful should become the victim of time and neglect. River View was an architectural gem filled with treasures—even if it did look spooky from the outside. One of Ed's recent sermon passages came to mind then—one from Matthew. "For where your treasure is, there will your heart be also." She hoped the Oglethorpes had been storing their real treasures in heaven. River View was just a house after all. Still, it was quite a house. "If only the walls could talk," she mused aloud.

"If only," Meredith agreed.

Together they followed Ed into the large music room. The baby grand piano in the center of the room was coated with dust, but the rest of the furniture had been draped with dust covers—some made of cotton and others of sheer plastic. Julia noted stacks of sheet music piled high on the window seat, the end tables, the book-shelves, and every other available surface.

"This is why I'm here." Ed made a sweeping gesture with his arm. "I was visiting Miss Dicey at the nursing home, and she asked me to come by to pick up some of her sheet music. Thankfully, she didn't specify any one piece of music in particular." He smiled. "She's been feeling puny-like, so she said, and wanted something to ease her days."

"This is a fine collection," Julia observed. "I knew Miss Dicey loved music, but I didn't know she played the piano." She pointed to the baby grand. "That piano is a Bösendorfer."

Meredith nodded. "She could have been a lauded concert pianist, but most women didn't pursue careers back in the day."

Julia picked up a sheet yellowed with age. "'Chickery Chick,'" she read. "The copyright date is 1945."

"Here's one with an image of Bing Crosby on the front." Ed held up another piece of faded sheet music. "'Zing a Little Zong,'" he read. "I'm not familiar with that one. Doesn't sound much like classical music, now does it?"

Picking up another sheet with ragged edges, Julia read the title, "'The Band Played On.'" She opened the page and read the copyright date. 1936. It was hard to imagine proper, straitlaced Laodicea Oglethorpe playing such lively popular tunes of the day rather than Mozart and Chopin. But it made sense that she would want her music with her at the nursing home. No doubt each tune brought back fond memories.

"I don't know much about music, except for hymns and country gospel," Ed volunteered. "And the occasional lively ragtime piece. Perhaps I should have y'all go through the stacks and pick out some of the classical music."

"No, she'll want these, I bet," Meredith guessed. "Just grab a handful from several different stacks and take them to her. You can tell just by looking at these sheets that the songs were played often. I'm sure they'll bring back happy memories for Miss Dicey, bless her heart. As she said, it will help to ease her days."

Heaving a sigh, Julia fanned her face with a piece of vintage music. "But surely you didn't ask us to come help you rummage through Miss Dicey's sheet music?"

Ed fished a snow-white handkerchief from his back pocket and wiped the perspiration dotting his face. Regarding them with an expression both sheepish and mildly eager, he said, "I want to show y'all something. It's a secret I need to share—just in case something...er...should happen."

Julia cast Meredith a sidelong glance. Her friend widened her blue eyes meaningfully.

"What might happen?" Julia wanted to know. "You're being mighty mysterious, Ed."

"And the suspense is killing me," Meredith piped up. "If the temperature in this room doesn't do me in first." She too had claimed a piece of music to use as a makeshift fan.

Ed cleared his throat. "All right then. Julia, would you come over here?" He stepped toward the fireplace with its handsome mantel made of green marble. A series of footed vases in various shades of blue and green made an eye-catching display across the top. Wedgwood jasperware, if Julia had to guess. Antiques, and quite valuable.

As she stepped toward the fireplace, Ed said, "Y'all watch closely now." He told Julia to place her hand on one of the carved rosettes on the side of the mantel. "Now push and turn it to the right at the same time."

Julia pushed and twisted. As she did so, she cast Meredith a questioning glance. There was a slow swishing sound, and suddenly, a dark gap appeared between two dusty bookshelves. Julia's pulse raced. "Stars and garters!" she exclaimed with bated breath.

"A secret panel!" Meredith declared.

Smiling, Ed shook his head. "Dear ladies, it's not the secret panel that's so amazing." His tone was now tinged with undisguised excitement. "Wait until y'all see what's inside."

Chapter Two

ED RETRIEVED WHAT APPEARED TO be an old leather-bound ledger. He opened it carefully, barely cracking the leather spine. Julia noted an ink stain in one corner as the musty scent of old paper and ink filled the air. With the flick of a finger, Ed turned a few yellowed pages until he found the one he wanted. Then he read aloud in his most solemn preacher's voice: "'*I found treasure. O intrigued. Fear trouble ahead.*' The entry is signed with the initials CW." In a hushed tone, he added, "I believe CW might stand for Charles Wesley."

"The hymn writer?" Julia arched her eyebrows. "'Hark! The Herald Angels Sing' Charles Wesley?"

Nodding, Ed added, "My personal favorite is 'Christ the Lord Is Risen Today.'"

Noting Julia's confusion, Meredith explained, "Charles Wesley served as General Oglethorpe's personal secretary for about six months when he and his brother John came to Savannah in the settlement's early days." She tucked a stray blond curl behind her ear.

"The same John Wesley as the statue in Reynolds Square?" Julia asked.

Meredith held out her hands for the ledger. "Yes. It's a shame to handle it without protective gloves, but that can't be helped now." She examined the page carefully.

Peering over Meredith's shoulder, Julia noted the faded ink, then the water stain on the opposite page. The leather cover was cracked and the pages brittle. Several of them seemed stuck together. Most of the notations, which appeared to be expenditures of some sort, were so faded they were practically illegible. A ridge of goose bumps prickled her arms. She sensed the historic importance of the old ledger. Glancing at Meredith, Julia wondered if her friend felt the same way. Meredith appeared to be concentrating on the short but cryptic notation, a frown pinching the skin between her eyes.

"How did you know about the secret panel, Ed?" Julia asked.

"I didn't," he confessed. "I tripped over my own two feet like a fool and reached out to steady myself. The next thing I know, *ta-da!* The panel opened just as it did now. I need to take this to Miss Dicey, but I wanted witnesses to see where and how I'd found it. I called Maggie Lu right off, wondering if she knew anything about it. She didn't, but she suggested I give you ladies a call right away. Just in case."

"Just in case," Julia repeated, with a knowing look. As a retired criminal court judge, she was all too aware of how something of this nature could lead to legal trouble of some sort. Her pastor was wisely covering his bases. She gave him an approving nod.

Ed nodded too. "Yes, just to be safe."

Meredith walked closer to the open panel in the wall and peered in. "I would love to find a letter or something that might explain the mysterious comment in here." She held up the ledger. Julia smiled to herself. Meredith might have vacated her position as director of the local historical society, but she still loved history—especially something as intriguing as this. And who could blame her? Ed was a history buff too, ever since discovering that one of his Ohio ancestors, a Captain Samuel Markham, died while helping to rescue slaves on the Underground Railroad.

"What we need is a map with a big X to mark the spot where the treasure can be found," Julia threw in. "Maybe it's a cache of silver coins or more pirate booty." She grinned. "Maybe this time we'll actually find something," she added, referring to one of the agency's previous cases.

Meredith laughed. "I love your enthusiasm, but don't get carried away. Remember what happened last time we set out looking for buried treasure."

"How could I forget?" Julia said. Meredith had inherited a diary that supposedly revealed the hiding place of Blackbeard's booty. The diary had been stolen, and Meredith had been abducted. Although she'd finally been rescued by Julia, the Coast Guard, and her sons Chase and Carter, they'd never located any treasure.

"We don't even know if it's *that* sort of treasure," Ed protested. "The Wesley brothers were devout men. They came to America to shepherd the flock here. Perhaps the treasure refers to something spiritual, like the pearl of great price."

Julia had her doubts about that.

"We won't know for sure until we can decipher the faded scrawl in here," Meredith said. "We should get Miss Dicey's permission before we attempt to do so. She may know exactly what the strange notation refers to."

Taking the ledger from her, Ed said, "The matter is rather urgent, considering the condition and age of this thing."

"And Miss Dicey's age as well," Julia put in.

Ed nodded somberly. "There's no time to waste."

"You're right." With a rush of enthusiasm, Meredith exited the music room. Julia hurried after her. They meandered through various corridors until they located the kitchen. It appeared surprisingly cheery, even though the cabinets and appliances were a dismal shade of avocado green. Meredith rummaged around until she found a drawer containing clean dish towels. She snatched one up and handed it to Julia, then led the way back to the music room.

"Put that around the ledger," she said. "Let's not get any more perspiration from our hands on this than necessary. Truly, it needs to be examined and preserved by an archivist."

Julia did as she was told, taking the ledger from Ed and wrapping the soft dish towel around it before handing it back to him.

"C'mon with me now, Meredith," Ed urged. "I'm going to take the sheet music to Miss Dicey. You show her the ledger and ask for permission to examine it further."

Meredith's eyes lit up eagerly. Then her shoulders slumped with disappointment. "I wish I could, but I can't. Not now." Glancing down at her watch, she said, "It's Tuesday, and I have an appointment with a prospective client. It's been on the calendar for weeks."

"I'll speak with Miss Dicey," Julia volunteered. "I look forward to seeing her again. It's been years and years since I saw the old darling, and it will give me a chance to ask about the clematis."

"That's fine by me," Ed said.

After retrieving her purse from the settee where she'd left it, Meredith fished out her car keys. "All right then. I'll go back to the office. You talk to Miss Dicey about the ledger. In the meantime, I suggest we keep this little discovery to ourselves." She indicated the ledger with a thrust of her chin.

"I agree," Julia said. "If we don't, folks will be all over us like gravy on grits, as my granny used to say."

***

Ed and Julia found Miss Dicey in her room, sitting in a wheelchair. She wore a pale blue caftan that reached to her thin ankles. Her wispy white hair had been cut in a stylish bob. Her swimmy blue eyes lit with pleasure when they walked in.

"Why, it does me good to have young people around," she declared, her voice frail but animated.

Julia and Ed exchanged amused glances. "I love it when someone calls me young," Julia replied with a laugh. "Thank you. Do you remember me, Miss Dicey?" She stepped forward to take one of the elderly woman's blue-veined hands between her own. "I'm Julia Foley. I was Julia Waverly before I married."

"Why, of course I remember! You've got your mama's gray eyes. Yes, indeed, just the same. Your mama Betty Jean was a pretty gal, and smart too. I always said so. She knew how to take tarts when tarts were passing."

Julia's lips twitched. She glanced up and caught the merry look in Ed's eyes. "You're right about that, Miss Dicey. Mama was always smart. She still is."

An orderly came in quietly on soft-soled shoes to adjust a knob on Miss Dicey's oxygen tank. Short and burly, the man had an unfortunate black mustache—one so pencil-thin it appeared to have been drawn over his upper lip with a black Sharpie. The security badge hanging from his lanyard read G. TATE. He cast a curious glance in Julia's direction before slipping out of the room again.

Ed cleared his throat. "Miss Dicey, I brought that sheet music you asked for."

"I do thank you kindly, Reverend. I do indeed."

Julia smiled. Miss Dicey had a quaint courtesy that never failed to charm.

"Where shall I put the pile?" Ed asked.

While the two discussed the matter, Julia glanced around the room—a private room, of course. She noted the lingering scent of pine cleanser and something faintly medicinal and wondered if Meredith was happy to let her come in her stead because of her dread of hospitals and long-term care facilities like this one. Meredith had felt that way ever since the death of her mother from cancer a while back. Still, the room appeared quite cozy with potted primroses and African violets on a desk by the window. Miss Dicey apparently still loved her flowers. Framed sheet music—most with colorful covers—hung on the off-white walls. Julia peered at the closest ones. "Forever and Ever," Perry Como. "La Vie En Rose," Edith Pilaf. These must have held particularly warm memories for the old dear. A long-lost love, perhaps?

"We brought something else for you to take a look at too, Miss Dicey." Ed nodded at Julia, who reached into her tote bag to retrieve the worn ledger, still wrapped in the dish towel. She placed it on Miss Dicey's lap.

"Now what, pray tell, is this?" She glanced from Julia to Ed.

"We were hoping you could tell us," Julia replied. "Be careful. It's quite old. The pages are brittle, and many of them are stuck together."

Miss Dicey sighed heavily. "My eyes aren't what they used to be. I won't open it. Couldn't read a thing if I did." She placed a gnarled hand on the ledger's faded cover. "Where did it come from?"

"We found it at River View this morning hidden behind a secret panel," Ed told her. He cast an excited glance at Julia. She felt her pulse quicken at the possibility of learning the secret behind the odd notation.

Miss Dicey's blue eyes widened. "You found this upstairs in the old nursery?"

"There's a secret panel in the nursery?" Julia asked. This time her heart literally skipped a beat. Was there anything more exciting than secret hiding places and hidden passageways? Meredith would be thrilled.

"Indeed there is, up on the third floor. My grandfather had it put in during the Lost Cause to hide the silver and Grandmama's jewels from the invading Yankees. But I haven't ventured up there in ages. Too many stairs and no reason at all to climb them."

"Actually, Miss Dicey"—Ed cleared his throat again—"the secret panel we're talking about is in the music room near the fireplace."

Miss Dicey's expression registered genuine surprise. She turned her wrinkled face to gaze out the window. "Daddy never told me. He was worn out from work and worry most days. When I think on it, I believe Daddy was born tired. He never mentioned a secret panel downstairs. I sure never dreamed there was one."

Chapter Three

WHILE ED EXPLAINED HOW HE'D discovered the secret panel in the music room at River View, Miss Dicey touched the brittle cover of the old ledger, slowly lifting it with both hands. "Household accounts, I should imagine. Don't know why in the world it would be hidden away, especially after all these years have passed."

Julia leaned over her, gently turning the pages until she found the one with the cryptic message. "It's this entry that Pastor Ed wants to ask you about. Shall I read it to you?"

"Yes, please do." Miss Dicey gave her a wan smile.

Julia read aloud, "'*I found treasure. O intrigued. Fear trouble ahead.*' The entry is signed with the initials CW. Does it mean anything to you at all, Miss Dicey?"

As Miss Dicey shook her head, Julia noticed Tate slipping into the room again through the open door. He seemed to make a bigger deal than necessary out of swapping a clean drinking glass for a dirty one near the sink, and she had a niggling feeling that he was only pretending to do so. Did he want to eavesdrop? Had he been listening outside the door? Maybe he'd had the same reaction to the word *treasure* that most people tended to have. Intense curiosity.

"Any idea what it's all about, Miss Dicey?" Ed asked.

Julia reached over to place her hand firmly on the pastor's arm, shooting him a warning glance as she did so. She rolled her eyes in the direction of the listening orderly. Ed followed her gaze and waited until the man left the room before continuing.

"Could the O be for *Oglethorpe*?" he pressed in a quieter tone.

Miss Dicey shrugged a thin shoulder. "Why, I suppose so. I really couldn't say for certain."

Julia closed the door before resuming her seat near Miss Dicey's wheelchair. "Then perhaps the CW could be for Charles Wesley," she proposed. "He served as the general's secretary for a short while, Meredith said."

"So then the J could be for *John*—John Wesley," Ed prompted.

Miss Dicey frowned, shaking her head slowly. "To my knowledge, General Oglethorpe never found any treasure. I doubt the good John Wesley did either. He was much too busy evangelizing the colonists, marrying and burying them, that sort of thing—as you would know, Reverend."

"Miss Dicey, do you mind if I keep this for a while? I'd like to read it and see what I can discover." Ed regarded her hopefully.

"Why, I don't mind at all." Then with a hoarse chuckle, she added, "If you find the treasure, whatever it might be, you may keep it for your church roof fund. It's been my experience that a church is always in need of a new roof." She winked. Ed and Julia chuckled.

While Miss Dicey was graciously granting favors, Julia hastened to ask for one more.

"Miss Dicey," she said, "would you mind if I took a snip from the purple clematis on the side of your house? I've always longed to grow them."

Miss Dicey, seemingly delighted by the request, granted permission for Julia to help herself to whatever she might like from the garden.

"No one else is there to admire it anymore," the elderly woman said with a wistful sigh. "You may even want a bit of that pale pink climbing rose in the heart of the garden too. It came all the way from England with General Oglethorpe on one of his later voyages. Now that's what I call a treasure indeed."

Julia and Ed took their leave then, promising to keep Miss Dicey informed about whatever they might discover regarding the mysterious ledger entry. As they made their way down the corridor, they passed a tall, barrel-chested man with crinkly wrinkles around his eyes. Jubal Early Jones. Julia recognized him at once. A big man, one who could hunt bear with a stick, as her daddy used to say.

Jubal's eyes lit with pleasure when he saw her. "Why, Julia Foley, where have you been keeping yourself?" He looked admiringly at her, taking in her bright pink polo shirt and pink and white seersucker capris. Her mama always did say pink was one of her best colors. "You're looking like fine china today."

"Hello, Jubal." She smiled up at the older man, who was nearer seventy-five than not. Julia had known Jubal for years. He and Beau occasionally played golf together, and he'd once served with Julia on the same Neighborhood Watch organizational committee. "I'm a gumshoe these days, don't you know? Meredith Bellefontaine and I are the proud new owners of Magnolia Investigations."

Jubal shook his head disbelievingly. "I'd heard something about that and could hardly believe it. Lady detectives. If that don't beat all. Just like *Cagney and Lacey* on television." Then he turned his broad smile upon Ed. "Good to see you too, Pastor Markham."

As the two men shook hands, Julia observed the medical bracelet on Jubal's wrist. She remembered Meredith wearing one temporarily after her heart attack when she was still taking blood thinner meds. Julia wondered if Jubal was wearing his now for the same reason.

"Jubal, I've not seen you in a month of Sundays," Ed declared. "How are you?"

"I'm walking the chalk line, pastor. Walking the chalk line." Jubal grinned. "Doing my Christian duty this afternoon, as you can see. Visiting dear old Aunt Dicey—ministering to the widows and orphans, so to speak. Although strictly speaking, she's not a widow, but she is an orphan. The old darling is all alone in the world, except for me and my bit of a clan."

"That's kind of you, Jubal," Julia said, and she meant it.

They exchanged a few more pleasantries before Jubal bid them good day and headed for Miss Dicey's room. Ed and Julia made their way to the parking lot, where he unlocked the van doors and turned on the air-conditioning full blast.

As he backed the van out of the parking space, he said, "Julia, I want to read as many of the entries in the ledger as possible, but it'll be tough going. The ink is pretty faded."

"Let's give it a try anyway," Julia said. "I'm curious. We may never get it back if we turn it over to someone at the historical society."

"I'm more than curious," Ed admitted. "I'm concerned. What if the information implicates the general and the Wesley brothers in something...er...unsavory? I'd like to reassure myself that's not the case. I wouldn't like to think of John or Charles Wesley having anything to do with ill-gotten gains. And let me point out that if that's the case, Naomi and the choir won't allow us to sing any of the great Wesley hymns in church any longer. It would be a shame, a crying shame."

"Whoa there! You're jumping to conclusions, aren't you?" Julia asked.

Ed shrugged.

"I can assure you that in all the years I've lived in Savannah, I have never heard of any rumors implicating the Wesleys in any sort of scandal. If they had been, surely Meredith would know about it or someone else in the historical society."

"Or Maggie Lu might know," he mused aloud. Julia didn't doubt that Maggie Lu King might know something. The retired school-teacher was a walking compendium of Savannah facts and trivia.

"I wonder what kind of treasure they could have discovered," Ed mused.

"Perhaps pirate treasure," Julia suggested. "Blackbeard wasn't the only buccaneer to plunder his way up and down the coast."

Ed glanced both ways before pulling out of the parking lot onto the busy tree-lined street. "Could be."

"Next time you call on Miss Dicey, I suggest you advise her not to speak of this to anyone."

"I wish I'd thought of doing that before we left," he lamented. "In the meantime, can you keep the ledger at your office? Y'all have an office safe, I believe."

Julia considered this. Meredith had moved the safe from Ron's office to her own, and they also had the hidey-hole behind the heavy gilt-framed historical plat map of Atlanta hanging in Ron's office.

"That would be fine," she said. "In the meantime, I'm going to transcribe as many words as I can reasonably figure out."

"Would you?" Ed's expression lifted. "That would be wonderful. This sort of thing is more up your alley than mine."

"Take me to the office, and I'll get started right away." Julia settled back against the seat and tapped her tote bag containing the historic ledger with the side of her foot. As she glanced idly into the side mirror, she experienced a familiar tingling sensation, her suspicious nature now on high alert. She continued to stare with intense concentration. After a moment or so, she said, "Ed, I believe we're being followed."

He shot a glance in the rearview mirror. Chuckling, he said, "You really take this detective stuff seriously, don't you?"

"I'm not kidding, Ed. Don't take me to the office. Try to shake him."

"Do you have any idea who *he* is?"

With a frown, Julia peered into the side mirror. "I think it's that orderly who was hanging around Miss Dicey's room while we were there."

Ed's head snapped toward her. He gave her a brief but searching stare. "Are you sure?"

"Fairly sure." She turned to look over her shoulder. It looked like the orderly to her. "Try to shake him off our tail," she repeated.

With resolve, the pastor tightened his grip on the steering wheel. The corner of his mouth quirked up in a lopsided smile. "Hang on, Julia. This is going to be fun!"

Chapter Four

"Come away, Johanna. There is naught you can do for him now." Sister Reidel tugged at her sleeve.

Johanna Hus ignored her, a fixed stare upon her father's fresh grave. How could a fever so quickly take the life of a stalwart man—so strong in body and in faith? Who would now take on his responsibilities as blacksmith for the community? With a heavy heart, she glanced at the other grave mounds on the bluff overlooking the slow, muddy-green river that flowed past the marshes into the sea. Too many had died, mostly women and children. The New World had not been kind, especially to the weakest among them.

It was so very hot here. She had not imagined it would be thus. And the gnats! What a plague of them! And flies and lice as well. Surely they were every bit as bothersome as the plagues Moses brought down about Pharaoh! The little red vermin bit one's legs and raised blisters when scratched. Was it any wonder so many fell ill with deadly fevers? And what of those strange creatures along the oozing mud banks—alligators? What of them? It was rumored they spread diseases too. She'd not seen one of the fierce beasts and didn't want to. But some of the men of the Moravian community had talked about them in horrified awe.

Again Sister Reidel coaxed her away, but this time with more gentleness. Her hawkish nose and thin slash of a mouth gave her a severe expression, but Johanna knew her to be a gentle, softhearted woman. With another downward glance at her father's grave, Johanna sighed heavily. "I am an orphan." Her tone sounded flat, her words empty of emotion. Her heart felt empty too.

Sister Reidel grunted. Her flushed, wrinkled face contorted into a frown. "Orphan? Nein! You are no longer a child. It is time for you to marry. For surely you will not see twenty again." The older woman's voice softened when she added, "Your parents would want you to find a husband, Johanna. To have a home of your own and perhaps children."

"If Gott im Himmel wills it so." Johanna heaved another sigh and quickened her step to keep up with Sister Reidel, who had already turned away from the crude, windblown cemetery. If truth be told, Johanna didn't think of husbands or a household of her own so very often, only sometimes. It was unnatural, she knew. She dared not share her feelings with anyone—not with Sister Reidel or the other women in the community. Not even with her mother when the good woman was still alive, back in Bohemia, so far away.

Johanna had other hopes, a different dream. When Vati told her they would sail to the New World to settle in a British colony surrounded by the natives of the land, her heart had lifted with gladness. Perhaps her secret longing would be satisfied after all. Vati insisted the colony was a true Eden, situated in the fairest corner of God's universe. He said apples and apricots, lemons and oranges fell from the trees in such abundance that colonists fed them to the cattle. That hearty Indian chieftains, born in this rich land, lived to be three hundred years old!

But the circumstances here were proving to be...difficult. More difficult than she'd ever imagined and certainly more difficult than the trustees in London had led them to believe.

And now her father was dead. Dear Mutti also, long since. Johanna's chest tightened at the thought. Gone to heaven where sorrow, illness, and disappointment could no longer overwhelm them. In that moment, grief, like a chilly ocean wave, washed over her. Halting on the path, Johanna felt a tremendous loss. She shuddered and blinked back the tears that threatened to spill down her flushed cheeks. She'd never known life without her parents.

Sister Reidel stopped too, amid the tall grass, and turned to her. "Johanna, you should rest. No one will begrudge you time alone to grieve."

"I want to go to the school," Johanna replied with certainty. She smoothed the front of her linen apron with hands that still trembled ever so slightly.

The Yamacraw children were her constant delight. How she loved them—so bright-eyed and eager. Besides teaching them their letters and basic arithmetic, Johanna had taught them a simple hymn that Mutti had taught her back home when she was not much older than the youngest among them. It had given her great joy to hear their angelic voices raised in praise to the Father, the Maker of heaven and Earth—even if they did not yet know the Holy Father. She would not succumb to despair. She had her teaching duties.

More than once Chief Tomochichi had expressed his great pleasure at the Moravians' establishment of the school. He was a wise and grave man, with strange black tattoos across his bare chest. Johanna admired him. She felt certain that if Tomochichi stood in the midst of one hundred other tribesmen, all dressed alike in bearskin robes and a crown of feathers, she'd still be able to pick him out as the chief, for he had an unmistakable dignity, as did his wife, Senauki— queenly in her calico jacket and petticoat, her missing eye an injury inflicted by the Spaniards, so some said.

"A few of the older children can already recite the Lord's Prayer, did you know?" she asked Sister Reidel. They resumed walking.

"I hope the Word has fallen upon fertile soil. I greatly fear we will not be here to cultivate the field or bring in a harvest," the woman replied, tugging her close-fitting cap more snugly over her ears.

"But we've only just arrived," Johanna protested. They'd not yet been in the village for six months.

"The earlier arrivals in our community have had naught but trouble with the other colonists," Sister Reidel pointed out. "I fear it will be so with us as well." Then with an exasperated hand gesture, she declared, "The colonists—they should be ashamed! So much drunkenness! Have you heard? Brother Swartzberger went to the trading post and found two Englishmen lying there outside the door, naked and unconscious with drink. What must the natives think of such behavior?"

Johanna shook her head with disgust. But truth be told, the natives were often guilty of the same conduct. General Oglethorpe—respectfully called Father Oglethorpe by many in the colony—had assured everyone that strong spirits were not permitted to be bought and sold in the settlement. Ale and beer were allowed, within reason. Still, the demon rum could be obtained at Musgrove's trading post and others that were not under the general's authority. Rumors circulated that the Tybee lighthouse would never be constructed, because the workmen were always too intoxicated to carry out their duties.

"Herr Wesley says we Moravians are the most pious and industrious of all the settlers. I have heard General Oglethorpe feels the same. Yet the other colonists seem to resent us for it," Johanna put in.

"No." Sister Reidel waved her hand. "It is not our piety and industry they resent. My husband says it is because our men have continued to refuse to serve in the militia. He says the other settlers are angry and resentful. They insist our men are shirking their duty because they will not take up arms against the Spaniards."

"And why should we?" Johanna queried. "The Spaniards are no enemies of ours. Has it not been explained that our men do not take up arms against anyone? Even on board the ship while the other men drilled with muskets, bayonets, and swords, our men did not do so. It is against our beliefs."

Sister Reidel shrugged a thin shoulder.

Johanna sighed again and wiped the sweat from her face with the back of her hand. She had little patience with the other colonists' lack of understanding. Did not the community men take their turn to serve in the night watch—going the three miles to and from Savannah each day to do so? Herr John Wesley had been attempting to smooth ruffled feathers on both sides. Her heart went out to him. He seemed a young man most unsettled in his heart and mind, but she liked him all the same. They'd become fast friends on the ship during the voyage from England. He helped her with her English, and she taught him a handful of German phrases. They found they had much in common—particularly a desire to win the heathen to the true faith. More than once they had encouraged one another to cling to the Lord's promise—Seek and ye shall find.

His brother Charles traveled with him. A short, sturdy, round-faced man who appeared rather awkward in society. While John seemed intensely earnest and driven, Charles was more tender and indulgent. She'd liked them both and approved of their steadfastness in pursuing the Lord's will. She'd envied them too. How nice it would be to have a brother or sister. She had not been blessed in that way.

"*I spoke with Herr Wesley, asking if the Spaniards are indeed a looming threat,*" Johanna said. "*He could not say for certain.*" She knew that John wouldn't be as concerned as the general, because it was Oglethorpe who had the responsibility for the safety of the settlement upon his shoulders.

"*Herr Wesley has been tasked with our spiritual welfare,*" Sister Reidel insisted. "*The community has come to the New World to preach the Good Christ's Gospel to the natives, not to perform military duties. The trustees assured us that we need not compromise our beliefs in this way if we came to the settlement. We should be free to evangelize and serve Gott as we see fit. They promised.*"

Johanna nodded. *This was true.* And the community had made building the school a priority so that they might teach the Yamacraw children the Great Word. The men had cut down pine trees, hauled the lumber, and cleared the brush around the building site, beginning each work day with prayer and thanksgiving. They'd rejoiced when carpenters from Savannah, encouraged by General Oglethorpe, had ridden out to help build the schoolhouse near the river. But hostility simmered all the same.

At least the natives are not hostile, Johanna reflected with relief, striding quickly forward to keep up with her companion. *Neither was John Wesley, who came often to visit the Moravian community. He'd been out the day before yesterday to offer his condolences upon the death of her father and had done so in his stumbling German. Johanna smiled as she recalled his hesitant but heartfelt speech. At least he had made an effort to speak to her in her own tongue, and she appreciated it.*

Not everyone had the facility of learning languages that she did. Already she could converse in English and was quickly acquiring skill with the Yamacraw tongue. It was a gift, Vati had told her more than once. He'd been so proud of her ability, and it was proving to be a blessing in this new land where it was said that the Georgia colonists and natives together spoke sixteen different tongues. Sixteen! The New World was a veritable Tower of Babel.

The desire to learn the Yamacraw language bound her and John Wesley together, although there were women in the community who shared knowing glances and whispered that Herr Wesley might desire to court young Johanna. She knew it wasn't so, and was glad of it. He wanted to preach to the Indians, to convert them to Christ. But he had little aptitude with the difficult language, besides which, his time was consumed by multiple congregations of debtors, wastrels, and convicts. His was not an easy calling. Johanna knew he was frustrated and impatient. Sometimes she wondered if he might be spiritually at sea too, in a manner of speaking, tossed and churned on the waves of life, seeking something he could not name. She prayed he'd come into the clear light sooner rather than later. She prayed for her own spiritual longings too and hoped it was not selfish to do so.

Chapter Five

ED STEPPED ON THE GAS, taking a sudden turn at an alarming speed. Julia closed her eyes. Surely they were going to crash into something...or someone. She sent up a quick prayer before croaking out, "You're going to get us killed!"

But her pastor drove with surprising skill. After what seemed like an eternity but proved to be less than five minutes after Julia glanced at her watch, Ed triumphantly announced, "We've lost him."

Julia peered into the side mirror before turning to look around the back of her seat. There was no sign of the pursuing vehicle or the man with the mustache. With a sigh, she said, "I guess you can take me back to the office now." She took a deep breath and concentrated on slowing her pulse down.

"I will—after I treat you to lunch," Ed said. "It's the least I can do considering that you graciously interrupted your busy schedule to help me with this mysterious ledger business. How about a grilled cheese sandwich at the Little Duck?"

Julia couldn't say no. Even on a hot day, a Little Duck grilled cheese sandwich with homemade tomato soup was delicious. She selected the classic cheddar with sweet tea—and extra ice—while Ed ordered the Fancy Schmancy loaded with gruyère, cheddar, and havarti. While waiting for their food, they both took time to check their cell phones for messages and texts. Shoving her muted phone back into her tote bag, Julia glanced over at Ed, who was tapping away on his screen.

When Ed placed his cell on the table, Julia said, "So tell me what you know about that orderly."

"Not much, really," he said. "Just that his last name is Tate. I saw that much on his name badge." Peering over the rim of his iced tea glass, Ed added, "I'll be frank, Julia. I'm not at all sure he was following us. He might've been taking his lunch hour, that's all. Or maybe his shift had ended for the day. You sure you aren't taking this Nancy Drew stuff a little too far?"

"Oh, don't you start," Julia warned. "You sound like Carter Bellefontaine, Meredith's oldest son. He still doesn't believe she is entirely capable of taking over his dad's PI agency—despite our success so far. Once he even told her that we were too old to play Nancy Drew. That's what he called it—*playing Nancy Drew*." She took a long swallow of iced tea. Poor Meredith. Would she ever be able to convince her eldest son that she was a strong, capable businesswoman?

They remained silent while the waitress served their sandwiches and refilled their glasses. After a few satisfying bites, Julia said, "So, about the ledger."

"You want to take another look at it now?" Ed asked.

"I wouldn't dare." She held up half a sandwich and wiggled the greasy fingers of her other hand. "Meredith is already concerned about the poor condition of the ledger. If we get tea stains and buttery fingerprints all over it now, she'll have a hissy fit."

Ed chuckled. "You're right about that. When you get back to the office, you might want to put on a pair of gloves."

"I intend to. The old ledger really is in deplorable condition. There's no reason to make things worse. I plan on going through it page by page and writing down whatever I can read. Then I'll let you know what I come up with."

Ed gave an approving nod. "Sounds like a plan. Just keep me posted so I can let Miss Dicey know what's going on. I don't want the dear little lady to fret about this."

"I understand," she assured him.

"Call me tonight if you turn up anything really interesting," he urged. "I've got a premarital counseling session, so I may be at the church rather late. And, Julia, you can tell Meredith I'll pay y'all for your time."

Julia smiled at him. "I'll be sure you get the friends and family discount, Ed," she said. They'd have to charge him, but it wouldn't be exorbitant. The possible significance of what might be learned from the contents of the historic ledger gave her delicious goose bumps of anticipation.

After lunch, Ed dropped her off at the office. A blast of frigid air welcomed her as she stepped in through the office door. Carmen Lopez, their twentysomething receptionist, sat huddled at her desk wearing a heavy cardinal-red cardigan over a pale gray blouse. She tossed her glossy black hair and removed the earbuds from her ears at Julia's entrance.

"Meredith is here, I suppose," Julia said with a rueful smile.

Carmen snapped her gum and rolled her beautiful brown eyes. "Need you ask? It's *muy frio*. She likes it very cold in here—too cold." The young woman shivered.

Julia made her way to the thermostat. Ever since Meredith had come off her blood thinner following the heart attack, she tended to set the temp so low that Julia often teased her about causing their very own polar vortex right here in little ole Savannah. With three women sharing the compact office space, there seemed to be a never-ending tug of war over the temperature setting. Peering closely, Julia noted that the room temperature registered a chilly sixty-two degrees. Much too cold. She punched the button, resetting the thermostat to seventy.

Behind her, Carmen gave a loud, exaggerated sigh of relief. Julia chuckled. She'd always appreciated the young woman's wry sense of humor. Years ago, Carmen had ended up in Julia's courtroom for disorderly conduct and petty theft. But the young woman had turned her life around and had proven to be a more than competent receptionist and savvy judge of character.

"When your fingers thaw out, could you please make a fresh pot of coffee?" Julia asked as she moved past Carmen's desk on her way to her own office.

Carmen fairly sprang from her chair. "*Es una buena idea.* Hot coffee coming up."

Julia placed her tote bag on her desk and retrieved the ledger, still wrapped in the well-worn dish towel. It was mercifully quiet today since Arnold Mains and his crew had ceased remodeling the office. There were a few things that still needed to be done, but those had been temporarily put on the back burner as Arnold took his annual family vacation to Gulf Shores. Julia made her way to Meredith's office and tapped lightly on the partially closed door before entering. Meredith sat at her husband's old walnut desk with several open file folders arranged neatly in front of her. The remains of a takeout salad and a well-thumbed crossword puzzle book had been pushed to one side. Julia knew what her business partner had enjoyed for lunch.

Meredith glanced up. Noting the towel-wrapped ledger, she raised an eyebrow. "I see Ed was willing to part with it. I wondered if he would before all was said and done."

"I want to have a go at trying to read the contents—what's legible anyway," Julia told her. "Besides, Ed wants us to keep it in the office safe." She paused. "Do you think it's genuine? I mean, do you think the entries were really written by *the* Charles Wesley?"

Shrugging, Meredith said, "Perhaps, but we can have the handwriting analyzed just to be sure. We have numerous samples of his writing—letters and such. It shouldn't be difficult to authenticate. What did Miss Dicey say when you showed it to her?"

Julia plunked down in a chair in front of the desk. "Miss Dicey had never seen it before, nor did she know there was a secret panel in the music room."

Meredith widened her bright blue eyes. "Oh my. As Alice would say about matters in Wonderland, things get curiouser and curiouser. What did she say about the clematis you covet?"

"I may help myself," Julia answered with a smile. "Bless her heart. You'll come with me when I go back to get the clipping, won't you?"

"Why? You're not going into the house," Meredith pointed out. "The gate is open."

Julia shrugged. "It would be better if you came along. I need someone to keep me from temptation or I might plunder all of her vines and dig up the shrubs and rosebushes."

"All right. Let's go out there first thing tomorrow morning before it gets too hot. Right now I need to tackle these." Meredith indicated the array of file folders. "There's a deadline."

Julia arched an eyebrow. "Is this work for the new client you met with earlier today?"

Meredith nodded. "One of the local elementary schools has to hire some employees at the last minute. The principal wants us to do the background checks. With school starting in a matter of weeks, there's not much time to get them done, and she doesn't want to offer contracts to these individuals until we check their references, credit scores, and criminal backgrounds."

"Is this becoming standard practice for most schools?" Julia asked. Meredith nodded. "Good. Means a steady source of income for the agency." When Meredith nodded again, Julia added, "Give some of the responsibility to Carmen. She's quite capable. Just remind her that confidentiality rules apply."

"Good idea," Meredith said. She opened one of the desk drawers and handed Julia a clean but worn pair of white cotton gloves. "If you're going to work on that"—she indicated the ledger with a thrust of her chin—"you'll need these. Be as careful as you can."

"I will." Julia leaned forward to take the gloves. She started to tell Meredith about her wild ride with Ed and the determined orderly from the nursing home in hot pursuit but decided against it. For one thing, Meredith was super busy. Obviously. For another, Julia had begun to wonder if Ed might have been right after all. That

Tate guy might have been headed home after a long shift or on his way to lunch somewhere. Perhaps she really had overreacted. If that was the case, then it would be best not to mention it at all and let Meredith get back to work.

Carrying the gloves and the ledger, Julia rose from the chair. As she started to leave, Meredith said with a half smile, "Don't get your hopes up, Julia. I know you think this might lead to another treasure hunt, but it's really going to be more of a paper chase. Even if there had been a treasure back when the Wesley brothers lived here in Savannah, it's probably gone now."

"Not necessarily," Julia protested.

"Oh for heaven's sake, it's been almost three hundred years," Meredith pointed out. "Some mysteries are never solved. Take Virginia Dare and the Roanoke colony, for instance. Not to mention our recent misadventure with the supposed location of Blackbeard's long-lost booty." Meredith rolled her eyes.

Julia shrugged. Although she suspected Meredith was right, she still didn't want to give up trying to figure out the meaning of the ledger's cryptic notation. However, it had been a long, long time ago. She might have to content herself with discovering what the treasure had been and what Oglethorpe and the Wesleys had done with it—if she could.

"Okay, you're probably right," she acknowledged, "but I have to take a stab at it."

"Understandable." Meredith brushed aside a stray curl. "After work, why not come over for a BLT? Beau's off fishing with some of his buddies, isn't he?"

Julia nodded.

"I've even got some leftover sweet potato pie from when Carter, Sherri Lynn, and the kids came over Saturday for lunch. There's pickled shrimp too."

"I'm in," Julia declared. Frankly, she was surprised there had been leftovers. Carter had a good appetite, and so did Kaden and Kinsley, especially when it came to their grandma's desserts. Meredith was a fine cook and an even better baker. Julia considered her sweet potato pie a little bit of heaven on earth. She'd gladly lick the crumbs from the dish.

Fortified with fresh, hot coffee, Julia settled down at her own desk to peruse the ledger. She donned the thin white gloves before poring over the brittle pages—no easy task as the ink had faded considerably. She guessed it had been made from pulverized walnut shells or something else easy to obtain in the colonies. Charcoal? Blueberries? Iron gall? What entries she could read seemed to be a list of household purchases, just as Miss Dicey had suggested. Julia wrote down everything—even her best guesses—on a yellow legal pad. Page after page in the ledger appeared to be lists of payments made to individuals for their work for the colony trustees. She'd forgotten that at one time Oglethorpe and the settlement trustees had paid men to plant mulberry trees and paid women for spinning silk from silkworms, hoping to start a booming silk industry in Georgia.

There were no other exciting hints about treasure—at least not on the pages Julia could access. Several of the faded pages were stuck together, and she didn't dare attempt to separate them. She'd leave that to the experts. The only other intriguing entry appeared at the bottom of a page dated February 17, 1736: *J to Irene.* Did the J refer to John Wesley? And who was Irene? Did J go see her about something? Or did it mean that J gave her something? Julia copied the odd notation on her pad. Here was something else to look up. Again she realized that Meredith was probably right. Some mysteries were never solved, no matter how vigorously folks tried. As an afterthought, Julia took out her iPhone and snapped photos of each page of the ledger.

Then she typed up her notes on the computer. She'd always worked that way—everything handwritten on a legal pad first then typed up on the computer. With a weary yawn, she decided to call it a day. She'd give the ledger and her handwritten notes to Meredith to lock up in the floor safe she had in her office. Next on the agenda was a visit to the library to check with Rebecca Thompson, the resource librarian. A visit with Maggie Lu might prove useful too. Both women were founts of knowledge when it came to Savannah's history.

Julia stretched her arms high over her head and took a deep breath. When she heard the office phone ring, she was surprised to hear Meredith, not Carmen, answer it. Glancing at her watch, she realized it was nearly an hour past closing time. Where had the day gone? Just then the office door swung inward. Meredith stood on the threshold, her arms folded across her chest. Her blue eyes snapped with indignation, and her cheeks bloomed bright pink.

Alert and tense, Julia straightened. "What's the matter?"

"You'll never believe this. Beatrice Enterline just called. She wants us to come over to the conference room at the historical society right now. In fact, she insists upon it. She wouldn't take no for an answer. It's practically an emergency, she said, and she ordered me to bring the ledger."

Chapter Six

STANDING NOW, JULIA PROPPED HER fisted hands on her slim hips. "So, we've been summoned by the Queen Bee to attend an unscheduled meeting of the historical society. I wonder what's up."

"I have a sneaking suspicion this is about the treasure, although how she found out about it so quickly, I can't imagine—unless Jubal told her."

Narrowing her eyes, Julia said, "He must have." Earlier, she'd given Meredith a quick rundown about what had taken place at the nursing home and how she and Ed had bumped into Jubal Early Jones on their way out.

"They intend to grill us about the ledger," Meredith lamented.

"Why should we go?" Julia asked. "We can just say no."

Meredith shrugged. "We might as well get it over with. She'll pester us to death otherwise."

Julia chuckled. "Has anyone ever told you that you're just too nice?"

Meredith snorted. "I don't feel nice at all."

"All right then, we'll go see the Queen Bee after you lock all of this into the safe." When that was done, Julia snatched up her tote bag and took Meredith firmly by the arm. "Be brave, my lamb," she quipped as they closed the office door behind them.

The first person Julia noticed when she entered the meeting room at the society headquarters was Jubal Early Jones. *Yep, should have known.* And he did not look happy. Apparently, sweet old Miss Dicey had mentioned the ledger and the secret panel to her nephew. The cryptic comment in Charles Wesley's notation came immediately to Julia's mind—*Fear trouble ahead.* Trouble indeed…and a headache to boot. But why in the world had Jubal notified Beatrice, of all people?

She glanced around the long U-shaped tables. Ed sat at one end looking rather sheepish. Catching his eye, Julia raised her eyebrows. Ed raised his too and shrugged. He'd no doubt already received a tongue-lashing. Jeannie Bell Hansen, with her well-coiffed cap of silver hair, sat across from him. The recording secretary, her turquoise blue glasses slipping down her nose, appeared sullen and rather censorious. Beatrice's assistant director sat to Jeannie Bell's left. He was a small man with a smattering of whiskers on his chin. Julia couldn't recall his name but remembered that when they'd met previously he had boasted about being a direct descendent of Confederate General Braxton Bragg. Why anyone would want to claim a relationship to one of the War's worst officers, Julia couldn't imagine. Lovejoy Stewart, the junior archivist, was present too. Young and eager. She had strawberry blond hair and impossibly dark eyebrows and lashes. Her family had come over from the Scottish highlands in 1745, not long after Oglethorpe had established the colony. They'd been in Savannah ever since.

"If this don't beat all," Meredith muttered under her breath. She let her glance sweep around the table at the others in attendance. Then she pointed to a platter of assorted deli sandwiches that had been placed at one end of the nearest table. Julia walked over to help herself to half a pimento cheese sandwich before taking the empty seat next to Ed. After all the cheese she'd consumed today, she made up her mind to have several prunes as a bedtime snack and raisin bran for breakfast tomorrow morning.

Meredith took the seat farthest away from Beatrice. It was going to be a long evening. Julia's heart fluttered. She didn't like conflict. Who did? But she had the blood of spunky Nancy Hart flowing through her veins—one of Georgia's most famous heroines of the American Revolution. Julia was not about to quake under the Queen Bee's interrogation. *Not on your life!*

"Thought you had a counseling appointment this evening," she whispered to Ed before taking a bite of her sandwich.

"I did, but they canceled. Then Ms. Enterline called. She is very...er...persuasive. She wouldn't take no for an answer. She said you'd be here, so I came to lend moral support."

Julia gave an understanding nod. The word *no* was not in Beatrice's vocabulary.

"Meredith, Julia, so delighted y'all could join us," Beatrice gushed with forced amiability. She was dressed to the nines in a very feminine fuchsia-colored linen skirt suit with a matching shade of lipstick that set off her dark hair admirably. A silver brooch in the shape of an open parasol completed her expensive ensemble. Her fixed smile was coquettish. Beatrice just needed a flounce or two to be the perfect twenty-first-century Scarlett O'Hara.

"Did we have a choice?" Julia muttered.

Ed's mouth quirked up in a smile.

"I thought this was going to be an informal meeting." Meredith cast a meaningful stare at Jeannie Bell. "If it's an informal meeting,

I can't help wondering why Jeannie is here. Why do we need a recording secretary?"

Beatrice cleared her throat and tugged self-consciously at one sleeve of her jacket. Then she fingered the chunky pink and white beads around her neck. "Now, Meredith, don't get your bloomers in a twist. This meeting *is* informal. There was no announcement in the newspaper, and as you'll see, not all of our serving officers are present. Jeannie is here to take notes."

"Notes about what?" Meredith pressed.

Beatrice ignored the question. She cleared her throat again. "I call this..." She bit off those words to declare, "Let's get started, shall we?" She glanced around the table, eyes snapping with purpose. "So, Meredith, Julia, it's come to Jubal's attention that you and Pastor Markham are in possession of a valuable artifact from the River View estate."

Meredith glanced from Julia to Ed, who arched his eyebrows.

Taking the bull by the horns, Julia sat up straight and replied, "Yes."

A quiet murmur rippled around the table. Ed squirmed beside her. "We didn't steal it, you know," Julia said. Then she fixed her gaze on Jubal. "Miss Dicey knows we have it. She encouraged the two of us to see what we could make of it. And frankly, I don't see what it has to do with you, Jubal, or"—she fixed each person around the table with a questioning stare—"any of the officers of the historical society."

"Why, it has everything to do with me, Julia!" Jubal boomed. Gone was his gallant manner from earlier in the day. "I am Miss Dicey's nearest relation and presumably her heir."

"Don't you know for certain?" Julia retorted.

He flushed. "I should have been informed about the ledger, that's all I'm saying."

"I don't see why," Julia insisted.

He opened and closed his mouth several times like a catfish gasping for air before rolling his pale blue eyes in Beatrice's direction, seeking help.

Beatrice flapped a well-manicured hand at him in a dismissive manner. Fixing her gimlet gaze upon Meredith, Julia, and Ed in turn, she asked, "Now, tell me, which one of y'all has the ledger in your possession? I believe you've discovered something of historical significance, and I feel—er—*Jubal* feels that it is important for the society to take possession of it at once."

"I have it," Meredith said. "It's locked in my office safe. Miss Dicey has given Julia permission to examine it at her leisure."

Lovejoy spoke up then. "I'd very much like to see the ledger myself, Mrs. Bellefontaine." She smiled brightly.

"You shall," Beatrice declared before Meredith had a chance to respond. To Meredith, she said, "I must say I'm surprised at you, Meredith. You of all people must surely know the protocol for examining historical artifacts. You were president of the society for many, many years."

Julia cast a sympathetic glance at Meredith. Beatrice's tone was not only chastising but also rather insulting. *Many, many years?* Meredith must be feeling rather ancient.

"The ledger is private property at this time," Julia hastened to point out. "As yet, it has not been donated to the society for its collection and won't be until Miss Dicey says so. So technically speaking, it's not an artifact."

Jubal bellowed out, "I have a right to know what it says." He eyeballed Julia accusingly.

"Do you?" Julia arched her eyebrows. She could feel her annoyance growing. "Why didn't you ask Miss Dicey?"

"I did. She mumbled something about the Wesley brothers and General Oglethorpe and a journal entry mentioning an unspecified treasure." His flashing eyes lit from person to person. "She's a bit muddled on the best of days. I'm not really sure what she was going on about."

Julia couldn't help noticing that the word *treasure* had caused all eyes to glimmer just a little brighter.

"It's not a journal. It's a ledger," Ed said. "From what I saw it merely contained a listing of household expenditures and monies paid out to those performing tasks for the colony at large. There are a few personal notations written in the margins. That's what Julia has been attempting to read, but it's difficult, as the ink is quite faded."

"But what does it say about the treasure? Is it pirate treasure?" This question erupted from the new assistant director. Julia suddenly remembered his name. Joseph McGibbons. He had a surprisingly deep voice for such a thin little man. An ardent lover of all things piratical, McGibbons often dressed like a pirate and gave creative monologues for tourists at the local pirate pub. He had a deeply lined face from many years of leisure sailing and messing about with boats.

"Why not hand it over now?" Beatrice asked. "You did bring it with you, right?" She looked from Meredith to Julia.

"No, I'm not done looking through it," Julia said. She had no intention of giving up the ledger until she was ready to do so. "Some of the pages are stuck together," she said. "But from what I've read so far, there's no mention of what the so-called treasure might have been. So far there's only the one mention of it in the margin, just as Ed stated. For all we know, it refers to a stash of seed or shipment of sugar or coffee or other commodity precious to the settlement at the time."

"Maybe even a shipment of Bibles," Ed suggested. The others regarded him with incredulous disbelief.

"Charles Wesley was the personal secretary to General Oglethorpe," Beatrice threw in, as if that explained everything. Heads nodded. With a loud huff, Beatrice glared at Meredith, Julia, and then Ed as though daring them to disagree.

"Yes, we are well aware that Charles Wesley was Oglethorpe's secretary for a brief time before returning to England and better days," Meredith said. There was a pause as though everyone waited for someone to pursue the topic or change it. The silence stretched on.

Jubal broke it. "So, Julia, when will y'all be done looking it over?"

Julia sighed. How many more times did she have to explain? "The ledger is not in good condition. The ink has faded, and much of the writing is illegible. Several of the pages cannot be separated without risking serious damage to them."

"And that's why we should take possession of the ledger and allow Lovejoy or one of the other archivists to handle it with kid gloves—literally," Beatrice insisted.

Suddenly, everyone began talking at once. Jubal berated Ed for abusing his role as a minister. Lovejoy lamented the damage humidity and perspiration could do to old documents. Jeannie Bell, scribbling frantically, told everyone to slow down, she couldn't keep up. The raised voices droned on.

Julia closed her eyes. *Lord, give me strength.* She felt a wave of exhaustion wash over her. It had been such a hot day. She tired easily in this weather. It was one of those not-so-fun aspects of aging, she supposed. Aging, certainly, but weak—absolutely not! No manner of coercion would induce her to surrender the ledger until she was ready to give it up. A sudden image of a scene in *The Wizard of Oz* came to her, the one with the witch skywriting the smoky words, SURRENDER DOROTHY. Julia chuckled. Then she giggled.

The room grew quiet. She became aware of glares and frowns aimed in her direction. Meredith and Ed stared at her as though she'd lost her mind.

"You find this matter amusing, Julia?" Beatrice bristled. Her cheeks turned pink with indignation.

Julia shook her head. "No, I do not find this amusing at all, merely exasperating."

Lovejoy cleared her throat. "Perhaps we could offer to buy the ledger from Miss Dicey right now and take immediate possession." She cast a questioning look at Jubal and then Beatrice.

There was a dry cough from Joseph McGibbons. "I'm not sure there is adequate funding for such a purchase."

"We can't know how much it's worth until we examine it," Jeannie Bell pointed out. "And we can't see it until Julia and Meredith allow us to do so."

"Or my aunt gives us permission," Jubal jumped in.

Julia sighed, lacing her fingers in her lap beneath the table.

Beatrice pushed. "What do you intend to do now, Julia?"

"Just what I told Miss Dicey," Julia said. *Stand firm. Be strong.* "I'm going to attempt to read as much of the ledger as possible. Keep in mind, it is just that—a ledger, not a journal or diary. Once I've done that, I'll report back to Miss Dicey and let her know what I've discovered. She can take it from there."

"And just how soon do you think that'll be?" Jubal pressed, eyes blazing, jaw clenched.

"I could be working on it right now, but we were called away to attend this inquisition," Julia said, trying to hold her temper in check.

Beatrice rolled her eyes. "Inquisition, oh my! Aren't we being a little overdramatic?"

Julia cast a sidelong glance at Meredith, who gave her a wink.

"Will we all be able to have access to the contents of this so-called ledger-not-a-journal-or-diary after Mrs. Foley has given it the once-over?" Joseph asked, addressing his question to Jubal. "If it says anything about buccaneer booty, I want to know."

Jubal cleared his throat. "I suppose you could look at it too, after I do."

"This is too much!" Lovejoy declared, surprising everyone with her impassioned outburst. "The ledger is over two hundred and seventy-five years old. We can't go passing it around like last month's copy of the *Savannah Tribune*. It must be protected and preserved to ensure no further damage. The very information you want may be on the pages now stuck together."

As murmurs circulated around the table, Julia held her tongue. This wasn't her circus, and these certainly weren't her monkeys. She caught Meredith's eye, giving her a nod. Then, pushing her chair away from the table, she rose to her feet. Meredith did the same. "We'll be going now. I've answered your questions. The sooner I get started on deciphering the Wesley notations, the better it will be for all of us."

Ed rose too, an eager expression on his face as he no doubt anticipated an escape.

Jubal called after her, "Julia…"

"You'll be hearing from me, Jubal." Then mustering her last dab of wilting dignity, Julia stalked out of the room, with Meredith and Ed close upon her heels.

Chapter Seven

"I JUST DON'T UNDERSTAND JUBAL going behind our backs like that," Meredith muttered as she slammed a dish of watermelon rind pickles onto the small kitchen table.

Julia flinched. Her friend continued to pull leftovers from the fridge, placing everything in front of Julia, who had lost her appetite following what she'd come to think of as the Inquisition.

"What did he hope to accomplish, I wonder?" Meredith mused. "Did he think we would knuckle under Beatrice's authority as head of the historical society?"

Julia shrugged. "I don't know," she confessed. After the three of them had stalked out of the meeting and they'd said good night to Ed in the parking lot, Meredith had driven her back to the office to pick up her car. Meredith then insisted that Julia follow her home to have a late supper. Twilight had fallen by the time they reached Meredith's house. She tried to convince Meredith not to bother with making BLTs.

"But we have to eat something," Meredith insisted and thus, the abundance of leftovers heaped upon the kitchen table.

"This is an awful lot of food," Julia observed, helping herself to a pickled shrimp.

"Leftovers," Meredith reminded her.

Julia nodded. She knew that on many Saturdays, Meredith entertained Carter and his family for a leisurely lunch. But from the looks of things, Carter and his wife, Sherri Lynn, and their adorable youngsters, Kaden and Kinsley, hadn't had much of an appetite this past weekend.

"It's perplexing," Julia said. "The meeting, I mean."

Meredith shoved a piece of sweet potato pie across to her. "You can say that again. Sweet tea, ice water, Diet Dr Pepper?"

"Diet Dr Pepper," Julia said. Something furry swept by her leg, and she heard a familiar "mrrow" sound. Looking down, she caught a glimpse of Meredith's Russian blue with the mesmerizing green eyes. "Hey there, GK." The cat had been named after the witty Christian apologist, G.K. Chesterton. Upon consideration, the feline did look rather scholarly, if not good-humored. The cat, having satisfied his curiosity about Meredith's visitor, gave another disinterested "mrrow" and slinked out of the kitchen. Julia watched him go. Maybe it was true what they said—dogs have families and cats have staff.

"It took some nerve calling Ed to attend the meeting too," Meredith said, placing a glass of ice and a soda in front of Julia, along with a small dish containing three-bean salad.

"Sit down, Mere, for heaven's sake! Your face is flushed, and you're probably having a blood pressure spike. We don't need any more food." The table fairly groaned with everything from cold ham and leftover biscuits to pineapple marshmallow Jell-O salad and pie. Meredith plopped down in the chair across from hers. "Besides, the whole thing is over and done with," Julia added.

"No, it isn't," Meredith said. "It won't really be over and done with, as you say, until we return the ledger to Miss Dicey. But you'll have to go through it from cover to cover before we do that."

"As a matter of fact, I've done that already." Julia smiled and helped herself to a piece of ham.

Meredith raised an eyebrow. "You're done?"

"I'm done. I went through every single page—the ones that weren't stuck together from moisture or whatever. It was tedious. The handwriting was small and sometimes too faded to read. Lots of figures too. I told the board it was a list of expenses for the Oglethorpe household and the colony at large, but they didn't believe me. I'm not even sure what the currency was back then, so the entries don't even make sense to me. I'm guessing the *p* stands for pence or pounds?"

"I would guess as much, but I don't know for sure," Meredith confessed.

"I used my iPhone to take photos of all the pages so someone else can take a look and see if they can read the figures. If Charles Wesley was indeed Oglethorpe's secretary, I don't think he enjoyed the job. His handwriting appeared rather sloppy and hurried—as though he was eager to get the data entered and be done with it."

"Charles Wesley didn't enjoy the job," Meredith said. "I remember reading that somewhere." She reached for a cold biscuit, cut it in half, and smeared it with peach preserves. "He only stayed in the colony for a matter of months. John Wesley stayed a bit longer. Both of them seemed disillusioned and disgruntled with life in Georgia, so they returned to England, pursued ministries there, and became famous. So it's a good thing they left Georgia, I suppose."

Julia reached for the other half of the biscuit and spread it with the peach preserves also. After taking a bite, she gave an appreciative groan. Meredith made the best preserves and freezer jams. There was no end to her friend's many talents. "I absolutely refuse to be bullied by Jubal Jones or Beatrice or anyone else on that board. I'll wait a few days and then give Ed a call. He can come get the ledger and have a talk with Miss Dicey to find out what she wants to do with it."

"Encourage him not to promise to hand over the ledger to Jubal or anyone else," Meredith urged. "It's Miss Dicey's property. She should have a say in what happens to it."

"The poor old dear must have told Jubal all about it when he went in to visit with her."

"I thought we agreed to keep its discovery between the three of us," Meredith said.

"We did, but then Ed and I forgot to suggest to Miss Dicey that she do the same." Julia gave a helpless shrug and reached for another piece of cold ham.

"Did something happen between you and Jubal at the nursing home—something that might have provoked his unexplainable behavior?" Meredith asked.

Julia shook her head. "No, he was pleasant. I was pleasant too." She took a sip of her soda before adding rather hesitantly, "But something did happen after Ed and I left. At least...I think it happened."

Meredith wiped her fingers on a napkin. "You're being rather mysterious. What happened...or didn't happen, exactly?"

Julia told her all about Tate appearing to listen to their conversation with Miss Dicey and later tailing her and Ed out of the parking lot. She also mentioned that Ed thought she was being overimaginative, that they weren't being followed at all. "But Ed lost him. I had no idea he was such a speed demon. He handled that van like a NASCAR driver."

Meredith chuckled. "Maybe Ed's right. Maybe this guy Tate was going home after his shift or meeting someone for lunch. There could be a dozen possibilities. Why should he be following you anyway? If it makes you feel any better, I could do a background check on him. What's his first name?"

Julia gave her a sheepish grin. "Don't bother. You and Ed are probably right. His being behind us must have been a coincidence, that's all. I think the whole possibility that we're starting out on another treasure hunt has made me suspicious."

Meredith gave her an understanding nod. "So, what will you do next, in regard to the ledger?"

"I want to show my notes to Rebecca at the library and see if she has any input or suggestions for resources I might consult her about the Wesleys' activities here in Savannah—diaries, letters, journals… anything," Julia told her.

"Oh, please don't mention diaries," Meredith pleaded with an exaggerated eye roll.

Julia chuckled. The Anna Coles diary that Meredith had recently inherited had hinted at the location of Blackbeard's buried treasure. That was a misadventure best forgotten.

"I also want to have a talk with Maggie Lu. I'm certain she'll have some valuable insights into the matter. She's a walking almanac of Savannah history and trivia."

"Good idea. Sounds like a plan. You've got it all under control." Meredith grinned and sat back in her chair.

Julia snorted. "Come with me to River View in the morning so I can get that clematis clipping. I want to go early before it gets too hot."

"It's August. It's always too hot—even at dawn. And I have no intention of going out that early," Meredith told her. "I'm not even civil until I've had a cup of coffee—or two."

Before Julia took her leave, they settled on a time. The following morning, Wednesday, Julia swung by at the designated hour, dressed in pale blue Bermuda shorts and garden clogs dotted with bright pink flamingos. She'd slathered herself with sunscreen, and she reeked of insect repellent. The combination might not prove effective against sunburn and bug bites, but it would definitely keep other people from getting too close.

"We're going to have to hurry, I think," she told Meredith when her friend opened her door. "It's going to rain—again." Meredith snatched her sun hat from the dining room table and a bottle of water before following Julia to her car. Julia took one sidelong glance at her friend's pale face and declared, "You didn't sleep well last night."

Meredith snorted. "I admit, I'm feeling rather sluggish, and my nerves are a bit frayed around the edges. Last night, after you left, I started thinking about that inquisition and could feel my blood pressure inching its way up to a dangerous level."

"Hey, let's not have any of that," Julia cautioned. She'd been so distressed when Meredith had her heart attack. She'd realized then how precious their friendship was to her and had sent up many a heartfelt prayer of thanksgiving when Meredith had come through her surgery with flying colors.

As Meredith snapped her seat belt, she said, "I think I'm most upset at Jubal for going behind your back like that to Beatrice—of all people. I don't like it, not one bit. Why couldn't he have come by the office or even my house or yours to discuss the matter? Or why not call one of us on the phone if he didn't want to discuss it face-to-face? I just don't understand it."

"My suspicions are aroused," Julia admitted. "All those years on the judicial bench have made me skeptical about people's motives. Why didn't Jubal simply go to his aunt to demand that she call me and ask for the ledger back? The fact that he went to Beatrice is suspicious, to say the least."

Meredith nodded. "I don't trust the old goat, not now."

As Julia considered her friend's comment, she silently admitted that Meredith had a good point. Why *hadn't* Jubal gone to Miss Dicey first? Jubal's betrayal in going to Beatrice had not only angered her, but it hurt too—more than she cared to admit. They'd been friendly acquaintances for years—or so she'd thought. Julia knew she'd get over the snub in time, but it still stung now.

"They've all made a great fuss over nothing, I'm afraid," Julia pronounced. "The entire committee is going to be disappointed. Other than one cryptic entry about a treasure and the trouble its discovery might cause, the rest of the legible entries all have to do with household and colony expenses and salaries paid out to settlers who were helping with the silkworms and other communal tasks required by the trustees." She paused as she stopped for a red light. When it turned green, she added, "That ledger is in horrible condition. The handwriting is faded and the pages are brittle."

"Lovejoy was right," Meredith said. "We really need to get it to an archivist as soon as possible for preservation. The pages should be digitally scanned, and the ledger stored in an acid-free box that will protect it from mildew, dust, and moisture. I'm anxious to pass it on."

"We need to be careful." Julia gave an emphatic nod. "Jubal may go to any lengths to get his big sweaty hands on it."

"Actually, any one of them might try to get their hands on it," Meredith told her. "Last night after you left, Lovejoy called me at home. She begged to take possession of the ledger immediately. She even promised not to tell Jubal that I'd given it to her, but I told her no. I said you were still looking it over."

"Did you notice the ripple of excitement in the room at the mere mention of the treasure?" Julia asked.

Meredith nodded. "I warned them not to get their hopes up. Like Ed said, the treasure might not be pirate booty at all. What the colonists would have considered valuable, we might not think so today. Back then, sugar, tea, and coffee, as well as other commodities, were kept in locked chests. Only the master or mistress of the house had the key. Even pies were kept in a locked pie safe. It could be something that simple—not exotic strings of pearls or antique gold coins."

"That's true, but on the other hand it really *could* be pirate loot," Julia insisted.

"I think that's what Joe McGibbons is hoping for." Meredith shook her head, blond curls swishing against her cheeks. "He's into everything pirate. Sometimes he even grows a beard and dresses like Edward Teach."

Julia chuckled. "Good old Blackbeard."

Again, Meredith nodded. "If indeed General Oglethorpe or John Wesley discovered buried pirate treasure, they may have mentioned it in a letter or journal, explaining where it was discovered and what became of it. It's just that in all my years with the historical society, I never even heard a whisper about any of this. So if John Wesley discovered a treasure and showed it to General Oglethorpe, the discovery couldn't have been common knowledge. To be honest, I'm not up for another so-called treasure hunt."

By the time the two friends arrived at River View, the sky loomed gray and ominous. Meredith cast an apprehensive glance at the lead-colored clouds overhead. A flash of lightning flickered in the distance. "We'd better hurry. That storm is heading this way."

Julia snatched a blue straw gardening tote from the back floor of the car and quickly followed Meredith up the flagstone path and into the side yard, where the once-lovely garden now appeared to be a neglected tangle of vines and flowering shrubs. From the looks of it, the stone fountain had stopped running ages ago. It held only a bit of rainwater from the last summer shower. The grass fronds around it reached more than knee-high in some places. The sultry air was heavy with the scent of late-blooming roses. Nothing moved.

This portion of the old house looked even gloomier than the front entrance. In some places the paint had blistered and peeled away. The windows appeared shrouded with closed curtains. Sighing, Meredith murmured, "It would break Miss Dicey's heart to see it like this."

Julia opened the tote and produced a pair of gardening gloves and secateurs. "I've come prepared. It won't take long." She then strode off in the direction of the clematis vine. With careful snips here and there, she took her desired cuttings. As she rambled through the neglected garden, Meredith indicated a climbing pink rose clinging to a portion of a sunbaked brick wall. "This was always one of Miss Dicey's favorites." Looking around, she added, "I'd forgotten just how big her garden is."

Julia wiped the beads of perspiration dotting her forehead. It was already quite warm despite the early morning hour. She was craving a tall glass of sweet tea with extra ice or better yet, a frosty Diet Dr Pepper. "I imagine you've been here many times over the years," she said, dropping her gardening sheers into the tote bag.

Meredith nodded. "Miss Dicey occasionally held garden parties here as fundraisers for the historical society. They were the most talked about social events of the year. As president, I presided over the festivities. You should see this place in March when the azaleas are in bloom. It's a little bit of heaven."

She sighed, apparently lost for a moment in reminiscing. Julia looked around. Despite its neglect, the garden was still beautiful and rather peaceful. She'd always felt close to God in a garden. But as she wandered around to the back of the house, pausing to admire an ancient pine looming overhead, she silently admitted that there was something rather creepy about the deathlike stillness here and the way the hoary evergreen shrubs appeared to sneak up on the screened back porch of the vacant mansion.

Even though she heard another ominous roll of distant thunder, Julia felt reluctant to hurry Meredith along. Her friend was so obviously enjoying herself, likely remembering days gone by. Julia studied the flower beds along the ivy-covered brick wall that hemmed in the property at the back. She caught a glimpse of what appeared to be a tall, narrow wrought-iron gate. "Mere, come here!" she hollered. "There's another gate. Look!"

With purposeful strides, Meredith joined her. She frowned. "I've never seen this before."

"Does it open into another portion of the garden or onto a path to the river?"

"I have no idea." Meredith wriggled her hand through the clinging ivy, giving the gate a tug. It opened inward with a screech of protest. She stepped through cautiously into what appeared to be a small oasis of flowering shrubs. Julia followed closely upon her heels, clutching her tote bag of clippings. Another lifeless fountain hunched in the middle of the secluded garden. It seemed a pocket of eerie silence. Tall grass prickled the back of Julia's legs. A lizard scuttled away at their approach. Julia's skin tingled with heat and the rising humidity.

"Oh, look." She pointed to a weedy bed of lily of the valley. "My great-aunt Blanche in Virginia had lily of the valley along the north wall of her home. I've not seen any since I was a girl. I simply must have a pip or two."

"Miss Dicey will consider it a kindness that someone took an interest in her garden," Meredith replied absently. She stood surveying the tiny enclosed space. "I never knew this was back here. They all look so sad, don't they? The little statues, I mean."

Julia, squatting beside the plants, looked around at the collection of grim cherubs, gloomy angels, and flop-eared rabbits. "They remind me of the hauntingly beautiful statuary in the Bonaventure Cemetery. Maybe Miss Dicey or someone in her family used this quiet corner as a place to pray."

Meredith didn't answer. She walked over to a concrete bench, crumbling on one edge, and sat down, momentarily lost in thought. Julia retrieved a trowel from her tote bag and quickly became absorbed in her task among the small, bell-shaped lilies. The tiny garden was sinisterly quiet. No bees droning or birds chirping. Not even a breeze to rustle the leaves. But the gnats were plentiful and annoying as usual.

"Do you think it's a place of mourning?" Julia asked, addressing Meredith over her shoulder. "Maybe the Oglethorpes buried their pets in here."

Before Meredith could reply, a low, menacing female voice demanded, "Now just what do y'all think you're doing?"

Chapter Eight

JULIA GASPED. MEREDITH JERKED TO her feet. They found themselves confronting a woman in a pale pink cotton dress, brandishing
a broom in a threatening manner. Her iron-gray hair stood out
around her head like a halo. Behind her loomed a very tall, broad-
shouldered young woman, frowning fiercely, wearing denim shorts
and a bright yellow tank top. She had the same high cheekbones and
bold nose of the older woman, who repeated her demand. "What are
y'all doing out here?"

As Julia caught her breath, Meredith said, "Ruth? Ruth
Simms? I'm Meredith Bellefontaine, a friend of Miss Dicey's. Do you
remember me?" She removed her sunglasses, squinting now against
the glare.

Ruth lowered the broom. "Meredith Bellefontaine? Why, of
course, now I remember you. Didn't recognize you at first in that hat
and those dark glasses, that's all."

"You gave us a bit of a fright, I must say," Meredith confessed.
"It's so quiet in this part of the garden. We didn't hear you come in
through the little gate."

With a chuckle, Ruth admitted, "Seeing that car out front gave
us a bit of a fright too. We thought somebody was robbing the house,
but when we didn't find anybody inside, we decided we'd better

check round the garden." Her dark-eyed gaze slid over in Julia's direction.

"This is my friend Julia Foley," Meredith said by way of introduction. "Miss Dicey gave her permission to take a few cuttings from her flower garden." To Julia, she said, "This is Ruth Simms. She's been cleaning house for Miss Dicey for as many years as I can remember."

"And my mama before me," Ruth added, with a touch of pride. "This here is Tamika—my granddaughter, the youngest." She tipped her head toward the towering teen, who gave a shy smile now that she realized Meredith and Julia were not intruders.

"I love your earrings," Julia commented, noting Tamika's large silver braided hoops hanging from her ears. Tamika smiled. Now that her pulse had resumed its normal pace, Julia realized she'd experienced a déjà vu moment. She wondered if Meredith remembered that it hadn't been too many months ago that they'd been scared to death in the garden at the old Besset place when the caretaker had loomed out of nowhere to see why they were snooping around.

Julia felt the first plunk of rain on her arm when Tamika said, "Meemaw, I think we'd better go on inside. It's beginning to rain."

"Let's make a run for it," Meredith declared.

"The back door to the kitchen is open," Tamika announced before sprinting ahead, as graceful as a young gazelle. The others hurried after her, Meredith keeping pace with Ruth's slower gait and Julia dashing ahead with her tote bag full of flower clippings, pips, and gardening tools.

Once inside, Ruth tucked her broom in a corner of the kitchen and put on a kettle for tea. "Need to brew us some fresh iced tea," she said, reaching for a glass pitcher from one of the kitchen cabinets. "Cleaning this old place is thirsty work."

Tamika threw open a window to allow the slightly cooler air from outside to circulate through the stuffy kitchen. Meredith and Julia plopped their totes and hats on the Formica-top kitchen table. A crack of thunder boomed nearby, and the raindrops pelted against the windows. Julia shuddered. She wasn't fond of storms.

"When I saw y'all's car I was mighty thankful I had Tamika with me," Ruth said as she slipped on an apron. She retrieved a package of Oreo cookies from her voluminous straw purse sporting bright yellow pineapples on both sides. "She lends a hand nowadays. I never come out here alone anymore and never at night now that Miss Dicey is no longer in residence. Makes me jumpy. This old house creaks and groans—it's got old bones, like me."

Julia asked, "Have you seen any trespassers?"

"Just y'all," Ruth replied, smirking. Meredith and Julia exchanged a grin.

Ruth opened a small utility closet. She retrieved a long-handled duster. Thrusting it at her granddaughter, she said, "Go on now. You know the routine. You can come back for sweet tea in a little bit."

Tamika heaved a bored sigh as she slouched from the room, duster in hand.

Ruth shook her head as she stood staring after her granddaughter. "That girl—she's like the lilies of the field."

Meredith arched her blond eyebrows and swiped a hand through her curls, now frizzy from the humidity. "How do you mean?"

"She toils not and neither does she spin." Ruth chuckled, clearly pleased with her own joke. "Doesn't like to work, that one. Just wants to play basketball. Night and day. Basketball." She shook her head. "Plays on the high school girls' team. Probably thinking about playing right now. The team is already practicing even though school doesn't start for a few more weeks. She's not the best player, but she's sure got heart. That's what the coach told her." Ruth fetched bright-colored aluminum drinking glasses from a cupboard near the sink.

"We came out here yesterday with Pastor Markham," Meredith said.

Ruth arched an eyebrow. "To fetch more of Miss Dicey's belongings?"

"Yes, she wanted some of her sheet music," Meredith replied.

"Well, there's plenty of that, for sure," Ruth said, nodding.

"It's a fine old house," Julia said. "Secret panels and everything."

Meredith jabbed her in the side with her elbow—hard. Julia winced.

"I know about the secret hideaway upstairs in the old nursery," Ruth said, giving them a sage smile as she opened the package of cookies, placing them on an old china plate with a floral chintz pattern.

"Mr. Jubal showed me that years ago when we were little chips together. He and his friends—when they were children—liked to hide in there and jump out at the unsuspecting. Scared everyone out of their wits every time."

"I'd love to see that," Meredith declared.

"Me too," Julia put in. "Would you show us?"

Ruth shook her head. "I'm not inclined to do those stairs anymore, but I'll have Tamika take you up. She knows all about it." Stepping out of the kitchen, Ruth called out for her granddaughter, who eventually glided into the room with an athlete's easy grace.

"You calling me, Meemaw? Time for sweet tea?"

"Not yet, child. You take Miss Meredith and Miss Julia up to the nursery and show them the secret hideaway up there."

Tamika gave her grandmother a lazy smile. "Okay, if you say so." As Meredith and Julia followed the girl down the corridor and to the staircase, Tamika said over her shoulder, "It's way up on the third floor."

When a flash of lightning lit the stairway from a window above, Meredith twitched. Julia did the same. "My poor cat," Meredith said with a sigh. "GK takes it as a personal affront when the weather is not to his liking."

The inside of the mansion was gloomier than ever in the storm, and the heat was stifling. Julia felt sure it was hot enough to melt crayons. She took labored breaths as she mounted the steps behind Tamika. She wiped the sweat from her forehead and upper lip with the back of her hand and tried to imagine what it would have been like to climb these steps burdened with a corset and a half-dozen heavy petticoats. She could hear Meredith huffing and puffing behind her. Her friend wasn't out of shape, she knew. Months of cardiac rehab had taken care of that. But she hoped the heat wasn't too unbearable for Meredith.

When they reached the nursery—a large, sprawling room— Tamika snapped on the light switch. A wobbly floor lamp glowed dimly to life. Julia had noticed already how few ceiling lights there were in the old house. "I loved playing up here when I was a kid," Tamika told them. "My sister and I came with Meemaw sometimes. While she did the cleaning, we'd play in here. Miss Dicey didn't mind." She made her way to the large, yawning windows and yanked up the dusty shades, now brittle and yellow with age. Rain streaked down the windowpanes.

Unlike the rooms below, this one did not have dust covers flung over the furniture—what furniture there was. A large table with six hard-back chairs dominated the middle of the room. One corner boasted a cane-bottom rocking chair and the other a battered pine chifforobe with an assortment of drawers on one side and small closet on the other. A dilapidated dollhouse had been stashed under the window. The bookshelves were mostly empty except for a few tattered volumes and some wooden puzzles. The green and pink striped wallpaper appeared faded and curled off the wall in places. There was no fireplace in this room, Julia noted.

"This must have been a lovely nursery once upon a time," she declared. She walked over to a bookshelf and retrieved a dusty volume. "It's *Little Women*. My favorite. I'll bet Miss Dicey read it more than once." She pulled out a second one. "*Treasure Island*— another classic. I can almost imagine generations of Oglethorpes playing in here and learning their ABCs."

"It's sad that Miss Dicey never married and had children of her own. I don't know what's going to happen to this old place when she passes away," Meredith said.

"Did the Oglethorpes hang on to their wealth?" Julia asked.

Meredith shook her head. "After the War, their fortunes took a turn for the worse, as you can imagine. When slavery was eradicated, Mr. Oglethorpe took on sharecroppers. Then came the crash of 1896 followed by the Great Depression in the 1930s. Miss Dicey's daddy sold off all the farmland. I'd heard he'd invested in telephone stock way back when, and I suppose that's how she's been able to hold on to the house for so long."

"I think Miss Dicey should open this old place for tours like they do those castles in England," Tamika put in. She'd been standing patiently near one of the windows while Julia and Meredith chatted.

"That's a great idea," Meredith agreed.

"With a little fixing up, it would make a lovely B and B or a venue for wedding parties," Julia added.

Tamika crossed the room. Placing one hand flat against the faded wallpaper, she rapped the wall with her knuckles. "Here's what you want to see," she announced, pressing on the wall. "The pattern of the wallpaper hides the door." There was a slow swooshing sound as the secret panel slid open.

Julia and Meredith moved closer to peer inside. There was nothing to see, of course. But this hiding place was much bigger than the one downstairs in the music room. Two youngsters could easily squeeze in together and an adult could kneel or squat safely inside. There was a rusty lever, which served to open the panel from the inside. "I wonder what this secret hiding place was used for," Julia mused.

Tamika shrugged. Meredith just shook her head. "Thanks for showing us this," she said, turning to the teen with a smile. "Julia and I want to look around a bit. We don't want to keep you from your chores, or your granny will never let us hear the end of it. We'll be down shortly."

With a slow gaze at the two women and then a sidelong glance at the open panel, Tamika gave another shrug and walked out. Julia watched her retreating figure. When she was gone, she tiptoed over to the open door of the nursery and peered into the corridor. There was no sign of Tamika. "What's up?" she asked in a low voice, just in case Tamika had paused on the stairs to listen.

"Nothing," Meredith answered. "I just want a bit of time to explore up here. I've never been in this portion of the house."

"But it's hotter than blue blazes," she complained.

"Yes, but I may never get another chance," Meredith insisted. "I won't take long, I promise." She made her way into the corridor to explore the other third story rooms, and Julia joined her.

Together they peeked into the various rooms and linen closets on the third floor. There wasn't much to see, not even old bed frames. Julia wondered if Miss Dicey had been selling off the upstairs furniture to help make ends meet. As they descended the stairs, Julia rubbed the back of her hand across her perspiring forehead. "I need a shower, and I need to get those cuttings and pips into some water. Then I want to get to the office and make a list of questions to ask Rebecca and Maggie Lu."

"Good idea," Meredith agreed. She attempted to smooth her frizzy curls. "I've got lots of phone calls to make—verifying references and all that. But I'm glad to have had the opportunity to see the other hidden panel. Beatrice would be green with envy if she knew what we'd been doing this morning."

"Surely you're not going to tell her?" Julia choked out.

Meredith chuckled. "Not on your life."

In the kitchen they found Ruth and Tamika enjoying sweet tea and cookies. Ruth invited Meredith and Julia to join them. Out of politeness, Meredith accepted. Julia reluctantly took a seat at the kitchen table. She was eager to get on with her day but remembered all too keenly Pastor Ed's recent sermon on kindness, gentleness, and the other fruits of the Holy Spirit. So she graciously accepted the glass of sweet tea and helped herself to a cookie. After the morning's adventures in the garden and the sweltering old mansion, she was thirsty and even helped herself to a second cookie. They chatted a little about Miss Dicey and then inquired about Tamika's upcoming basketball boot camp. As soon as it was polite to do so, they gathered up their belongings, said their goodbyes, and headed out the kitchen door into the rain-soaked yard.

"When you see Miss Dicey next, tell her hello from me," Ruth called after them.

"We'll do that," Julia promised. After checking her phone quickly for any important messages, she drove back to town, dropped off Meredith, and headed home.

Julia showered and changed into khaki-colored slacks and a peach-colored blouse—one with long sleeves, just in case Meredith had beat her to the office and turned on the air-conditioning full blast. She gulped down a small carton of strawberry yogurt and headed for the office. Meredith's car was not there.

Carmen sprang to her feet when Julia entered. "You have a visitor," she said in a low, conspiratorial tone. "In there." She jerked her dark head to the side, indicating Julia's office. The door was ajar. "Insisted on waiting," she added. "Insisted!"

"A client?" Julia asked in a low voice as she passed Carmen's desk. Carmen shook her head.

Julia took a deep breath. She feared it was Jubal Early Jones, come to pressure her into releasing the ledger into his care. Well, he would go home empty-handed. She would not be intimidated. She'd stood up to meaner bullies than Jubal in her days as a criminal court judge. Jubal didn't know who he was dealing with. She thrust her chin forward and pushed open the door. Seeing her visitor, she froze on the threshold.

"Why, Lovejoy Stewart, what brings you here this morning?"

Chapter Nine

Johanna Hus
Georgia Colony, February 1737

Johanna stirred the bubbling stew. Her legs quaked beneath her light woolen skirt. She could hear the raised, angry voices of the men outside the main cabin. There had been strong differences between the men of the community and the Savannah colonists—always centered upon the militia. Now matters had to come to a head. She'd stared out the window earlier at the men gathered outside. She'd seen tempers flare, jaws clenched—and some fists too.

Fear not, the Lord is with thee. Johanna silently repeated the comforting words over and over again. A few other women stood watching out the windows, their arms folded across their bosoms. One or two exchanged worried glances. How many times must their husbands repeat to General Oglethorpe that they would not take up arms to join the militia? It was against their religious principles. They would not be swayed.

Johanna, hearing a strangled whimper, cast a quick glance at Rachel Dober. The young mother, not much older than Johanna, stood staring out the window. Two small boys clutched at her skirts. Johanna left the long wooden spoon in the cook pot to move to her side. Placing an arm around the other woman's quivering shoulders, she whispered, "Fear not, the Lord is with us." Perhaps the words she found so comforting would be of comfort to Rachel too.

Rachel received this encouragement with a curt nod. Then thrusting her chin in the direction of the window, she said, "Behold, Ephraim, my husband. His face is flushed. His hands fisted. The man has such a temper. It is a cross to bear. What if he should strike out at one of the Savannah men?"

"Your husband had better hold tight to the reins of his temper," one of the other women warned from across the room. "Have you not heard? There is already talk of casting us out of the colony."

"And taking away our land grant," another threw in. "Then where shall we go? What shall we do? We must have a care."

An appalled hush followed this impassioned pronouncement. Johanna felt a sick stirring in the pit of her stomach. Fear was difficult to quench. But she would have to try. "They cannot cast us out," she declared with as much confidence as she could muster.

All eyes swiveled in her direction now—the argument outside ignored for the moment. She could tell by their expressions that some of the women were surprised that she'd spoken out at all upon the subject, for she had no husband to explain such matters to her. Others, like Sister Reidel, gave her a knowing glance. Johanna guessed her friend now wondered what Herr Wesley had perhaps told her in private. The English minister spent time in her company—at the school and following song services on Saturday evenings when he rode out to join them. He'd made no secret that worshipping with the community and studying the Holy Word with the elder brethren had been a great comfort to him. No doubt the women now assumed Johanna knew something.

"Why say you this?" one of the older women asked, a frown furrowing her brow.

Johanna shrugged. "Think on it. The Savannah colonists did not give us the land nor did they pay our passage on the ship. The trustees did so. We are in debt to them only. We cannot leave this place until our debt is paid. Think you the men of Savannah will pay it to be rid of us?"

A murmur followed Johanna's explanation. She returned to stir the stew, toying with the idea of joining the men outside so she could more readily listen to their conversation. But no, that would be too bold. Still, after a year in the colony, her English was adequate, and she could translate the conversation—nay, the argument—for the women to understand. Everyone in the community had encouraged her to learn English, but she was more intent upon studying the Yamacraw tongue so she could better teach the children in the school.

Returning to the window, she focused her gaze upon Herr Wesley, who stood halfway between the English and the men of the community. How like him! He seemed always to serve as a bridge between the two. No, she would not go out. She did not look her best. Her skirt hem was dragging, and her apron was soiled from preparing the meal. She did not want John to see her in such disarray and frown his disapproval. Johanna knew she should not be concerned with earthly attire. Their beloved God had given them a wardrobe of a different nature—they should be clothed in Christ, in spiritual garments. She needed to remember to don a tender heart, kindness, humility, and forbearance. These were far more important than a comely dress with a lace collar.

She turned, studying the faces of the other women—her sisters. Some appeared anxious, flushed, hopeful, and even tearful. They all knew the very existence of their settlement depended upon the goodwill of General Oglethorpe and the trustees. Before coming, the elders had made sure the congregation would be allowed to live in peace and stand upon their convictions. As soon as they arrived, they'd put in crops and built small cabins and even a school for the Yamacraw children. Johanna didn't want to leave now. And in truth, the Good Lord knew they could not afford to pull up stakes and go elsewhere. They had spent all their funds to get this far.

She again turned her attention to the men outside. This time John saw her at the window and acknowledged her with a slight nod of his head. She mustered a weak smile. He was a champion for them she knew, trying to make the other settlers understand their religious viewpoint. It wearied her to think upon the same old battles. Had they not fought them in the homeland too? Would they never end? And now she did not have her parents to speak to about her feelings, to comfort and encourage her. Mutti was long dead and now Vati gone after.

How exhausting settling in the New World had proven to be. She fought back a sudden urge to cry. She must not! She was a woman grown with duties to fulfill. She had no time to cry.

Johanna swallowed hard as she removed her soiled apron and tossed it over the back of a crude wooden chair. She slipped unnoticed—or so she hoped—out the back door, intent upon making her way to the river. The afternoon was unusually hot and sultry for late February. The perspiration trickled down the back of her neck. Her garment stuck to her back. She longed for evening, which would bring respite from the heat. She hadn't gone very far when she became aware that someone had followed her, with hurried, heavy steps. Without slowing her stride, she turned to look over her shoulder. Recognizing John Wesley, she came to a halt on the path. Embarrassed by her untidy appearance, she straightened her white cap, poking strands of golden brown hair that had escaped its tight coil up underneath. She smoothed her skirt. It was the best she could do.

"Where are you going, Miss Hus?" he asked, catching up to her. He'd removed his outer coat and rolled up the sleeves of his linen shirt. His dark waistcoat was stained with sweat underneath his arms.

"I needed a breath of fresh air," she replied. *If one could call anything about this day fresh.* Still, she'd needed to get away from the clutch of anxious women fretting in the cabin, away from the raised voices of angry men.

"Do you mind if I join you?"

"No," she lied. *God forgive me.* She wanted to be alone, to treasure a few solitary moments—moments to think about *anything other than chores and angry men and the uncertain future.*

"You are distraught," John observed. "It is the matter of your brethren and their reluctance to serve in the militia."

"That worries me not," Johanna told him. In a way, it was true. The brethren would not be moved by threats or even violence. They would stand firm on that point. There was no sense in worrying about it. "I worry about what will happen if the enmity between the other colonists and our community continues its course."

John nodded. "There is cause for worry," he admitted, matching his steps to her own. "The Savannah colonists are angry. They feel the community here is not pulling its weight as it regards the safety and security of the colony. They have urged the general to force the brethren to join in with the weekly marching and drilling."

Johanna shook her head. "They will not. Nothing could induce them to do so. My sisters know this, and so we are fretful."

Again, he gave an understanding nod. In a low voice, as though he feared he might be overheard, John said, "It has come to my attention that there are those who insist your congregation leave at once if your men are unwilling to participate fully in ensuring the success of the colony."

"But we are willing!" Johanna felt indignant. "We have worked hard. We have planted crops. The women spin silk. The men take part in the watch. We do all that is asked of us…except joining the militia."

"I know this." John touched her arm lightly, by way of reassurance.

"If they make us leave, where will we go? We have no funds, no resources. The Good Lord brought us here to serve the heathen, and that is what we do." Anger and frustration made her quicken her pace as she walked toward the river's grassy bank.

With a shrug, John said, "I agree. And so does the general. He has told everyone of his admiration for your community's zeal and industry. He has written to the trustees as well. He is greatly pleased with the brethren."

Johanna swallowed hard. She would not cry in front of this man.

"Although I am not your pastor, I would admonish you in the words of Paul to allow Christ's peace to rule in your heart." John reached out and pulled her arm this time, forcing Johanna to cease her walking. "On the ship during the voyage I witnessed for myself numerous times the faith and steadfastness of your congregation. I admired it greatly. I still do. On one occasion, I feared we would all perish. Your prayers and hymn singing were a comfort to us all. Never have I witnessed such faith in God's providence. The Lord has and will continue to make a way for you here in this new country."

Johanna sighed raggedly. She pushed another loose strand of hair under her cap. She turned her gaze to the glistening river and swatted at the gnats that beleaguered her face. "I fear we face an even greater storm than we did then."

"I wish there was something more I could do," John said.

"Are you not their pastor?" Johanna asked. "Can you not remind them to love their neighbors?"

John hung his head. "I do try. But I confess, I have never met a more stubborn set of malcontents in my life."

Johanna folded her arms across her chest. She'd heard rumors about the other congregations, that they were not as dedicated as the men who ministered among them. And truly, John Wesley had his hands full. His many duties took him miles in all directions, for he did not pastor one flock, but several. And with so many languages to contend with, it could not be easy to shepherd such diverse parishioners.

There had been rumors too about women. It was said that both John and Charles had spurned the bold and romantic attentions of certain women, and suffered the consequences with regard to their offended families.

"Then promise me—if we are indeed forced to leave and to abandon the colony, you will try to find someone to keep the school going." She looked at him hopefully.

"Truth to tell, the other colonists do not see it as important," he told her, his expression grim. "Perhaps you should take up the cause with the general. He has always approved of your efforts there."

She nodded. "The children are so willing and eager. If we leave, someone must take over their care—and the care of the orphans, for we could surely not take them with us wherever we go."

"I am trying to learn their tongue—it is not an easy one," John admitted. "You have the gift of languages, Miss Hus. I would that I did also."

"Perhaps your brother Charles would be willing to take over the school?"

John frowned. He tugged at his waistcoat. "I cannot say. He is unhappy here. He has already spoken with the general about returning to England. The general has become quite displeased with him, I fear."

Johanna turned away. She experienced a flash of anger toward Charles Wesley and did not want his brother to recognize it in her countenance. "Returning to England? How can that be? He has responsibilities here. Besides, did he not hear God's call to come?"

John responded with a shrug before saying, "One can be mistaken in hearing God's call—especially when eager to serve."

Her head hung, Johanna heaved a sigh. Had her father been mistaken in thinking God had called them to the New World? In her eagerness to be a teacher, to win the hearts of heathen children to the Lord, had she overlooked her true path of service? It was too upsetting to contemplate.

Chapter Ten

LOVEJOY SPRANG TO HER FEET. She looked very young in her white-strapped sandals and a cute seersucker sundress dotted with small hand-embroidered daisies. The garment must have cost the earth. Her freckled face and french braid made her look barely sixteen, but Julia knew Lovejoy already had a master's degree. Meredith had told her so. Of course, now that she was in her sixties, Julia thought everyone looked ridiculously young, especially doctors and professors. Meredith's handsome son Chase—a history professor—was a case in point.

"May we speak privately, Mrs. Foley?" Lovejoy cast a meaningful glance at the open door. Carmen sat at the front desk sorting the morning mail. In a lower voice, she added, "It's about the ledger."

"Certainly." Julia smothered a sigh. The rest of her morning, apparently, was not going to play out as she'd planned. She took a step into the outer office. "Carmen, hold my calls."

Carmen raised her eyebrows. "*Sí.*"

As Julia closed the door behind her, she paused. "Where are my manners? May I offer you a cup of coffee? Or something cold?" Meredith had purchased a small dorm fridge for bottled water and cans of Diet Dr Pepper and Coca-Cola.

Lovejoy shook her head. "Nothing for me, thank you." She waited for Julia to be seated behind the desk before resuming her own seat. There was a large paper shopping bag with handles beside her chair.

Julia wondered what was inside. "Now what can I do for you?" She gave the young woman a polite, professional smile.

Lovejoy reached into the shopping bag and removed a slim gray box with metal edges and a large sheet of thin gray paper. "This is an archival storage box and archival tissue. I brought them from the museum for you to store the ledger in." She handed these items to Julia across the desk. "After what happened last night at the meeting, I couldn't sleep a wink thinking about that historic ledger. I just couldn't. What a marvelous bit of Savannah history! It needs to be stored properly. I can't understand Meredith Bellefontaine's cavalier attitude toward it." Lovejoy blushed then to the roots of her hair. "No offense intended," she hastened to add.

"None taken," Julia replied. She was actually thankful for these items, because she too realized that every time the old leather-bound ledger was handled, it became more deteriorated. The thing was in bad enough condition as it was. "Does Beatrice know you brought this to me?"

Lovejoy shook her head. The blush on her freckled cheeks bloomed an even brighter shade of crimson. "But I'm sure she wouldn't mind. After all, she wants the journal protected too. Anything we can do to ensure its safety and historic integrity—that's a good thing."

"It's not a journal," Julia reminded her. "It's a ledger." How many more times would she have to repeat that before people finally believed her? If they truly thought it was a journal and not a ledger of household accounts, she and Meredith would have no peace as long as the ledger was in their possession.

"By chance, is it here in this room?" Lovejoy's gaze swept the office with a bright eagerness, her eyes gleaming with hope.

Julia shook her head. "But it's in a safe place," she assured her. Emphasis on the word *safe*—Meredith's office safe.

"Oh, Mrs. Foley, could I...would you be willing to let me have one little peek?" Lovejoy wheedled, leaning forward toward the desk.

Julia gave her an apologetic smile. "No, I think not."

Sitting up straighter in the chair, Lovejoy said, "Why not let me wrap it in the tissue and place it in the box? That's all. I won't even ask you to let me take it back to the museum, although I really should. You know I could take digital photos of the pages and keep the journal—I mean ledger—protected from dust and dirt and humidity and all the rest of it. That's my job, and I'm good at it."

"I'm sure you are," Julia said, smiling. The ledger was not leaving her possession until Ed and Miss Dicey had had time to discuss what to do about it. For the briefest of moments she considered allowing Lovejoy to have a look at the ledger. She was a professional, committed historian. But Julia quickly squashed the thought, realizing that if she allowed the young woman a peek then everyone else on the committee would swarm her office like cockroaches to ask for the same privilege. She explained this briefly to Lovejoy, who gave an understanding nod, but her shoulders slumped.

With a disappointed sigh, Lovejoy said, "Well, I do hope it's in a safe place." Again, her keen-eyed glance darted around the room.

"Yes, it's quite safe," Julia assured her once more.

Lovejoy remained quiet for a moment, fixing her glance downward toward her sandals. "Well, in any case, I should warn you that

I am not the only one who intends to plead for a glimpse of the Wesley ledger. Beatrice is going to implore you to allow her to see it and also Joe McGibbons. They both said as much before the meeting broke up last night."

"Thank you for the warning. I'll be on my guard." Julia gave Lovejoy an amused smile. Did this sweet young thing really think she couldn't handle Beatrice and Joseph McGibbons?

Rising, Lovejoy smoothed the skirt of her crisp sundress. "You might put Beatrice off, but Joe will trick you into showing it to him. He's quite clever."

Arching an eyebrow, Julia asked, "Trick me? How does he propose to do that?"

"I don't know how exactly," she confessed, "but he's sneaky." She rolled her eyes. "You'd be surprised how he takes advantage of Beatrice and others when he wants to borrow something from the museum collection. He's the clever one all right."

Sneaky and clever. A dangerous combination. Julia felt determined all the more not to fall for any of his shenanigans. She'd encountered his sort many times in her courtroom. He might be a smooth talker, but she refused to budge no matter what he might say or do. No one was going to handle or see the ledger again until she'd spoken with Ed and Miss Dicey. And that was final.

Lovejoy swished her way to the door, pausing as she opened it. "I do hope the ledger is safe—for your sake and that of the agency. I surely do. Goodbye and thank you for your time."

Julia frowned as she slumped back into her swivel chair. Did Lovejoy's parting words sound like a threat, or had Julia only imagined it? First, she suspected she was being followed by a nursing home orderly, and now she was imagining that sweet little Lovejoy Stewart had threatened her. Ridiculous! She needed to get to the library.

After turning to her computer, she opened the electronic ledger file and printed off a copy of her meticulous notes regarding its contents. Thrusting this into her tote bag, she checked her cell for messages from Beau. Not that she was expecting any. He was off on a fishing trip with some old college buddies. She guessed they were having a roaring great time. She smiled, wondering just how much fishing they were doing. She suspected they were enjoying a male gabfest around the campfire, recalling the good old days when they all had more hair and less money.

Stepping through her door into the outer office, Julia paused at Carmen's desk to pick up the pink "while you were out" message sheets. "Anything important?" she asked.

"*Nada*," Carmen replied with the shrug of a shoulder. "That Mrs. Enterline—she called twice—and a man named McGibbons. They refused to leave messages so it cannot be too important," When Julia arched an eyebrow, Carmen added, "They asked to speak to Meredith too but didn't leave messages for her either. I think they want to get their hands on that old ledger."

"Carmen, your intuition never fails to amaze me," Julia said truthfully. "The ledger stays here in Meredith's safe until we are ready to part with it."

"So I thought," Carmen replied with a knowing glance.

As she drove to the historic Carnegie Library on Henry Street, where Maggie Lu volunteered and where Rebecca Thompson worked, Julia realized that Beatrice and Joe were wasting no time in their campaign to seize the ledger. She wondered if theirs was a joint effort or if they were working separately without one another's knowledge. Keeping an eye on traffic, she noted that the tourists were out in droves today, especially near Forsyth Park, but the pan-handlers seemed few and far between. Too hot, she supposed. August in Savannah, what could she say? Julia found a parking space as close to the entrance as she could get and hurried up the library steps, hoping Maggie Lu could shed some light on the cryptic remarks in the old ledger. She'd been a teacher before retiring. In fact, she'd even won Savannah's prestigious Teacher of the Year Award some years back. Maggie Lu had also been volunteering at the library for ages and was a voracious reader. Julia guessed that whatever Maggie Lu didn't know something about wasn't worth knowing at all.

She found her pushing a cart with nonfiction books that needed to be reshelved. Tall and straight, not completely gray, Maggie Lu certainly didn't look her age. She wore a loose brown and black shift with cap sleeves. A matching headband completed her attractive ensemble.

"Hard at work as usual, I see," Julia greeted her.

Maggie Lu glanced up, her face beaming with pleasure. "I thought I'd be seeing you or Meredith soon enough." She gave Julia a sage look. "I presume you are here to tell me what Pastor Ed found at Miss Oglethorpe's."

Julia nodded. Noting a few library patrons strolling the stacks, she asked, "Is there some place we can talk privately?"

"Follow me." Maggie Lu pushed the book cart to the side and led the way to a small private study room. Small, windowless, and cramped, the room was hardly conducive to study, Julia thought. But it was certainly free of distractions—only a table with four plastic hard-bottom chairs, not even a cheap painting or framed print on the cream-colored walls.

With a winsome smile, Maggie Lu said, "Take a seat and tell me all about it."

Julia did, quickly summarizing yesterday's events at River View. "Ed said he'd called you when he discovered the ledger, and you recommended he call Meredith and me."

Maggie Lu smiled. "Of course. You're Savannah's finest sleuths."

"And you're a storehouse of knowledge when it comes to Savannah history. I'm hoping you can help me out."

The older woman's smile broadened. "Why, I'd be happy too, if I can."

Julia rummaged in her tote bag and retrieved the pages she'd printed before coming to the library. "I want to talk to you about treasure," Julia said. She handed the clipped pages to Maggie Lu and then rested her elbows on the table.

"Now, what kind of treasure do you want to talk about?"

Julia took a deep breath. "Something that might have been discovered back in 1736 or 1737 during General Oglethorpe's time."

Maggie Lu asked, "Why don't you talk with Miss Dicey Oglethorpe? If it involves the general, surely she would know."

"But she doesn't and that's the problem." Julia laced her fingers together.

"Mercy me." Maggie Lu quirked an eyebrow. "Maybe you'd better start at the beginning."

"I know I can trust you to keep this to yourself, Maggie Lu. It's important. We found the old ledger in Miss Dicey's home behind a secret wall panel, a secret panel even Miss Dicey knew nothing about." As she expected, Maggie Lu was surprised to hear this. "I've gone through the entire ledger, page by page, and written down everything I could read. Then I typed up my notes, and that's what you've got there. I've highlighted the one mysterious mention of treasure."

Maggie Lu flipped through the pages until she found the page with the highlighted portion. "You're thinking pirate booty, aren't you?"

Julia shrugged. "Blackbeard and pirate treasure are the first things that come to mind, I'll admit. I honestly don't know what it could be. You've lived here most of your life. But I don't recall any tales about the Wesley brothers and old Oglethorpe discovering any treasure—pirate booty or anything else. Do you?"

Maggie Lu pursed her lips, then slowly shook her head. "No, can't say I have. But then it all depends on what you call treasure." She paused a moment before adding, "I don't suppose it would have anything to do with the Moravians?"

Moravians? Julia couldn't recall much about them at all. She knew they'd been some of the first settlers in Savannah. They spoke German, came from eastern Europe somewhere looking for religious freedom, and were intent upon evangelizing the Indians. *Note to self: research Moravians.*

"No, I doubt the Moravians had anything of value," Maggie Lu said after a moment's reflection. "Unless they brought something rare and valuable from the Old World. No, why would they? I'll bet they were as poor as church mice." She chuckled. "And not popular with the rest of the colony, as I remember."

"Why was that?" Julia frowned.

"The men wouldn't serve in the militia. They did a bit of farming and opened a school for the Yamacraw children, which greatly pleased Chief Tomochichi."

Julia nodded. Some of her early Georgia history was coming back to her now. But the Moravians hadn't stayed long in Savannah. "Didn't they move north to Pennsylvania? I doubt they had anything to do with treasure."

"Maybe they found Spanish loot," Maggie Lu suggested. "Yes, that could be it. Something valuable washed ashore."

Julia considered this for a moment. "You mean items from shipwrecks?"

Maggie Lu nodded. "Exactly. Keep in mind that Spain had already settled much of Florida and Cuba long before the British settled Georgia. It's a known fact that several galleons sank off the coast during hurricanes and other storms in the early 1700s."

While Maggie Lu explained, Julia listened without comment, her attention riveted to the other woman's narrative. "The lost 1715 fleet carried millions of dollars' worth of silver plate and gold coins. Much has been recovered in recent times. Back in 2015, divers recovered hundreds of gold coins, an emerald ring, pearl earrings, and a valuable rosary made from coral beads. Now, as you know, General Oglethorpe established the Savannah colony after 1715." Maggie Lu looked at Julia inquiringly.

"Yes, that's true."

"Then it's not impossible that some of those sunken treasures washed ashore, and John Wesley, making his way from one parish to the next, could easily have discovered something on the beach."

"Yes, that's quite possible." More than possible, Julia realized. Even today folks walked the beach with metal detectors looking for stuff that had washed ashore from the so-called treasure ships. Finding a handful of gold or silver coins, a ring or even a rosary in the sand—such items could easily be concealed in saddlebags and would hardly ignite a frenzied treasure hunt, especially if John Wesley kept the discovery to himself. Digging for buried pirate treasure would attract attention. Rumors would fly, and those rumors could circulate for years and even centuries, as she and Meredith had discovered. There were no such rumors that the Wesleys discovered pirate loot.

Maggie Lu, her eyes bright, disrupted Julia's reverie with a throaty chuckle. "Maybe your treasure mystery is not such a mystery after all."

"Maybe," she agreed. "I'd forgotten about the Spanish treasure ships. You've been a big help, Maggie Lu. I appreciate it." She realized what a great teacher Maggie Lu must have been back in the day. Even now she had a way of bringing history to life.

"Happy to oblige. You're not responsible for discovering what exactly those items were, are you? Have you been hired to do that?"

Julia sighed. "No, I've not officially been hired at all. I guess you could say I'm doing this as a favor for Ed and Miss Dicey. I think the best thing for me to do is return the ledger to Ed along with my notes and have him ask Miss Dicey what she would like to do with them. Unfortunately, now that the words *lost treasure* have been uttered, a bit of a firestorm is raging through the historical society. It's hard to quench that sort of thing."

Maggie Lu shook her head. "Some folks can only imagine treasure as something with monetary value—gold, silver gems. Might be something else. You know, when I found out the Besset estate had been left to me, I was mighty surprised and donated it to the historical society. But I did take one thing for myself."

"What was that?" Julia asked, curious.

"I wanted the old chifforobe from little Harriet Basset's room. It's a pretty thing, and I think of her—my long-ago friend—whenever I see it. It's not very big—suitable for a child's things, but I keep my grandmother's linens in the drawers. That chifforobe is a treasure to me."

Julia nodded. "I understand. I consider my grandma Gertrude's cookbook, with her handwritten notes in the margin, to be a treasure, but it has no monetary value at all."

"It's a treasure all the same," Maggie Lu insisted. She pushed back her chair and rose. "I need to be getting back to work, but I'll think on it some more. If I come up with anything, I'll let you know."

Rising, Julia said, "Thanks, Maggie Lu. Ed is a bit concerned that the Wesley brothers might have been involved in something illegal. I want to be able to assure him that there's no evidence of that at all. I'm going to talk with Rebecca to see if she can direct me to diaries or letters or anything related to the Wesleys' time here in Savannah. Whatever they found, they disposed of it in some way. You've been a big help."

"You're more than welcome. May I keep this?" Maggie Lu indicated the printed pages.

Julia nodded. "Yes, that's your copy."

When Maggie Lu opened the door, she added, "I'm thinking that Mr. Charles Wesley was a bit of a prophet."

"How so?" Julia asked, turning.

"Regarding the treasure—whatever that might have been—he feared there'd be trouble. That's what the notation in the margin says. Don't know how much trouble he and his brother had on their hands because of it, but it's certainly causing trouble for you and Meredith."

Chapter Eleven

JULIA FOUND REBECCA THOMPSON AT the reference desk staring intently at her computer monitor. "I need your help with something," she told the librarian, who greeted her with a smile.

"That's what I'm here for," Rebecca said. Julia knew she could count on Rebecca's help as well as her discretion. Without revealing any specifics about the ledger or the events that had taken place in the past two days at River View, Julia explained what she was looking for in regard to the Wesley brothers possibly discovering treasure of some sort.

Rebecca arched an eyebrow. "I've never heard of anything along those lines, but I could suggest some possible sources for you to use in your research."

"That would be great," Julia said.

"Have you consulted the archives at the historical society?" Rebecca asked.

Julia wrinkled her nose. "Not yet. I'm saving that as a last resort." She knew if she showed up asking for information about the Wesleys and General Oglethorpe, word would get around. Before she could say "boo," Beatrice would be dogging her heels to find out exactly what she'd been researching.

Rebecca slipped her stylish red glasses down her nose and peered over the top at her. "You've piqued my curiosity, I must say."

"Anything you can suggest regarding the brothers' contact with the Moravian settlers would be helpful too."

"This is getting more interesting by the minute," Rebecca said, scribbling a few notes on a pad of paper.

"And if John Wesley kept a journal regarding his pastoral calls, I'd like to know how to access that too," Julia threw in. She knew Ed kept a log of sorts regarding the people he called on and those who came for counseling. Perhaps John Wesley had paid a pastoral call upon a dying buccaneer who confessed the whereabouts of a buried treasure while on his deathbed. Anything was possible. Her phone vibrated then, and she reached into the outer pocket of her tote bag. She guessed it might be Meredith, but it was Ed. "I'm sorry, I have to take this," she apologized.

"Come back in an hour or so," Rebecca told her. "I'll have something for you then."

Julia gave her a thumbs-up before stepping away from the reference desk. "Ed, hi," she said quietly into the phone. "Everything okay?"

"It's about the ledger." His tone sounded anxious. "I think I should come get it and take it to Miss Dicey. I had no idea its discovery would cause such a firestorm. Naomi and I don't feel right about getting you and Meredith muddled up in this matter. We've been praying for you—for both of you."

"Thanks for the prayers, Ed. I'll take them all day every day."

"So, I can come get the ledger and there won't be any hard feelings?"

"The ledger isn't mine," Julia reminded him. "If you and Naomi would feel better keeping it for Miss Dicey, that's fine with me—and no hard feelings."

"Have you had time to make all the notes you wanted to?" he asked.

"Almost." Julia made her way to the foyer. There was no one in sight. "I've written down everything that's decipherable. But those pages that are stuck together—I couldn't tell you what's written on them. Probably nothing important. As I told the Inquisition, other than that one cryptic notation about J finding treasure and O being intrigued, there's nothing other than lists of expenditures. Well," she paused hesitantly, "there is one other curious notation. Do you know anything about John Wesley and a woman named Irene?"

"Couldn't say," Ed told her. "Something else to research, I suppose. Why do you ask?"

"There's a single notation that reads *J to Irene*."

"That's it?"

"That's it."

"I have no idea who she might be. Ask Maggie Lu." Then with a heavy sigh that came out loud and clear over her cell, Ed said, "Send me an invoice, Julia. I want to pay you for your time."

"Don't worry about that. We can discuss it later," she assured him. "When do you want to come by and pick up the ledger?"

"Later today or maybe even tomorrow," he told her. "Naomi has given me quite a scolding over this."

Julia chuckled. The pastor's wife was as efficient as she was kind and a fierce protector of those in the church flock.

"Call before you come. Meredith or I need to be there to remove it from the safe for you."

"I'll do that, and thanks so much for understanding, Julia." He sounded relieved.

"Not a problem," she assured him. "Oh, by the way, Meredith and I got a look at that secret hiding place upstairs in the old nursery this morning, the one Miss Dicey mentioned."

"Oh?"

"Tamika Simms showed it to us. She was at the house helping her grandmother with the housecleaning," Julia explained.

"Was it bigger than the secret panel downstairs in the music room?" Julia could hear the hint of excitement in his voice.

"Yes, much bigger, but there were no forgotten treasures or even old ledgers inside. Just cobwebs and dust."

"What a shame. I wish there had been something stashed away that would have shed further light on Charles Wesley's mysterious comment about the treasure."

"I know. Me too." After a pause, Julia asked, "Do you think Miss Dicey would let me go back to the house sometime to poke around a bit? When the weather is cooler perhaps—that place is hotter than blue blazes in this heat."

"I could ask her," Ed offered. "I could also let Ruth know so she could turn on the air-conditioning and the overhead fans ahead of time."

Julia thanked him and said she'd see him later. Glancing at her watch, she realized how late it was. And her stomach gave a rumbling reminder that she hadn't had lunch yet. She punched in

Meredith's number on speed dial. When her friend answered, Julia asked, "Have you eaten lunch?"

"No, I'm just now heading into the office," Meredith told her. "Carter called. He knows about the ledger."

"What?" Julia could hardly believe it. "Meet me at the Downhome Diner. I'm starving. I want to hear all about what Carter had to say, and I have something to tell you too."

***

Charlene Jackson greeted them warmly as she seated them at their favorite table. "Talked with your mama this morning," Julia told her. "She's helping me out on a little project of historical significance."

The diner's owner, tall and lithe with iron-gray hair curled tightly against her head, gave Julia a bright smile. "Mama is a walking almanac, that's for sure, and she has more energy than most people half her age."

"I'll agree with that," Meredith chimed in.

Over Greek salads with quinoa, Julia pressed Meredith to tell her about the phone call she'd had with her eldest son Carter.

"He's still worried about me, even though I told him there's no need," Meredith insisted. "He thinks I've revived Ron's old agency because it's my way of keeping his memory alive. He's also annoyed that I have a gun permit."

"That's what the law requires," Julia said, taking a stab at a black olive.

"I reminded him of that, and then he asked if I'd ever fired a weapon before." Meredith gave a mild snort. "I was married to a cop, for heaven's sake. Ron took me shooting before the boys were ever born."

"Maybe it was his way of trying to find out if you've fired the weapon since reopening the agency," Julia suggested.

"Happily no, and I pray the Good Lord won't put me in a situation that I might have to." Meredith shrugged. "I accused him of watching too many late-night *film noirs*—those old black-and-white films about hard-boiled private investigators starring Humphrey Bogart and Victor Mature." She took a swig of iced tea.

"Did you tell him that most of our business these days is frankly boring and routine—other than your recent kidnapping escapade? That our main source of income is conducting background checks for businesses that are hiring new employees? Even churches and schools do that now. We have a very respectable clientele."

"Yes, I told him, and that's when he mentioned the ledger." Meredith shook her head. "When I asked him how he'd heard about that he simply said he had his sources." She fixed Julia with a sharp stare. "You don't think he's pumping Carmen for information, do you?"

Julia pointed her fork at her friend. "You can put that worry right out of your pretty blond head. Carter may try to pump Carmen for information about the agency's business, but that gal is too sharp to fall for it. Trust me."

"Carter also wanted to know if we're off on another treasure hunt, and I told him no. We aren't." Frowning slightly, Meredith added, "We aren't, are we?"

"No, we're not," Julia assured her. "I am merely doing some historical research into the Wesleys' time here in Savannah. That's my story, and I'm sticking with it."

After a quick, piercing glance, Meredith said, "Good." She poked at her salad. "Carter reminded me that people kill for gold, and he didn't want me to get involved. Honestly, he thinks I'm a helpless baby. I was a history major in the good old days. I know all about people killing—and being killed—for gold. But everyone is making a mountain out of a molehill. There's no gold, no treasure. I'm certain of it. Mostly." Her shoulders slumped.

Julia reached across to pat Meredith's hand. "I know you're frustrated by Carter's concern, but think of it this way—he loves you. He cares. He doesn't want you to get hurt or to bite off more than you can chew."

"I know. But he must surely know that if we need help I can touch base with Ron's old colleagues with the police. He was popular, and they remember him fondly. I run into some of them now and then at the supermarket, and we still exchange Christmas cards."

When her friend lowered her gaze and fell suddenly silent, Julia said, "You still miss him, I know."

"Every single day," Meredith replied, her blue eyes watering. "Not a day goes by that I don't thank the Lord we were married for so many wonderful years." Then straightening, she said, "Now what did Maggie Lu have to say about the ledger?"

"Not much—yet," Julia replied. "I gave her a printout of what I'd been able to glean from the ledger and asked her to look it over. She did suggest that John Wesley may have found gold doubloons or something washed ashore from a Spanish shipwreck. She said there'd been a notable one in 1715. That would fit the time period."

Meredith nodded. "There have been lots of shipwrecks along the coast in the past centuries. Think of all the Spanish treasure ships that sunk when caught in a hurricane. We've had enough of those too over the years."

"She also mentioned a group called the Moravians."

"What about them?" Meredith wanted to know.

"Haven't a clue. They were part of the group of colonists here in Savannah during the Wesleys' time," Julia said.

Meredith chewed in silence, apparently contemplating any connection between the two.

Julia added, "Ed called. He's stopping by the office sometime today or tomorrow to pick up the ledger. He and his wife are beside themselves for involving us in such a ruckus. I also asked if I could get back into Miss Dicey's place and have another look around."

This time, Meredith put her fork down. "Do you realize how big that mansion is? All sorts of things could be hidden all over the place—under loose floorboards, tucked away in bookshelves, and even buried in the garden."

Julia shrugged. "Why was the old ledger hidden away in the first place? Who'd put it there?" She glanced at her watch. "Oh, look at the time. I've got to get back to the library. Rebecca is putting together a list of possible resources for me to consult. I've gotta dash."

"Go on then," Meredith told her. "I'll get this." She indicated the remains of their salads with a whirl of her fork. "I'll see you back at the office. I'll be intrigued to see what Rebecca suggests."

When Julia returned to the library, she pounded up the front steps and raced to the reference desk. She'd promised to be back in an hour, but it had been a lot longer than that. Rebecca rose from the computer station when she saw her approach. Breathlessly, Julia apologized, "I know I should have been here earlier. I hope I didn't inconvenience you."

Rebecca shook her head. "It's fine, Julia. I'm running a bit behind myself, and so I told your associate when he stopped by asking for the information I'd promised you. He seemed pretty disgruntled when I told him I didn't have it ready yet, but I sent him on his way all the same."

Julia's shoulders tightened. Her stomach did an awkward flip, and she suddenly felt uncomfortably queasy. "My associate? A man, you say?"

It was Rebecca's turn to look alert. "Yes, a man." Her brow knit with worry.

"He told me you'd sent him over to pick up whatever I was putting together for you."

"Thank goodness you sent him away empty-handed." Breathing heavily, Julia asked, "Can you describe him? Tall? Short? Young or old?" She couldn't help wondering if Jubal or Joe McGibbons had been following her for some nefarious reason to do with the ledger.

Rebecca wrinkled her brow as though trying to remember details. "A white man, short and on the stout side, with a thin mustache."

"Oh my word!" Julia's hand flew to her chest. It had to be that Tate guy—the orderly from Miss Dicey's nursing home.

"So I take it you don't have a male associate working with the agency?" Rebecca looked troubled.

Julia shook her head. "Just Meredith and Carmen Lopez, our receptionist. But I'm fairly certain I know who he might be." She just wasn't so sure how she was going to handle it.

Frowning, Rebecca said, "I won't ask you exactly what you're researching. Obviously it relates to General James Oglethorpe and the Wesleys, but I hope one day you'll fill me in. I have the distinct feeling there's a delicious secret or conspiracy or *something* very intriguing going on."

"There is, sort of, but I'm not at liberty to discuss it yet," Julia admitted. "I appreciate your help and your discretion more than I can say. When I'm able to do so, I'll spill the beans. I'll tell you everything over lunch at the Olde Pink House—my treat."

Rebecca's eyes lit up. "You're on. I love their shrimp and grits and the crab cakes." She returned to her desk to retrieve a neatly typed list. "Here's a list of books, articles, and digital resources that may prove helpful in your research."

"Thanks so much." Julia glanced over the list quickly before slipping it into her tote bag. She could hardly wait to get back to the office to begin her research.

"You be careful," Rebecca warned. She glanced around the library, her frown returning. "I don't like the idea of some guy following you around."

"Neither do I," Julia replied. "And I intend to do something about it."

Chapter Twelve

"HE DID WHAT?" MEREDITH'S CHEEKS flushed brightly. She appeared both shocked and angry when Julia told her about the man with the mustache following her to the library.

"I guess he's been following me all day, and I didn't even realize it," Julia told her. "What kind of PI am I?" She slumped into the chair across from Meredith's office desk. She'd kept the door open as Carmen had left early for a dentist appointment. She reached into her tote bag and retrieved the typed list Rebecca had given her. "This is what he was after, apparently." She thrust it forward.

Taking it, Meredith gave the list a quick perusal. Glancing up, she huffed, "The nerve of that guy! Pretending to be a part of our agency." She handed the list back to Julia. "I wonder why he was so eager to get his hands on this list. There's no harm done though."

"Except to my nerves," Julia pointed out. She was not normally a nervous or high-strung person, but this incident had left her feeling a bit skittish. It had thrown her off her stride. She had to admit that.

Meredith fiddled with the tape dispenser on her desk. "So what are you going to do about him?"

Julia shrugged. "I'm not sure. My first inclination was to head straight to the nursing home and demand an explanation. Then I thought better of it. You know the old maxim about acting in haste.

Besides, I doubt if I asked them for his name and contact info they'd willingly provide it."

Meredith pursed her lips and asked, "Do you think Jubal put him up to it?"

Julia cocked her head. "I hadn't thought of that. Maybe." After a moment's silent consideration, she added, "Maybe Jubal offered him money."

Meredith gave a mild snort. "I hope he didn't promise this Tate guy a portion of the nontreasure."

"Nontreasure?" Julia grinned. Her friend had such a way with words. "Wasn't it good old P.T. Barnum who insisted there was a sucker born every minute?"

Nodding, Meredith added, "If this guy is teaming up with Jubal in hopes of becoming rich on long-lost pirate treasure, he's going to be mighty disappointed. We'd all do well to remember all those Sunday sermons about laying up treasures in heaven and not worry so much about earthly treasure."

"Amen," Julia replied.

"The thing is," Meredith went on, "even if you could discover exactly what Charles Wesley was referring to, and even if you could confirm that a treasure was found and disposed of in some way, it will be hard to quash the rumors. Sometimes this sort of thing takes on a life of its own—you know, like the Spanish conquistadors and their search for the Seven Cities of Gold."

Julia sighed. "Heaven help us if this turns into one of those endless treasure hunts, like the one going on up on Oak Island in Nova Scotia. Two hundred years and counting." She shook her head and sat up a little straighter. "I am not going to let this slide. I'm going to confront our Mr. Tate and demand an explanation."

"I just don't understand why he's involved in the first place," Meredith said.

"I told you he was eavesdropping when Ed and I were talking with Miss Dicey, and I know for certain he saw the old ledger in her lap." Sighing, Julia added, "And perhaps you're right. Jubal may have put him up to something."

Meredith leaned forward. "Speaking of ledgers, Ed stopped by to pick it up right after I got back after lunch. I was a bit surprised to find it had been placed in an archival box with tissue and everything. How'd you get hold of that?"

"Lovejoy Stewart stopped by with it," Julia told her. When her friend arched her eyebrows in surprise, she added, "She was hoping to take a sneak peek at the ledger, but I refused to allow her to do so. I feared she'd brag about seeing it and then Beatrice and company would all come traipsing in here demanding the same privilege."

"Maybe Beatrice sent her over with the box hoping you'd give in," Meredith suggested.

Julia shook her head. "Lovejoy said no one knew about her coming."

"Did you show her the ledger?"

"No, but she tried her best to persuade me to do so," Julia admitted.

Meredith laced her fingers on her desk. "She's not the only one in a persuading mood. After Ed left, Beatrice called asking to stop by to see the ledger too. So did Joe McGibbons. Jubal called twice.

When I told them we no longer had the ledger in our possession, I got varied responses."

"I'll bet you did," Julia said with a half smile. Meredith giggled.

"Beatrice sputtered and chuffed. Joe went silent. I did tell Jubal that I'd handed it over to Ed. He seemed rather pleased, I'd say."

"So you didn't tell Beatrice and McGibbons what you'd done with the ledger?" Julia probed.

Meredith shook her head. "I only told Jubal. I figured he's related to Miss Dicey and had the right to know."

"I can't say I'm sorry to see it gone. The ledger is Ed's headache now."

"Oh, don't say that, Julia," Meredith protested. "You make me feel guilty."

Julia laughed. "That's just what Ed said. His wife, Naomi, told him he should be ashamed of himself for saddling us with the burden of that old ledger and getting us involved in the matter in the first place. If he didn't feel guilty after last night's so-called unofficial meeting, he sure felt that way when he called me."

Meredith sat back in her chair. "He seemed rather relieved to have it back in his possession but also a bit concerned about what to do with it now. Surely he won't give it to Miss Dicey? Oh, Maggie Lu called wanting to take a look at it too. She said she'd gone over the transcription you'd given her earlier this morning and just wanted to see for herself what all the fuss was about."

"What did you tell her?" Julia asked.

"As Ed had already picked it up, I told her she'd have to ask him. I'm sure there won't be a problem." She paused briefly before adding, "She mentioned something about sunken ships and Moravian colonists too. Then she said the ledger was a bit of a hot potato. There was a lot of *tsk-tsk*ing when I mentioned last night's meeting with Beatrice and the gang. She said she thinks a lot of people are going to be disappointed before all is said and done."

"I think Maggie Lu is right—as usual." Julia rose and smoothed the front of her slacks. "I'm going back to see Miss Dicey and talk to her about sunken ships and Moravian colonists—not that I think she will know a thing about them, but all the same, I'll leave no stone unturned."

"And what about Mr. Tate?" Meredith asked, looking up at her.

"I'm going to have a word or two with that gentleman too!" Julia declared.

"Do be careful, Jules." Meredith pushed her chair away from the desk. "Do you want me to come with you?"

Julia shook her head. "No, you're up to your earlobes with employee background checks." The agency needed the money, she knew. Meredith was still paying for the office remodeling. "I can manage. And don't worry. The home is a very public place—plenty of residents and staff members to see and hear what is going on, should our Mr. Tate decide to get ugly."

Meredith accepted this with a shrug. "Are you going to come back here when you're finished? I want to show you something."

Julia cocked her head to one side. "Can you show me now?"

"No. It's something I found in Ron's office, tucked away at the back of a drawer in that old battered file cabinet I want to get rid of."

"Something related to one of his cases?" Julia probed.

"I'm not sure. It's rather puzzling, to tell the truth." With a wave of her hand, Meredith said, "Go on. It can wait. I'll show it to you later."

Julia gave her friend a penetrating glance. She remembered their conversation at lunch, how Meredith had choked up a bit when mentioning her late husband and how much she still missed him. Julia had a hunch it was going to be another long day—maybe even another long evening. It didn't matter. She was used to those ever since law school. Who wanted a sit-around-do-nothing retirement anyway? Not her, thanks. No, ma'am. She wasn't the rocking-chair-on-the-porch sort of person.

***

The late afternoon heat was merciless as Julia pulled her car into the nursing home parking lot. How grateful she was for air-conditioning! How did the folks in the Old South ever survive the summers here? She dropped her keys into her tote bag and slipped the straps over her arm. Then she reached for the box of specialty chocolates she'd purchased for Dicey Oglethorpe. Julia loved Adam Turoni's chocolate shop on Bull Street with its clever library ambiance. The truffles were arranged by alphabetical order on bookshelves, along with novels and reference books. Even the candy boxes were shaped like hardcover books. She'd selected a few choice pieces for Miss Dicey along with a honeycomb dark chocolate bar—filled with fresh wildflower honey from the Savannah Bee Company—to give to Meredith later. She'd even indulged herself, selecting one divine milk chocolate peanut butter cup out of the refrigerated display case.

Seeing the pleasure on the elderly woman's face when she slipped off the ribbon and opened the box made Julia so thankful that she'd gone to the shop on the spur of the moment. Grateful she'd given in to the impulse.

"I can't remember the last time I received a box of candy," Miss Dicey drawled. "Why, I do declare they are almost too pretty to eat. Almost," she added with a playful smile.

"You can eat them or not, Miss Dicey," Julia told her. "They are yours." She noticed the dark shadows under the older woman's eyes, the paleness of her skin. With trepidation she wondered if Miss Dicey was losing sleep over the discovery of the old ledger. Julia surely hoped not. Maybe she was coming down with something. She had a white knobby sweater tossed around her shoulders and a long-sleeved mint-green and white striped shirt over white gauze slip-on slacks. She looked more frail than she had the last time Julia had seen her.

"Oh lands, where are my manners?" Miss Dicey declared. She held out the open candy box. "Help yourself, Julia."

"No, thank you. I helped myself at the candy store," she confessed, "and enjoyed the treat immensely."

Miss Dicey chuckled. "Well, I may just enjoy looking at them for a while before I eat one. I must say, they are works of art."

"They are indeed," Julia agreed. She leaned forward in the blue vinyl chair she'd occupied the last time she'd visited. "I want to thank you again for allowing me to plunder your garden. I did go out there and help myself to a snip of your glorious clematis. I dug up a few lily of the valley pips too."

"Oh, I am so glad." Miss Dicey's face lit up. A strand of snow-white hair grazed her cheek. "You go on back any time you like. No one's there to bother you."

"Except for Ruth Simms," Julia told her with a laugh in her voice. She explained her encounter in the garden with the house-keeper—armed with a wooden-handled broom.

Miss Dicey chuckled. "Ruth's a gem. I miss her. She comes by now and again. Not as often as I'd like. But then, she's no spring chicken either, and she has a big family to look after."

"I'd like your permission to go out to River View again sometime to explore the house," Julia said. She would not disturb the older woman's peace of mind by explaining that she hoped to snoop around for anything that might be connected to the ledger or the one curious notation about treasure.

"Why, of course you may," Miss Dicey said. Then, sighing, she added, "It's a grand old house, if I do say so myself." Her stooped shoulders slumped lower still. "Or it was in its day."

"It's still grand," Julia told her. "It just needs a little TLC—some tender loving care will put it back in tip-top shape."

Miss Dicey said nothing, but gave her a wan smile.

Julia returned her smile. "I couldn't help wondering if someone in your family—in days gone by—boasted of discovering gold coins or other artifacts washed up on the shore somewhere."

Appearing slightly discomforted, Miss Dicey frowned. Julia felt a twinge of guilt for putting the elderly woman on the spot like this. Miss Dicey might feel embarrassed if she couldn't remember or even reluctant to share if she did remember something pertinent to the question. Miss Dicey wasn't on the witness stand, and Julia silently reminded herself of that.

Raising a frail hand to her withered cheek, Miss Dicey asked in a quavering voice, "What sort of artifacts do you mean?"

Julia felt bad for the old dear. Was it cruel to push her to remember something that she might not be able to? And what if the Oglethorpes knew nothing about any shipwreck bounty? Would

Miss Dicey worry herself into a lather trying to remember something that had never happened?

"To be honest, Miss Dicey, I don't really know what sort of artifacts, if any, might have washed up on the beach long ago. Maybe a jeweled pendant or a rosary strung with pearls, or perhaps even Spanish coins."

Miss Dicey's frown deepened. "I never heard of such—not in my lifetime certainly."

"What about back in the day when General Oglethorpe was here in Savannah?" Julia pressed.

"Why, how could I know that?" Miss Dicey asked, one hand fluttering.

Julia hesitated. Just how far should she push? If the general had never written anything down, Miss Dicey wouldn't know anything at all. But if he had kept a journal or diary or even old letters, those could prove useful. Still, she could see that the woman was agitated. She would let it drop. "It's nothing to fret about, Miss Dicey. I'm curious, that's all."

"Is it important?" Miss Dicey asked, turning watery blue eyes upon her.

"Not in the least," Julia assured her. She hoped that was true. "I'm intrigued by family stories that get passed down through the years, that's all. After seeing your secret panels, my imagination has run amok." She gave Miss Dicey a broad smile. "I love old family tales and mysteries."

The tension eased from Miss Dicey's thin shoulders. Her frown slipped too. Julia realized that the woman must have been quite pretty in her youth, with her wide blue eyes and fair hair.

"We have many old family tales, as you call them," Miss Dicey told her, "but not all of them are pleasant, to be sure. My daddy put down his favorite hunting dog, Old Fly. She got the bloodlust, don't you know, and went after the chickens. And then one day, she plucked my cousin Eddy Belle's three-month-old infant right out of her cradle. Scared us all half to death. That dog carried the baby halfway to the riverbank before Daddy caught up with her. He came back with the baby but not the dog."

Julia's heart lodged her throat. What a horrible story! "Was the baby all right?"

Miss Dicey nodded. "But Daddy stomped around the rest of the week, silent and grim-faced. He wasn't just sad, you see. He was angry because Old Fly had betrayed his trust. Daddy never could abide disloyalty." She turned her head then to gaze out the window, lost in old memories. "I remember the man who tried to sell Daddy a piece of land on Tybee Island. Daddy didn't like him." She stopped abruptly. "But that's a story for another time."

Julia said nothing for a while before changing the direction of the conversation. "Do you have any family tales about the Moravians?"

Miss Dicey looked at her, astonishment evident in her expression. "Moravians?"

"The early colonists from Germany, I think," Julia tried to explain. "They were rather like the Amish."

With her head cocked to one side, Miss Dicey said, "You are mighty full of questions today. Can't say I know a thing about Moravians or Amish either. You'd better talk with Maggie Lu King or your friend Meredith Bellefontaine. They know everything there is to know about Savannah's history, between the two of them. I never was much into history. Music was my love." She lifted a blue-veined hand to indicate the framed sheet music on the walls. Sighing, she added, "I'm rather tired."

It was a polite dismissal, Julia knew. She rose immediately. "Thank you for your time, Miss Dicey. I've enjoyed our visit."

"And thank you for this." Miss Dicey indicated the elaborate candy box in her lap. "Bless your heart." She gave Julia a half smile.

"Goodbye." Julia slipped the straps of her tote bag over her shoulder and left. She hoped her questions hadn't stirred up unpleasant memories. She knew she'd be haunted by the story of Mr. Oglethorpe's dog for some time. As she passed through the corridor, Julia stopped at the nurses' station. "I'd like to speak with Mr. Tate," she said to the middle-aged woman in a white uniform behind the counter. Her flame-red hair was obviously from a bottle and her blue eye shadow had been smeared on with a heavy hand. Her nametag read SHILOH HOLMES.

"He's not working today," the nurse replied with a polite smile. "May I take a message?"

Not working? Oh yes he was. He just wasn't working at the nursing home, which allowed him plenty of time to dog her heels, Julia thought with a spark of anger. "No message," she replied with a polite smile of her own. "I'll speak with him another time."

As she made her way to the exit, she noted several residents milling around near the door to what appeared to lead to a dining hall. She quickly glanced at her watch. Yes, it was nearing five o'clock. Almost suppertime, she supposed. Pushing her way out the double front doors, she heaved a sigh. Still too hot outside. She could already feel perspiration beading across her forehead and her upper lip. As she made her way to her car, she glanced around, searching for any sign of Tate. It made her feel distinctly uncomfortable that he'd followed her to the library earlier that day. She couldn't figure out how, and she certainly didn't understand why.

❧ Chapter Thirteen ❧

Johanna Hus
Georgia Colony, March 1737

Johanna felt a stirring of joy as she lifted her voice in song. Joy was truly a gift of the Holy Spirit and so much richer than mere happiness. The small congregation stood in good voice this evening. John Wesley had joined them, as had become his habit the past several weeks when his pastoral duties allowed. His bold voice blended in harmoniously with the others. He enjoyed the brethren's Saturday evening song service and had said as much to Johanna and others on more than one occasion.

Earlier there had been hot sassafras tea and cake. Cake! This luxury had been a result of General Oglethorpe's most generous gift of twenty pounds of brown sugar—a treasure, to be sure—come all the way from the Barbados on the supply ship sent by the trustees. Sister Katarina had baked two cakes in her large, heavy skillets. She'd laced the batter with gratings from her prized nutmeg, the size of a shriveled apricot pit. She then sprinkled brown sugar on the top of the batter to caramelize in the heat of the hot, well-stoked oven.

General Oglethorpe had delivered a young pig too, which had lifted everyone's weary spirits. Johanna tried not to complain about the monotony of the food—rice, salted meat, and the ever-present cornmeal mush. Sometimes she found herself repeating the mealtime blessing with an ungrateful heart. She missed bread mostly, but wheat was rare and butter too costly. Even fresh meat was an infrequent treat, although Chief Tomochichi occasionally provided them with venison or grouse in appreciation of their work at the school.

Katarina's cakes served to make the Saturday song service a festive occasion. Johanna was thankful John had been able to join them. She delighted in their friendship but tried not to appear overeager for his company, fearing others would mistake her feelings of friendship for something more romantic and tease her shamelessly.

They were in the midst of a rousing rendition of "All Creatures of Our God and King," following light refreshments, when young Elias flew into the main cabin, eyes wide, hair wilting from the heat, hat askew. "Riders coming with torches," he gasped.

Johanna's gaze flew to the window. She instinctively placed one hand over her pounding heart. A feeling of dread settled upon her shoulders like a heavy woolen cloak. It must surely be after six o'clock, she guessed. The daylight had faded, but it was not yet dark. She shifted her anxious gaze to John Wesley. He stood watching her with a concerned frown pinching his brow, yet from the depths of his fine clear eyes flashed fire. He shared her worries about the school and the

*children, she knew. Had colonists come with bad news?
Perhaps an attack by the troublesome Spaniards? Or did they
intend mischief of their own making? Johanna could think of
only two reasons why riders should come at such an hour—to
relate important news or to do wickedness. But in the twilight, surely they would be recognized and a report would certainly be made to the general.*

"I shall go out to meet them," John volunteered.

*"You'll not go alone, Herr Wesley," one of the carpenters
said, stepping up beside him.*

*Sister Katarina clasped Johanna's elbow with a trem-
bling hand. Johanna feared her own hands shook also, but
she forced herself to give the other woman's a reassuring
squeeze.*

*"Shall we step outside, Herr Wesley?" Brother Konrad
asked. He gestured toward the open door.*

*Johanna rose without thinking. She needed to know what
the men were going to talk about. But Brother Konrad had
noted her rising. "Remain seated, Sister," he said, not ungently.*

"But I—"

*"Remain." His stern look brooked no protest. Obediently,
Johanna sat down again, watching the men step outside,
shutting the door behind them.*

*A low murmur rippled through the congregation.
Johanna felt several pairs of eyes fixed upon her. She noted a
frown or two as well. Sister Reidel would no doubt chastise
her later for being too forward. The woman had taken over
what she considered to be a mother's role in Johanna's life.*

She meant well, Johanna supposed, but at the age of twenty-one she did not so much need a mother as a friend.

The prickly heat rash that had broken out under her arms and along her waist earlier in the week now felt unbearable. She realized her spirit felt just as prickly. The peace that surpassed all understanding eluded her. What would happen if the disgruntled men from Savannah forced them to leave the colony? It caused her pain to think about it.

Brother Hansbeck stepped forward to lead the congregation in another hymn, but the effort of those assembled seemed half-hearted at best. Then the door opened once more, and Brother Konrad and John Wesley reentered, looking concerned. A hush fell.

Brother Konrad cleared his throat. "I believe it is a deputation from Savannah. They may force us to leave—this very night."

"To demand that you do so," John said, so no one misunderstood.

"Oglethorpe knows of this?" one of the men asked.

"I am certain he does not," John admitted. "And he would not condone such actions if he did know of it. I would ride back to alert him, but I think it best that I stay to bear witness to"—his glance swept around the room—"what shall happen here this night."

"We appreciate your concern," Konrad told him.

"Should we prepare for violence?" one of the women asked. Johanna could hear the fear in her strained voice.

John shrugged. "I cannot say for certain, but I fear it may come to that."

"*Then let us meet them outside and have the women and children remain here,*" *Konrad suggested. There were murmurs of assent from the men and quiet moans of despair from some of the women. Johanna's pulse raced. She could not help being fearful. Even the Lord's disciples had been afraid at times. She knew fear was a normal, human reaction. Courage, however, was a choice. She silently prayed with great fervor for courage and steadfastness.*

One of the men protested, "They cannot ask us to leave. We have a right to be here."

"Is it only because we are not willing to serve in the militia?" Brother Reidel asked.

John Wesley spoke before Konrad had time to answer. "It is true that the others have no legal right to ask you to leave, but I feel certain they will cause such mischief that you will wish to go sooner or later. I know these men. They are malcontents with little Christian spirit. They are likely to burn your homes, your crops."

"And the school?" Johanna heard the despair in her own voice. The neat little schoolhouse with its benches and her desk made of crates and smooth planks—how she loved it!

"They may well start with the school," John replied, giving her a look of heartfelt sympathy. It took all her resolve not to cry. How could they? What right did they have to destroy something the community so proudly built without asking for their help? "I will do all I can to prevent any destruction," he promised. Johanna wanted to believe that his efforts would prove fruitful.

The sound of thundering hooves grew louder. Johanna could see wavering torchlight through the gap in the window curtains. How many men had come to terrorize the little community?

"We must prepare," Konrad said. "Let us first pray for the Lord to help us."

One at a time heads bowed. Brother Konrad prayed, then Brother Reidel. Even John Wesley prayed, asking for God's protection and for the Holy Spirit to soothe the savage hearts and minds of the intruders. Johanna's throat felt dry. Her head pounded, and her heart raced. She was still afraid.

"Give thanks to the Lord, for He is good," intoned Brother Reidel.

The congregation responded in unison, "His loving-kindness endures forever."

Outside, the dogs barked a warning as the men and horses clattered into the heart of the community. Brother Konrad said, "Herr Wesley, Brother Reidel, come with me. We shall meet them outside. Turning to the rest of the congregation, he said, "You shall resume the service, dedicating yourselves to prayer and hymn singing. Those of you with small children feel free to leave through the back door."

Johanna glanced around the room. There were precious few children now of any age. The ones who did not die shortly after birth did so later from one fever or another. Young Rosina Wetzel had been the most recent casualty of Georgia's harsh climate, and she not yet three years old. Her grave was now located beside that of Johanna's own father. The three

Yamacraw orphans no longer lived among them either, for Chief Tomochici had taken them back to be raised by the tribe.

"Shamed him into it," Sister Reidel had commented dryly when he'd come to the school to collect them. He'd seemed puzzled by the colonists' kindness toward the youngsters who had been left to fend for themselves when their parents had died from illness. Johanna had resented the chief's decision, but perhaps it had been for the best, considering the trouble the congregation had been having with the other colonists. Still, Johanna missed the youngsters, their round, dark-eyed faces smiling up at her shyly as she shared with them her favorite Bible stories.

"I think it would be safer for us to stay together," Sister Reidel spoke out. She turned her worried gaze upon the mothers present. The women nodded.

"As you wish," Brother Konrad agreed. He opened the door then and stepped outside to meet the men on horseback. John and Brother Reidel followed him. Johanna pulled away from Katarina's fearful grasp to make her way to the nearest window, which contained no glass but only simple linen curtains. Tugging one aside, she could see a dozen mounted men, most of them carrying torches. Were those solely to light the way between here and Savannah? Or did they intend to use them to start fires? She noticed how straight and tall the brethren stood near the door. They did not appear daunted by the intruders. Surely the Good Lord was with them. With a surge of pride, she pressed closer to the window to be able to hear the conversation.

"*Why have you come? What is your purpose here at this time of night? Where is General Oglethorpe?*" *Brother Konrad called out.*

The first man dismounted. His white stockings seemed to glow in the torchlight. His long leather vest strained across his barrel chest. With his sneering lips and beak of a nose, he appeared cruel to Johanna. "*We don't need the general for what we have to do,*" *the man replied in a gruff tone.* "*We came to demand you clear out. You don't deserve to be part of the settlement. You won't take up arms against the enemy.*"

"*We have no enemies,*" *Brother Reidel spoke up.*

"*What of the Spaniards?*" *one of the mounted men called out.*

"*The Spaniards are not our enemies,*" *Brother Konrad reminded them.* "*And neither are the English. I believe the feud between the two is longstanding.*"

There was a ripple of humorless laughter among the Englishmen. Johanna knew the settlers in Savannah feared the Spaniards. John had explained that there existed a treaty between the two, but it was not respected by either side. The settlers in Savannah lived in a constant state of uneasiness, fearing an attack from the sea. Every plausible report of a Spanish vessel off the coast caused panic.

"*Every man must go to war and fight for the safety of the settlement,*" *the barrel-chested man spoke up.* "*If you do not agree to do so, we will burn down your houses and kill you—if the Spaniards don't kill you first.*"

"You may indeed do so, if your consciences permit," Brother Konrad said quietly, "but it is against our conscience to join in battle."

"Have you forgotten that General Oglethorpe has promised these good people exemption from the military?" John spoke up. "They only claim that liberty which he pledged to them."

One of the other mounted men spoke up in a more conciliatory tone. "Come, sir, give us the names of the men among you who might be called upon in case of an attack."

"I refuse," Brother Konrad said boldly.

The barrel-chested man shouted, "You are cowards!"

Johanna heard no more of the conversation, for Brother Dober began singing, "A Mighty Fortress Is Our God" in his rousing baritone. The others joined in, making a valiant effort. Johanna, keeping her position beside the window, squeaked out a verse. Her throat felt so dry, her lips chapped. She could hear the continued murmur of men's voices out front, the barking of a single hound. As an unmarried woman without a father, Johanna had little to say in the matters of the community. She must abide by the decisions of the elders. She must leave Georgia if the elders determined they must leave.

As she swept the room with her anxious gaze, she wondered if perhaps they should leave before they all became too sick, slighted, and cast down. The prospects of success here seemed to become less and less. They had come to America to

pursue religious liberty and to evangelize the heathen. If not allowed to do either, why should they stay?

She turned away from the window as Brother Dober began the second verse of the hymn. Then she heard a gunshot.

Chapter Fourteen

"ARE YOU SURE YOU HAVE time to take a look at this stuff?"

Meredith regarded Julia with a questioning frown as she wiped the empty coffeepot before leaving the office for the day. "It's Wednesday. Don't you have a prayer meeting at church this evening?"

"I'm not going tonight. Too frazzled," Julia admitted. "It's been quite a day." She'd already shared with Meredith her conversation with Dicey Oglethorpe and told her, with a disappointed slump of her shoulders, that the mysterious Mr. Tate had not been at work. "Beau's not due back for a few more days, so I don't need to get home at any particular time." She thrust her chin toward Ron's old office. "Is what you want to show me in there?"

Meredith shook her head. "It's on my desk." She led the way to her office and indicated a cardboard banker's box. "As you know, I took a lot of stuff out of Ron's office before the remodel, trying to decide what needed to be kept—like tax papers and client files— and what I could pitch. Carmen's done a great job digitizing all of the old phone records and some other things as well. But this"—she placed her hand on the lid of the box—"this has me stumped. I don't know what it is, and I don't know what to do with it."

"Let me take a look," Julia offered, removing the lid. Inside she found dozens of manila file folders stuffed with old newspaper clippings about an incident that had taken place decades ago in Pickens County. Noting the dates on some of the clippings, Julia realized the incident had occurred long before Ron had become a cop. He must have been just a kid at the time. The case involved two men and two women living together in a tumbledown house with a veritable zoo of goats, dogs, rabbits, chickens, and cats. Authorities couldn't determine exactly what had happened. Trespassers had discovered the bodies in the dilapidated ballroom—complete with piles of dried animal dung and cobwebs in the corners. The sheriff suggested it had been some sort of murder-suicide pact.

"Have you shown these files to the boys?" Julia asked. Carter and Chase were fine young men. They'd been a big help and a comfort to their widowed mother. She knew Meredith valued their insights.

"Yes, not long after Ron died," Meredith told her. "Neither of them had any idea why their dad saved all this. But we agreed it seemed odd that Ron would save so many old clippings about one particular crime. As you can see, the incident happened a long time ago."

"Do you think Ron had been working on a cold case? Or maybe he'd known the victims when he was a boy," Julia suggested. "Relatives, perhaps?"

Meredith shrugged. "I didn't recognize any of the names when I glanced through the cuttings, and Ron never mentioned any relatives living in Pickens County." As Julia continued to peruse the contents of the files, Meredith added, "Ron occasionally talked to me about his cases—without violating confidentiality, of course. He always valued my insights and suggestions. But he never breathed a word about this one."

"The amount of clippings and notes is rather surprising if he only had a casual interest," Julia observed. There were even county road maps and crime scene photos. Had Ron made copies of the originals when he was on the force? It seemed quite obvious that Ron Bellefontaine had been consumed by the case. But why? And for how long? "Do you think someone with the police turned these over to him and asked for his input?"

"I don't know," Meredith admitted, "but no one has ever called to ask for the files back. Maybe it's going to be one of those mysteries that never gets solved. Maybe the Charles Wesley notation will be another one."

"Not if I can help it," Julia said, thrusting her chin forward with determination. As she rummaged through the clippings, notes, and old photos, a thousand ideas ran through her mind, sparking her imagination: who, what, when, where, and why? The journalist's five Ws. Giving her friend a sidelong glance, Julia noted a sadness in her expression. She knew Meredith still missed Ron and occasionally wondered aloud why the Lord had taken him so soon. Julia never knew what to say.

She didn't know what to say about this collection of clippings and case notes either. Ron Bellefontaine had certainly been intrigued by the crime. Why else would he have gone to so much trouble to collect all this stuff over such a long period of time? She wondered if Meredith hoped she'd offer to look into the matter, perhaps to solve the case—if in fact there was a case to solve. After so many years of law school and serving as a criminal judge, Julia knew she was good at this sort of thing. She had connections too. If she and Meredith solved a cold case—one that Ron had considered important for some reason—would Carter cease hassling his mother about reviving the agency? Julia knew he'd prefer to see Meredith as president of the local crocheting club rather than heading up a detective agency.

"Meredith, I don't know what to say," Julia confessed. She dropped all the clippings she'd removed back into the box. "I have no idea why Ron would have saved all these. Is this something you think we should pursue?"

Looking slightly flustered, Meredith answered, "I don't know. I really hadn't thought about that."

"Good," Julia declared. "We're too busy to tackle this now. For all we know, the case has been closed since Ron's passing."

"Perhaps." Meredith shrugged and fell silent.

After a pause, Julia said, "Hear that? It's my stomach growling. Let's go get something to eat. My treat. How about fish tacos at that little place near Jones Street?"

"I'm not really very hungry," Meredith told her, tucking a blond curl behind one ear.

"You need protein," Julia said. "*I* need protein," she amended. "Besides, if you wither away from not eating, Carter will say the agency is too much for you to handle. You don't want to face that argument again, do you?" She arched an eyebrow.

Meredith shook her head. "All right. Fish tacos it is." She replaced the lid on the banker's box and shoved it to the corner of her desk. "I'll drive."

"Fine. You can bring me back here afterward so I can pick up my car," Julia said. Outside, she glanced over her shoulder once or twice before opening the passenger's door of Meredith's SUV. Not observing anyone suspicious lurking around, she opened the door and slid across the hot vinyl seat. She'd sure be glad when the cooler fall weather arrived.

On the way to the tiny hole-in-the-wall restaurant, Julia and Meredith talked about the background checks Meredith had been doing and what a big help Carmen was proving to be. Julia wondered if she shouldn't give their able receptionist some of the research responsibility on the Wesley-Oglethorpe case. Rebecca had provided a long and thorough list. It might be wise to ask for Carmen's help. And perhaps it would also be wise to alert Carmen to the possibility that someone might be following her or Meredith. Was that likely?

Julia was still pondering this possibility when Meredith found a parallel parking space near the eatery. Lost in thought, Julia nearly stepped into the path of an oncoming car as she and Meredith attempted to cross the busy street. Meredith seized her arm, jerking her backward. As the vehicle whizzed by, Julia's heart jolted with fear. "That was a close call," she muttered, embarrassed by her carelessness. She glanced at Meredith. Her friend's face was pale.

"Julia, watch where you're going," she gasped. "You scared me half to death."

"I was thinking about Tate," Julia admitted, dashing across the street in Meredith's wake. "It gives me the creeps to think he might be following us around." She glanced over her shoulder, staring up and down the street. The sidewalks appeared thronged with the usual summer tourists. A young father pushed past them with a toddler in an umbrella stroller.

"Female intuition?" Meredith asked with humorless smile, as she opened the restaurant door for her friend. A small bell tinkled overhead, and a blast of frigid air wafted toward them.

"Call it what you will. It's just a feeling I can't shrug off."

"It's not like you to be so skittish. You're one tough cookie, Julia," Meredith told her after they'd been seated at a table near the window. "I don't doubt your feelings or your intuition. If you think you're still being followed, then you probably are." She glanced around the restaurant as though looking for some suspicious character. "If you want to stay in my guest bedroom while Beau is out of town, you'd be more than welcome."

Julia gave her friend a broad smile. How like Meredith! Always looking out for others' comfort and safety. "Thanks, Mere, but I'll be fine."

They sat at an empty table and perused the menu. Julia had begun to feel rather sheepish. She'd been letting her imagination run wild. Then the uncomfortable thought surfaced again. "Meredith, if I'm being followed, maybe you are too. And Carmen. People do crazy things when it comes to long-lost treasure. The mere mention of it can bring out the worst in people. Look what happened with the Blackbeard treasure case. You were kidnapped, for heaven's sake. Promise you'll be careful?"

"I promise." Meredith gave her a reassuring smile.

Julia decided to put business aside during their meal and talk about something other than their current caseload and Ron's odd collection of newspaper clippings. Instead, she asked about Meredith's grandchildren, knowing how much her friend loved nine-year-old Kinsley and her brother Kaden. She'd chosen the right topic, for

Meredith quit brooding while she happily shared the latest news about dance recitals and soccer practice and an upcoming shopping trip with her daughter-in-law Sherri Lynn and the kids for back-to-school clothes.

When they paid their bill and left the restaurant, Julia was more relaxed than she'd been in days. She paused to smile at a tall, red-haired woman walking a tiny white teacup poodle. Someone brushed against her and tugged at her tote bag. Startled, she whirled around. A teenager in a navy blue hooded sweatshirt attempted to pull her bag from her arm. She gasped as he tried to shove her off balance in an attempt to make her drop the tote bag. Immediately, she went into self-defense mode, thrusting an elbow sharply at the attacker's chin and throat and kicking at his knee-cap with her foot. This time the teen grunted, released the bag, and raced off.

Meredith hurried forward and clutched Julia's arm. "Julia, are you all right?"

"Yes, I'm fine. That kid tried to snatch my bag." Her heart pounded, but she realized she was more outraged than scared. "Did you get a good look at him? I noticed the dark sweatshirt and blond bangs in his face. Who wears a hoodie in this heat?"

Julia allowed Meredith to take her by the elbow and move her out of the pedestrian traffic on the sidewalk. People had stopped to see what the commotion was all about. A man hurried up then, red-faced. He had snow-white hair and wore a bright yellow polo shirt. "You all right, lady?" he asked, addressing Julia.

She straightened her shoulders. This was embarrassing. "Yes, thank you. I'm fine. No harm done."

"I saw what happened. That kid ran right past me. I tried to grab him as he raced past, but he was too fast for me."

"How kind! And they say chivalry is dead." Julia gave him her warmest smile.

The man flushed an even deeper shade of scarlet. "I got a pretty good look at him though. Shaggy blond hair, faded jeans, navy blue hooded sweatshirt. Something on the front of it, but I didn't have time to make it out. Might have been a logo of some sort."

"So it was definitely a boy?" Meredith asked. "I couldn't be sure—not in those baggy jeans and the loose sweatshirt. The bangs made me wonder if it might have been a girl. And she couldn't have been more than fifteen or sixteen years old."

"Hard to tell," the man admitted. "The kids these days go in for that unbecoming androgynous look. Don't know what the younger generation is coming to." The man caught his breath and shook his head before pulling out his wallet. He handed Julia a business card. "The name is Riley—Sev Riley. If you file a police report, they may want to speak with me. I own a print shop down by the river. They can reach me there."

"You think you could identify the kid in a lineup?" Julia asked.

Riley nodded. "I'm pretty sure."

Julia thanked him, and then she and Meredith made their way to the car. "Are you going to file a police report?" Meredith asked.

"No," Julia told her. "Nothing was actually stolen. Besides, we don't even know if the would-be thief was a boy or a girl. There isn't enough information for the police to follow up on."

"My thoughts exactly," Meredith said, unlocking the car. "That kid must have been desperate, but for what? It isn't that dark out and the streetlights have come on so he could have been easily identified, especially with all the people on the sidewalks. What was he—or she—thinking?"

Julia said nothing. She wasn't so sure the would-be thief wanted money at all. When Meredith demanded to know what she was thinking about, Julia said, "What if that kid tried to snatch my tote because he thought I had the Oglethorpe ledger in there?"

"What?" Meredith gave her friend a quick, disbelieving glance as she pulled out slowly into traffic. "How on earth would he know that?"

"Somebody could have told him. Someone could have offered him money to steal my tote bag," Julia proposed.

They remained silent, lost in their own thoughts for most of the ride back to the office. Finally, Meredith spoke up. "I wonder if the man with the mustache bribed the kid to steal your bag, hoping to get his hands on Rebecca's list. After all, he did attempt to coax Rebecca into giving him the list—pretending to work with you in the agency."

Julia chewed the corner of her bottom lip. "You're right. It could be him."

"Are you carrying the list in your bag?" Meredith wanted to know.

Julia shook her head. "I left it on my desk at the office. But the would-be thief couldn't know that, nor could the man with the mustache. If that's what the kid was after, then I've been followed just as I suspected."

An uncomfortable silence followed before Meredith said, "The Lord was watching over you today."

Nodding, Julia felt a bit of a lump in her throat. Yes, the Lord had been watching over her. She uttered a silent prayer of thanksgiving. "First thing tomorrow morning I need to go back to the nursing home and confront that guy Tate. I need to get to the bottom of this before something worse happens."

Chapter Fifteen

JULIA WOKE UP EARLY THURSDAY morning, ready to tackle the elusive Mr. Tate in his den—or at the nursing home, if he was working there today. She opened her double closet doors to peruse her wardrobe. She needed to do some power dressing—no cute capris or feminine frills this morning. Mr. Tate had a lot to answer for, and she intended to see that he did. She would wear one of the many suits she'd accumulated during her career days. But what color? That was the dilemma. She placed her coffee mug on top of the dresser and looked over her clothes. Charcoal gray was certainly businesslike, but red was a power color. She had two black suits, which might make her appear rather intimidating. Did she want to intimidate the mustache man? Maybe. On the other hand, her cobalt blue suit was very becoming, and blue was said to be a friendly, disarming color. Did she want to appear friendly and disarming when she approached the mustache man? Julia wasn't so sure.

She wasn't even sure what she was going to say when she finally met the man face-to-face. She hadn't slept well last night because she'd been rehearsing the imagined conversation in her head. Besides, she still felt mildly outraged about the attempt to steal her tote bag. Julia had almost called Beau on his cell last night to tell him what had happened. She changed her mind immediately. Beau would abandon his buddies quicker than she could say Rhett Butler. He'd speed all the way home to make sure she was all right, and Julia didn't want him to do that. No, Beau didn't get to spend time with these old buddies very often, and she would not ruin his vacation.

The landline rang then, startling Julia out of her reverie. Frowning, she glanced at the digital alarm clock over by the bed. It was just after seven. What early bird was calling her at this hour?

She answered the phone tentatively. "Julia, I'm so sorry to call so early, but there's been a break-in at the church."

It was Pastor Ed.

Julia let out a small gasp. "Ed, I'm sorry to hear that. Have you called the police? Is there much damage? Is anyone hurt?"

"No one's hurt, thank the Lord. It must have happened late last night or in the wee hours this morning. The police are here now. There's not much damage, but…" He paused significantly.

"But what?" Julia prompted, tucking the phone's receiver between her ear and shoulder.

"The burglar stole the Wesley ledger."

Julia felt her stomach begin to knot. "Oh no, Ed."

"And last night's offering was taken too. A little cash and a few checks. I don't know how much all total. Greta hasn't come in yet this morning to prepare the deposit."

Julia could hear his heavy sigh. The church secretary would be horrified by the theft. Julia hoped Ed would call Greta to warn her so she wouldn't be startled at the sight of squad cars in the church parking lot. Longing for a fortifying gulp of coffee, Julia glanced around for her abandoned mug, saying, "I'll be right over. Call Greta and give her a heads-up. You don't want the poor woman to have a panic attack when she arrives for work and sees the police there. I'll call Meredith."

"Thank you, Julia. You can't imagine how awful I feel about this," Ed mumbled.

With all thoughts of the nursing home orderly dismissed from her thoughts for the time being, Julia tapped out Meredith's number. Her friend answered with a demanding, "What's a six-letter word beginning with O that means futile or functionless?"

"Otiose," Julia replied after a moment's thoughtful consideration.

"Spell that, would you?" Meredith asked. Julia did so. There was a brief silence while her friend penciled in the letters.

Then Julia shared the news. "There's been a break-in at my church. Ed said the burglar took some cash and the ledger."

"The Oglethorpe ledger?" Meredith asked. Julia could hear the shocked disbelief in her friend's voice.

"Yes, I'm going over there now. Thought you might want to come too. The police are already there."

Meredith groaned. "Give me half an hour before you come by to pick me up. This is awful! Beatrice is going to pop her cork, and I shudder to think what Jubal will say or do."

Julia pondered that uncomfortable thought as she dressed hurriedly in peach seersucker pull-on pants and a white roll-sleeved T-shirt. Never mind the business suit this morning. Mr. Tate would have to wait. She swallowed a hasty breakfast of yogurt and blackberries sprinkled with flax seed before heading over to Meredith's.

Outside it was overcast and muggy. The weatherman had predicted a 60 percent chance of rain. Julia hoped the police would quickly investigate the outside of the church building to locate the point of the burglar's entry before a rain shower washed away any likely clues.

"Looks like it's going to rain," Meredith said, opening the passenger side door of Julia's car and sliding into the seat. She looked fresh and crisp in turquoise capris with a coordinating white and blue notch-neck tunic. "I hope the police can get their investigating done before it does."

"I was thinking the same thing," Julia admitted.

"Do you think it's a coincidence that someone tried to snatch your tote bag yesterday and today your pastor calls to tell you the ledger has been stolen?" She gave Julia a questioning glance.

Julia shrugged. "Honestly, I don't know what to think."

By the time they reached the church, the police were wrapping up their preliminary investigation of the crime scene. They'd located the point of entry, dusted for prints, and taken photos, the pastor informed the women. "I'm not sure if any of this is really going to help retrieve the ledger." He led them through the church foyer and into the church office and then opened the door to his private office.

Meredith gasped, and Julia exclaimed softly, "Oh no." The room had been ransacked and no mistake. One glance at Ed's distraught face, and Julia knew just how shaken he was.

"The doorknobs—inside and out—were wiped clean. No prints." He indicated the damage to the main door of the outer office.

"Where was the ledger?" Julia asked.

Ed lowered his head. His shoulders slumped. "It was lying right here on my desk." He turned to point. "I'd been looking through it—wearing a pair of disposable gloves, like you suggested, Meredith. I wanted to have a quick look before turning it over to Miss Dicey or Jubal. I never suspected someone would try to steal it."

"Was your door locked?" Meredith asked, glancing around at the pastor's small office.

"No," Ed admitted, his tone apologetic. "I usually don't lock my office door. Greta keeps the main office locked when we're out, and of course the church entry doors are locked when we leave."

"How did the burglar or burglars get in?" Julia wanted to know.

"Through the back door in the fellowship hall," Ed replied. "I can tell you, I'm flummoxed, simply flummoxed. Who would do such a thing? I feel just sick about it." He ran a hand through his closely cropped hair. His dark brown eyes appeared troubled. "Nothing like this has ever happened during my tenure as pastor. I'm so sorry."

"You needn't apologize to me," Julia said. "It didn't belong to me. It belonged to Miss Dicey. I guess we'll have to tell her."

"I suppose so." Suddenly, his face lit up, as though he'd had an unexpected idea. "What if the thief sends a ransom note? We could buy it back, perhaps?"

Meredith gave him such a look of pity that Julia laughed out loud. "Don't hold your breath, Ed," she told him. "I can't imagine anyone stealing an old ledger and holding it for ransom. One look at all those monetary entries and they'd realize the ledger has little other than historical value."

"What's this?" Meredith pointed to broken bits of a shattered blue glass on the corner of the secretary's desk in the outer room.

"A broken vase. It was donated to the church by Miss Dicey upon the occasion of the congregation's fiftieth anniversary," Ed explained. "It's the only thing damaged, that I've been able to see. I picked up all the pieces, but I'll have the janitor run the vacuum just in case there are small bits under the desk or behind the bookshelves that I didn't get. Otherwise, things are just topsy-turvy."

"It looks like one of those vases on display in Miss Dicey's music room at River View," Meredith observed.

"Yes, so you can imagine how valuable it is...was." Ed shook his head. "I guess it got broken when the intruder pushed his way in. Like I said, as far as I can tell, it's the only thing that got damaged. Most of this"—he indicated his office—"looks as though the intruder simply threw things around for effect."

Julia frowned. "Where was the vase kept exactly?"

Ed pointed to a bookcase on the far wall. A uniformed police officer entered the main office then and paused beside the secretary's desk. He held some forms in his hand. Seeing him, Ed said, "Will you ladies excuse me?"

"Certainly." Julia took Meredith by the elbow. "We'll be in the kitchen, Ed. I need a cup of coffee."

Julia led her friend down the corridor to the fellowship hall and into the kitchen. Someone had already brewed a pot of coffee, she noted. Ed apparently, as there didn't seem to be anyone else in the building. After retrieving two white mugs from one of the kitchen cabinets, Julia poured a cup for herself and one for Meredith. "I can't help feeling responsible for the ledger," she admitted. "Even though I don't think it has any monetary value, nor do I think we'll find the so-called treasure mentioned in it, the ledger dates back to 1735, which makes it historically significant. In a way, I feel like I've let you down—because I've lost it." She handed Meredith a mug of steaming coffee.

Meredith placed a hand on Julia's shoulder. "It's not your fault. Put that thought right out of your head." After taking a sip, Meredith added, "I suppose Miss Dicey will have to be told about the theft today, and Jubal as well."

Julia heaved a sigh. "I don't envy Ed that task at all." She took a gulp of coffee and placed the mug on the counter. "I want to have a look at that door to see how the perpetrator got in." She made her way to the back door. It was apparent that the police had already dusted for prints as the doorknob—inside and out—was covered with dark graphite-based powder. "The lock will have to be replaced," Julia observed. "No fingerprints. Someone had the forethought to clean up after himself, and yet he left a mess in Ed's office. That broken vase puzzles me too. The thief had to go out of his way to break it. It was nowhere near the door so it couldn't have been broken accidentally."

"I don't think kids would remember to wipe away prints," Meredith said. "There's no tagging with spray paint, no shattered windows. Someone went straight for the pastor's office. I think they knew what they wanted—the offering or the ledger or both. Kids didn't do this."

Julia opened the door and stepped outside onto the narrow paved sidewalk that led from the back door to a small parking lot. A pair of neglected lilac bushes hunched on either side of the door. It was just beginning to drizzle. Surveying the area, Julia supposed this was the perfect place to break in to the church building. No one would notice. There were no security cameras and no streetlights to illuminate this pocket of the property. Had the perpetrator done his homework ahead of time, casing the joint, as they used to say in the old detective movies?

As she turned to go back inside, a glint of something underneath one of the bushes caught her eye. Julia bent down. It appeared to be three small gold-colored links and a broken clasp. With her finger, she pushed around in the moist soil but couldn't find anything else. Someone had lost a necklace, perhaps. Or part of a chain? She pocketed the bits and went back inside. She and Meredith finished their coffee and then filled a cup for Ed. They carried it to his office and learned that the police had given the pastor a copy of their preliminary report so he could file a claim with the church's insurance company. Perusing it, Julia noted that while Ed had listed the broken vase and missing cash, there was no mention about the loss of the ledger. "Will you file a claim?" she asked.

Ed shrugged and took a sip of coffee. "I guess I should notify the deacons first. I'm not sure what our deductible is— pretty hefty, I'd imagine. They might not want to file a claim. We'll just absorb the loss of cash and the vase, I suppose. When Greta gets here, I'll have her call a locksmith right away. But the ledger…" He shrugged again.

"Who knew you had the ledger here?" Meredith asked.

"Naomi, my wife, of course," Ed told her. "My secretary. Any one of a dozen church volunteers who came in and out of the office yesterday might have noticed the archival box on my desk. Maybe."

"Jubal knew," Meredith reminded them. "I told him so on the phone when he called yesterday. And I'll bet he told Beatrice."

"If Jubal knew, he could have told any number of people," Julia pointed out. "And Beatrice could have mentioned it to Lovejoy Stewart or someone else on the committee who knew about the ledger in the first place. That means we need to include Jubal and the others on our list of suspects. Any one of them could have stolen the ledger."

"Surely not!" Ed nearly choked out the words. "I can't imagine anyone at that unfortunate committee meeting sneaking into my office to steal the ledger."

"I can," Meredith said with a vigorous nod of her blond head. "The lust for gold is a strong overpowering force."

Sighing, Julia dropped into the chair next to Greta's desk. Her thoughts buzzed like a swarm of bees. She needed to go someplace quiet and have a good long think.

Watching her, Ed gave a mirthless chuckle. "Julia, I can hear those wheels a'turnin'. Thank y'all for coming. I realize now there's nothing you can do, but it's nice to have your moral support all the same. We started out in this adventure together, but now it's come to an end."

"Why do you say that?" Julia asked.

"The ledger is gone. The thief might toss it in the trash, if it doesn't crumble in his hands first."

Julia noticed that the mention of the historic ledger disintegrating caused Meredith to wince.

"So now we'll never know what it was all about," Ed went on, hands shoved into his pockets.

"Don't forget, I made a copy of all the legible words and entries, and I took digital photos, so we still have that to go on," Julia pointed out. Still, she grieved the loss of the old ledger. If some careless person tried prying apart those pages that had been stuck together, valuable tidbits of Savannah history would be lost forever.

Ed let out a breath of air. "I'd forgotten about that. So we still have *something.*"

Then an unpleasant thought tickled the back of Julia's thoughts. If someone had ransacked Ed's office, someone might decide to ransack the agency's offices too. At that moment, the church secretary breezed in through the open door of the office. Her shirt and slacks appeared slightly damp. Raindrops speckled her dark hair. Greta Kinkaid took one look at the doorknob smudged with fingerprint powder and the broken vase bits on her desk before throwing up both hands. "I can't believe this! Nothing like this has ever happened before." Walking past Meredith, Greta peered into the pastor's small office. "Unbelievable! Someone needs a good spanking, that's what."

Julia rose from the chair beside the desk. "Greta, can you tell at a glance if anything else has been broken or taken from your office?"

"Not that I've noticed right off," Greta admitted. "I'm surprised they didn't take the pastor's laptop or any of the office equipment."

Ed chuckled. "I can't imagine anyone running off with that bulky paper cutter or the copy machine."

"It's not funny, pastor," the secretary said, dropping her purse onto her desk and plopping down into her swivel chair. "It gives me palpitations."

"You're right. I shouldn't joke about it," Ed admitted. "They stole last night's offering. By any chance do you know how much was in the envelope?"

Greta shook her head. "I didn't count the money or the checks. It wasn't a lot though. Mostly small bills and some twenties, for sure." Turning to Julia, she added, "I noticed those in particular because someone had colored in Andy Jackson's nostrils with red ink." She rolled her eyes. Then turning back to the pastor, she said, "I rolled them up and put a rubber band around them, just like I always do. Then I put the roll in a manila envelope and closed the clasp. I always do that too," she said, looking from Julia to Meredith. "I placed the envelope on the pastor's desk so we could count the money and prepare the deposit slip first thing this morning."

"For once I'm glad there wasn't a lot of money in the offering plate," Julia said.

Shrugging one shoulder, Greta said, "A lot of folks give online. We don't get as much in cash or checks as we used to. Maybe it's a good thing."

Meredith turned to Ed. "If there's nothing further we can do, Pastor, I need to get to my own office today. Keep us posted, won't you?"

"And if you need us for anything, don't hesitate to call," Julia added.

Ed shook their hands. "Thank you, ladies. I'll be in touch."

As they said their goodbyes, Greta leaned over to pick up something from under her desk. "Julia, did you lose an earring?" She held out her open palm to reveal a large braided silver hoop.

Julia hesitated for a fraction of a second before snatching the earring from her hand. "No, but I think I know who did. Thanks, Greta. Bye now." She waved briefly before grasping an astonished-looking Meredith by the elbow and hastily leading her out the front door of the church.

Chapter Sixteen

"SO WHOSE EARRING IS IT?" Meredith pointed to the silver hoop in Julia's outstretched palm. They sat in the car in the church parking lot. Rain dotted the windshield. It seemed the weather couldn't make up its mind if it really would pour or simply drizzle.

"You don't think it looks familiar?" Julia regarded her friend with one quirked eyebrow.

Frowning, Meredith peered closer at the piece of jewelry. "It does actually, but I can't think where I've seen it before." She picked it up with two fingers to examine it more closely.

"It's identical to the ones Tamika Simms was wearing yesterday."

Meredith's eyes widened. She dropped the earring into Julia's open palm. "Surely you don't think Tamika broke into the church?"

"No, I don't," Julia replied. "But that doesn't mean she wasn't here for some reason or another."

"So are you thinking...?" Meredith paused, giving Julia a frown. "Are you thinking she broke in to steal the ledger and the cash?"

Julia stared down at the earring. "First, we need to find out if indeed Tamika is missing an earring. If she is..." She left her supposition unfinished.

They returned to the agency's office without Julia dropping Meredith off at home first. "I can walk home later, or Carmen can give me a ride," Meredith had insisted. "Besides, I really want to finish up as many of those employee background checks as possible before the week is out."

Julia didn't argue. She was eager to get started on the list Rebecca Thompson had provided regarding connections between Oglethorpe, the Wesley brothers, and unspecified treasure—if in fact there were any connections. They found Carmen already at the office, updating client files. She'd made a pot of coffee and brought a box of fresh doughnuts.

"You're an angel!" Julia exclaimed, selecting a cream-filled one topped with chocolate. The yogurt breakfast had worn off long ago.

"I second that," Meredith chimed in. She helped herself to a cinnamon twist.

Carmen gave them a cocky grin. "Sí, I know it." She smoothed the front of her daffodil-yellow sundress with both hands. Over coffee and doughnuts, Julia explained what had happened at New Beginnings.

"I got Meredith's text," Carmen said. "She told me there'd been a break-in and you two would be late coming to the office."

Julia pulled the earring from her pocket along with the broken clasp and placed them on Carmen's desk. "Put these in a plastic baggie or an envelope, please. I may have use for them later."

"This is nice," Carmen said, picking up the earring. "It looks expensive. I bet whoever lost it will want it back."

"But what's this?" Meredith pointed to the clasp and links attached to it.

"I found it outside in the dirt by the back door where the perp entered the building," Julia explained. "It might be important, but then again, it might not." She licked a bit of chocolate from the corner of her mouth.

"So what are you going to do about the earring?" Meredith wanted to know. "It could belong to someone who attends your church."

"Perhaps," Julia acknowledged. "But Greta thought it was mine. That means she didn't easily recognize it as belonging to somebody else. Obviously, it wasn't on the floor yesterday when she left the office. Otherwise, she would have noticed. So, I'll start with Tamika Simms because I know she has a pair like this."

Meredith sighed. "I'm hoping—no, I'm *praying* it isn't hers. I like Tamika. She's a personable young woman. It would break Ruth's heart to discover her granddaughter is a thief."

"And who is this Tamika?" Carmen asked. She reached for her mug and filled it with coffee.

Meredith explained.

"You think she is a burglar?" Carmen asked, frowning.

Julia shrugged. "I have no idea, but I'm going to find out. I'm just not sure how to do it tactfully. I wouldn't want to offend Ruth."

"Why not call your pastor and find out if Tamika came to visit him yesterday?" Meredith suggested. "In all the flutter of excitement regarding the break-in and the police investigation, he may have forgotten to mention it."

"If the pastor says no, then call this Tamika and ask if she's lost an earring," Carmen added.

"And if Tamika admits she's lost an earring?" Julia asked, turning her gaze from Carmen to Meredith. She could already imagine the awkwardness that would follow Tamika's admission. Her stomach tightened at the prospect.

Carmen shrugged. "Then you tell her you found the earring at your church. Don't say anything else. The ball will be in her court. She'll have to give you an explanation of some sort, sí?"

"Carmen's right," Meredith agreed, wiping the cinnamon sugar from her fingers with a napkin. She walked over to tap the thermostat. "Our next move will depend on what she says." She held up one finger. "Either she'll say yes, she's lost an earring or..." Meredith held up a second finger. "Or she'll say no, she hasn't lost an earring."

With an elaborate eye roll, Carmen said, "This detective stuff—it's not so hard." She plopped down in her swivel chair and crossed her tan legs.

Meredith chuckled. Julia shook her head. The young woman was incorrigible. But she loved her. Julia slipped her cell phone from her tote bag and made the call to Ed. He quickly replied that Tamika Simms had not paid a visit to the church office the day before or at any other time. When he asked why she wanted to know, Julia avoided answering by responding with a vague, "Talk to you later." Turning to Meredith, she said, "Tamika didn't visit the church yesterday or at any other time." To Carmen, she quipped, "What now, Dick Tracy?"

Carmen frowned. "Who is Dick Tracy?"

Meredith laughed. "Now you will prove just what a valuable employee you are, Carmen. I want you to call Tamika. Tell her you work for our agency and let her know we've found her missing earning and that she may come by to pick it up."

With a gleam in her chocolate-brown eyes, Carmen asked, "Are we setting a trap?"

Julia felt a smile tugging at the corner of her lips. "Not exactly. But this is such an unusual piece of jewelry, I'm pretty sure it belongs to her. We'll just have to wait and see what she says."

Meredith threw her hands up in the air. "I just can't imagine Tamika breaking into the church to steal the ledger. The cash, maybe. But even that's doubtful. Why would she risk losing a possible basketball scholarship over a handful of cash? And she doesn't even know about the ledger, so why steal it? The whole idea is ludicrous."

Carmen held out her hand toward Julia. "Give me her number. I'll call. The suspense is killing me."

"I don't have her number," Julia admitted. "But I could get it from Ed."

"Wait a second," Meredith said, straightening. "I might have her grandmother's phone number in my old Rolodex from my historical society days." She ducked into her office. Casting a sidelong glance at Carmen, Julia took advantage of her partner's absence to readjust the temperature. Meredith returned a short while later with a small off-white card. She handed it to Carmen. "It's a landline number. I hope it still works. I called her once or twice when the committee needed to get into the mansion to decorate for a fundraiser and Miss Dicey wasn't home."

While Carmen made the call, Julia finished up her doughnut and went to her own office to drop her tote bag in the chair beside her desk. She retrieved the list Rebecca had compiled for her and gave it another quick glance. There was a lot of work to do. The burglary at the church had messed up her plans for the day. She felt a pulse of irritation. Who stole the old ledger? Surely not Jubal or Beatrice. They weren't stupid enough to commit a crime to get their hands on it, were they? Neither would Lovejoy Stewart. A sudden idea popped into her head then. Julia rushed into the outer office.

Meredith, seeing her, raised a finger to her lips. She stood next to Carmen's desk. The sassy receptionist was wrapping up the phone call. In her most pleasant professional tone, she said, "Yes, ma'am, the agency office is open until five o'clock." After a brief pause, she added. "Thank you so much. Goodbye now." Smiling, Carmen hung up the phone, saying, "That was Ruth Simms. She's going to have Tamika call regarding the lost earring—which she didn't know anything about, if that matters."

Julia sighed. "Now we wait."

Meredith sighed too. "I sure hope it's not Tamika's."

"Me too," Julia admitted. When Meredith returned to her office to place the phone card back in her Rolodex, Julia followed her. In a near whisper, she asked, "What if the burglar is the mustache man?" She folded her arms across her chest and waited for Meredith's response.

Meredith gave her a blank stare.

For a moment, Julia wondered if her friend had forgotten all about the elusive Mr. Tate, the nursing home orderly. Surely not! "You remember, don't you? Mr. Tate, who works at Miss Dicey's nursing home."

"You think he stole the ledger?"

"I'm simply picking your brain," Julia told her. "Do you think he could be a possible suspect?"

"I suppose so," Meredith said with hesitation. She dropped into her desk chair.

"Of course he is," Julia insisted. "He followed me to the library and tried to get hold of the list Rebecca prepared. He also followed Ed and me from the home after we visited with Miss Dicey. It wouldn't take a rocket scientist for the man to figure out where Ed serves as pastor." She began to pace. "I'm sure he was eavesdropping on our conversation with her. He must have heard us mention the ledger and ask about the treasure."

"This is getting to be a rather sensitive case that will require tact and discretion," Meredith said. She knitted her fingers together on top of her desk. "You can't just come out and ask the man if he robbed your church. Besides, how would he know Ed had the ledger?"

Julia pursed her lips. Stopping to place her hands on her hips, she admitted, "I haven't figured that part out yet."

"You were going to hunt the man down today, weren't you?" Meredith cocked her head to one side.

"Yes, I was." With a wry smile, Julia added, "I was trying to figure out which of my suits would be appropriately intimidating when Ed called to tell me about the break-in. I don't want to go to the home looking like this." She glanced down at her casual attire.

"Why not?" Meredith smiled at her. "You look nice. You always do."

"I don't want to look nice. I want to look authoritative."

"That's the legal eagle coming out in you," Meredith teased. Then on a different note, she added, "Have you considered Joe McGibbons as a suspect?"

"That's a thought." Julia frowned. She wrapped a strand of hair around her finger. "Maybe I should. Lovejoy did warn me specifically to beware that gentleman, that he's the sneaky sort."

"He's also clever," Meredith pointed out. "On second thought, I doubt he'd break into Ed's church and leave a mess. He'd have used a hairpin or screwdriver or some professional gadget to get in without anyone being aware that he'd done so. He'd be neat—like a cat burglar."

"You're right," Julia agreed. "And I doubt he'd steal that meager amount of cash from the offering either. The ledger, yes, money, no. Unless he thought that would throw everyone off his trail."

Carmen came to the door then, rapping lightly. "Julia, your cell is ringing."

Julia walked briskly to her office. She hoped it wasn't Ed. Had he told Miss Dicey or Jubal about the missing ledger? If so, she and Meredith had better brace themselves for a flood of phone calls. She shuddered imagining the harangue they would get from Beatrice when—if—she learned about the theft.

Surprisingly, it proved to be Maggie Lu. "Good morning, Julia. If you've got a bit of time, would you mind meeting me at Charlene's diner? I went through those papers you gave me yesterday, and I have a few thoughts I'd like to share with you. We can have lunch, my treat."

Julia glanced at her watch. It was later than she'd realized—nearly noon. She wasn't hungry after indulging in that decadent doughnut, but she couldn't afford to pass up a chance to pick Maggie Lu's brain regarding the ledger's contents. "I'll be right over," she promised.

***

Twenty minutes or so later, Julia was sitting across from Maggie Lu in one of the booths at the Downhome Diner. Her friend wore a striking black-and-white blouse that reminded Julia of zebra stripes—a pleasant contrast to the red seats in the booth. While patting the raindrops from her hair, Julia noted that the red stools at the counter and the red vinyl seats in the booths looked particularly cheery today. Someone had raised the solar shades to let in what feeble sunlight there was. Charlene took their order personally. Watching Charlene and Maggie Lu interact with one another gladdened Julia's heart. She and Meredith had played a part in reuniting the mother and daughter, and it felt good.

Maggie Lu had had a son too—Jacob. He died while serving in Operation Desert Storm back in 1991. Julia quickly shoved this sad thought from her mind when her cup of oyster stew and Maggie Lu's shrimp and grits was served.

"The aroma of oyster stew always takes me back to when I was a little girl," Maggie Lu recalled. "One of my uncles lived on Tybee Island. The family gathered there on Saturdays in the winter months on a rickety old dock along Oyster Creek. Uncle Marshall would go out along the wild oyster reefs in the marsh wearing his tall rubber boots and thick gloves. With an old roofing hammer, he'd chisel those oysters out and toss them in a battered metal bucket. All the men came equipped with shucking knives. They'd get a fire going and later roast the oysters and make oyster stew. The aunties would compete with one another to see who could bring the most savory sauces and pies. My favorite was buttermilk pie." With a sigh she added, "Life was tough in those days. My family survived hard times and heartaches and even a hurricane or two," she added with a chuckle.

Julia laughed. "Still, you have some fond memories, I can tell."

Maggie Lu smiled. "In a way that leads right in to what I want to tell you. I looked over the papers you gave me—the transcript of the ledger's contents—and I got to thinking about Spanish treasure ships again. Remember, I mentioned the shipwrecks?"

Julia nodded, taking a sip of sweet tea.

"As I recall, one of my ancestors found a couple of old Spanish coins—solid gold. Found them on the beach and used them to purchase his freedom. His name was Tiberius. My mother referred to him as Old Tib."

Raising an eyebrow, Julia asked, "So he was a slave?"

Maggie Lu nodded. "Yes, here in Savannah."

"But Meredith told me that Oglethorpe insisted there would be no slavery in the city—no lawyers or liquor either."

"Of course this was long after General Oglethorpe's days. It was back in 1863, if I'm remembering correctly." Maggie Lu speared a shrimp with her fork. "I'd forgotten all about Old Tib until after our conversation at the library brought him to mind. He bought his freedom, headed north to Pennsylvania, and no one ever heard from him again. It got me to thinking about the Moravians again. You know the ones here in Savannah pulled up stakes in a hurry too. And as I recall, they also moved up north to Pennsylvania."

"What does that have to do with Spanish treasure?" Julia asked, stirring her cup of oyster stew absently.

"Most of them had to borrow money from the trustees in England to make the journey here to Savannah," Maggie Lu said.

"In return, they had to perform certain tasks for the colony free of charge. I think that involved raising silkworms and spinning silk." She went on to explain Oglethorpe's desire to give the French competition in the silk trade. As she talked, Julia once again realized what a wonderful teacher Maggie Lu must have been before she retired from her classroom duties. She had a lovely voice and had a way of bringing history into the present. Julia could easily understand how the woman had been named teacher of the year back in 1998.

Still feeling a little muddled, Julia said, "But I still don't see the connection between Old Tib and the Moravians and the ledger. I must be dense."

Maggie Lu sat up a little straighter. "It's only speculation on my part, of course. I have no proof. But the treasure Charles Wesley mentions could have been just a few coins or something like it he found on the beach. He may have expected there to be trouble, if word got out that his brother John had found it. My early Georgia history is a bit murky," she added, "but I'm sure Rebecca Thompson could help you research them. She told me she gave you a list of sources to look up. Have you done so?"

Licking her lips, Julia said, "No. I haven't had time. The past twenty-four hours have been a bit...stressful." She proceeded to tell her friend about the attempt to steal her bag and the break-in at New Beginnings. "The ledger was stolen from the pastor's office."

Maggie Lu gasped. "Someone stole that old ledger?" Both her tone and expression were incredulous. "Was anyone hurt?"

"No, thank the Lord," Julia declared. She heaved a sigh.

"Yes, thank the good Lord for that," Maggie Lu agreed.

"You see, I can't help wondering if the break-in and the attempt to steal my bag are related somehow." In a quiet voice she explained about the elusive Mr. Tate. As she did so, Maggie Lu's eyes widened with concern.

Charlene strolled over then and placed a hand on Maggie Lu's shoulder. Refilling their iced tea glasses, she said, "Mama, is everything all right? The two of you are looking mighty serious over here." She frowned slightly at Julia before giving her mother a sharp glance.

Straightening, Julia quipped, "It's just sleuth stuff."

Maggie Lu gave her daughter a quick smile. "Nothing to concern yourself about, hon."

"Well, if you're sure…"

"We're sure," Julia and Maggie Lu replied in unison and then laughed.

This seemed to reassure Charlene, who walked away to greet several customers coming in through the front door, shaking out umbrellas and exclaiming over the drizzle.

"What are you and Meredith going to do now?" Maggie Lu asked, once Charlene was out of earshot.

Julia shrugged. "What can we do? Ed didn't tell the police about the missing ledger, and we have no idea who took it or why. We may never know what's on those sticky pages either." She heaved another sigh but became immediately alert as Maggie Lu sat up straight and fixed an intent gaze over Julia's left shoulder.

"Uh-oh," Maggie Lu whispered.

Julia turned in her seat. Joe McGibbons stalked over to their booth, a fierce frown marring his craggy features. Slapping both hands down on the table, he leaned toward Julia, saying, "You and that incompetent Bellefontaine woman have lost the Oglethorpe ledger, I hear." Straightening, he snarled, "Now we'll never find the pirate treasure. They ought to lock you up and throw away the key!"

❧ Chapter Seventeen ❧

Johanna Hus
Georgia Colony, March 1737

Had Sister Reidel not gripped her firmly by the wrist, Johanna would have bounded out the door. Who had been shot? She hoped fervently it would not prove to be Herr Wesley, for he had been more than kind to the brethren over the many months they'd known him. One of the other women started to weep. No one made any pretense to continue the worship service, although a few individuals clasped their hands in silent prayer.

Johanna tugged away from her friend's grasp and made her way to the window. The simple homespun curtains did little to keep the flies out and certainly allowed little of the evening breeze inside. Pulling back the curtains, Johanna peered out into the darkness. The light from the torches was bright enough to reveal the dead dog lying in the dirt at Brother Konrad's feet. The little yellow cur the men called Kip. At once she felt a surge of thankful relief but pity for the poor dead creature.

"They killed one of the dogs," she said over her shoulder. This announcement was followed by a quiet murmur. Apparently everyone else felt relieved too. Outside, the men's voices grew quieter, calmer. Perhaps the death of the dog had sobered them.

As Johanna strained to listen, she caught only bits and pieces of the conversation, something about building a fort and the loan of the brethren's oxen and wagons.

"What do they say, Sister Hus?" one of the men asked in German. Johanna translated as quickly and quietly as she could. She often forgot that most of those in the settlement could not understand English and relied upon her and Brother Konrad and one or two others who had acquired the rudiments of the language while they lived in England those many months before sailing to the colony.

She leaned closer to the window, straining to hear. There was something about a Spanish ship. Turning to Sister Reidel, who hovered at her elbow, she said, "The militia has spotted a Spanish ship off the coast."

When Sister Reidel shared this news with those standing closest to her, it ignited a burst of rapid questions: How many ships? Did they carry soldiers or cargo? How close did the ship sail along the coastline?

Johanna waved an impatient hand. She couldn't listen and talk at the same time. Holding her breath, she wondered what the elders would do or say if indeed the Spaniards attacked the colony. Any injuries or deaths of English settlers would be laid at the brethren's door, she feared, for they had staunchly refused to bear arms or serve in the militia. Now, if they refused to help build a fort to protect their neighbors, she could only imagine the bitterness that would be exhibited toward their community—and the school. Would it be so wrong to help the others fell trees and haul timber at least? Might not the brethren need to seek refuge in such a fort if indeed the Spaniards came ashore intent on making war?

While tension inside the communal cabin seemed to heighten, matters outside fizzled. Johanna heaved a ragged sigh. There was the murmur of voices followed by the jangle of harnesses and the clopping of horse hooves. "They are leaving," she announced, her heart lifting.

Brother Konrad, John Wesley, and Brother Reidel opened the door and came inside. John's gaze flicked around the room. He let his gaze settle upon Johanna briefly before turning his attention to one of the men hovering at his elbow. Everyone bombarded them with questions, while the men raised their hands for order. Brother Konrad tried to answer their questions calmly and concisely. Her knees weak from the ordeal, Johanna collapsed upon the nearest bench. She observed Brother Dober and young Elias going outside, she supposed, to bury the poor dog.

"If we are going to be abused in this manner, I say we leave here and go north," one of the men opined. "The colonists in Pennsylvania are friendlier. We've been told this more than once. We would be welcome there."

This statement was followed by an outcry of anger and dissent but a few voices of agreement too.

Johanna felt emotionally drained. She did not want to hear the discussion. Slipping out of the door—unnoticed, she hoped—Johanna sought a quiet refuge in the night air. She slipped around to the north side of the large cabin and sat down upon a crude wooden bench that had been placed there by one of the men. Women often sat here in the late afternoon to snap beans or shell peas. Turning her eyes heavenward, she marveled at the night sky heavily salted with stars. A whiff of pungent air from the nearby marshes drifted toward her on the breeze.

Sighing deeply, Johanna's thoughts turned to an Englishwoman who had lived long ago. A woman named Julian. While in England waiting for the trustees to approve their application to voyage to Georgia, Vati had borrowed books written in English for her to read. She'd always been a voracious reader, when circumstances permitted and when books were available. Julian had lived more than four hundred years ago in an enclosed room inside a church in the town of Norwich. It was said that she'd become seriously ill, had been miraculously healed, and later blessed with visions of Christ. Julian wrote eloquently about her spiritual experiences. Somehow, Johanna's father had managed to borrow a copy of the book, Revelations of Divine Love.

Johanna had found it most interesting for many reasons. She'd never read a book written by a woman before. That in itself was a marvel. She'd also found Julian's writing to be hopeful and optimistic. Over and over again, Julian urged her readers to trust in God's goodness and mercy, assuring

them that no matter their circumstances, "All shall be well
and all shall be well and all manner of things shall be well."

At the time, Johanna had wondered how it was possible
for a woman to live in a state of devotion to prayer, not forced
to marry or serve others but to be served herself and live a life
alone, apart from all others. It was fascinating to contemplate. She was doing so now when the sound of swishing skirts
and heavy shoes stepping across the gritty dirt came from
around the corner of the cabin.

"What are you doing out here alone, Johanna?" Sister
Reidel sounded anxious and weary. The woman limped as
though her hip troubled her. With a ragged groan, she seated
herself slowly on the other end of the bench.

"I am thinking," Johanna said taking care not to
sound irritated because her solitary reflections had been
interrupted.

"Thinking about what?" her friend probed.

"I am thinking it would be no bad thing to be a holy
woman living alone in a cell to read the scriptures and pray
without ceasing."

Sister Reidel gave a snort. "That's Papist talk. You think
too much."

"I think not," Johanna snapped back. In the dark, and
with only the faint gleam of candlelight coming from the
cabin, she could not see her friend's face, but Johanna did not
doubt that the other woman was frowning.

They shared a brief, companionable silence before Sister
Reidel said, "My husband has suggested they cast lots to

SAVANNAH SECRETS

determine whether or not they should help with the building of the fort."

Johanna felt a tight clutch at her heart. She felt certain that no matter the outcome, there would be no hope of peace between the community and the settlers in Savannah.

"I think they will also discuss the possibility of leaving here," her friend added.

Sitting up straight, her back stiff and rigid, Johanna declared, "I won't go!" She stamped a foot. The Yamacraw children could not be deserted. Clutching her knees with curled hands, she could feel the tears puddling in her eyes. "I'm sure the Indians will let me live with them."

Sister Reidel made a choking sound of indignation. "We could not leave you here, Johanna! It would not be possible." In a lower tone, she muttered, "Leave you with these sinners? Alone? What nonsense!"

"Is that what the men are talking about now?" Johanna demanded. "It's late. Such important decisions should not be discussed at this hour. Everyone is tired. Mutti always said important matters should be talked about in the glare of day."

"Sound advice," Sister Reidel agreed, rising to her feet and rubbing one hip. "Now come back inside."

Johanna obeyed, too tired to resist. Besides, she wanted to hear what the men had to say. Stepping over the threshold, she caught a whiff of cinnamon—the only remnant of the cake they had all enjoyed earlier. She noted the few children asleep in their mothers' laps. The women appeared grim with concern. Sister Dober had wide frightened eyes like a cornered doe. The men had rearranged the benches to face one another. They talked in low voices. Their bearded faces seemed stern in the candlelight. John Wesley stood near the hearth, his hands clasped behind his back. His German was not fluent enough, Johanna knew, to follow their conversation with ease.

"Let us cast lots then," one of the men said. "To be sure we are doing the Lord's will."

Brother Konrad stroked his chin. The men around him looked grim with resolve. One of them said, "I overheard some of the colonists at the grist mill last week discussing our habit of casting lots. They thought it odd. But one man said that if we always cast lots when making decisions, he would believe we are intent on following God's will, but if we make decisions without doing so, then it proves we do as we please when we want to."

This caused a mumbling of concern among the others. Some clenched their jaws. Others gripped their knees with splayed hands and shuffled their feet with discomfort. The tension increased.

"We shall cast lots regarding the building of the fort," Brother Konrad declared. Pieces of paper with various answers written upon them were put into a hat. First they prayed fervently for God's guidance. Johanna reflected upon so many matters decided by such a way. Even her parents' marriage to one another had been decided by the lot. After a half hour of fervent prayer, Brother Konrad reached into the hat and pulled out the answer: Absolutely not.

"*This is God's will then.*" *He passed around the paper.* "*We shall not help with the construction of the fort.*"

"*This will cause more dissention between us and them,*" *Brother Reidel said.* "*Matters will only worsen. We need to discuss going out from among these people.*"

"*I agree,*" *one of the carpenters spoke up.* "*If we remain, we provoke the anger and mistrust of the others. We will be a spiritual burden to them, for they are the weaker brothers, unable to forgive or understand. I say we remove from this place. We can catch a ship and sail north to Pennsylvania.*"

So the men cast lots again. Brother Konrad held up the paper. It read, Go out from among them.

"*But what of the debt we owe to the trustees?*" *one of the men pointed out.*

"*We have no funds to travel north,*" *another added.*

But it had already been decided. This was God's will, and they must obey. Johanna felt a chill and shivered. She also felt a pronounced loss—yet another one. First Mutti and then Vater, and now she was to leave the Yamacraw children she had come to serve and to love. It was too much to bear. She ran from the cabin, sobbing. Was she the only one who cared so deeply?

Chapter Eighteen

BACK AT THE OFFICES OF Magnolia Investigations, Julia told Meredith and Carmen what had happened at the diner. "You should have seen his face," Julia said. "Joe McGibbons scowling at me and growling. He said they should lock us up and throw away the key." She gave Meredith a wan smile.

Meredith snorted. "In keeping with his preferred pirate persona, he should have said throw us in the brig. Isn't that what they call jail on ships?"

"Or threatened to make you walk the plank," Carmen added. Then with an exaggerated roll of her dark eyes, she added, "I think he must be nuts."

Twisting her mouth to one side, Meredith let out a gruff, "Argh, you're right about that, matey."

Julia and Carmen laughed. "I certainly wouldn't want to be pushed off a plank," Julia insisted.

"On a more serious note," Meredith interjected, "Do you think Joe followed you to the diner?"

Julia shook her head. "No, he came in and seemed surprised to see me there with Maggie Lu. He decided to take advantage of the opportunity to vent his spleen."

"So he thinks the ledger is lost and not stolen?" Carmen asked. "That could be significant."

Meredith gave an agreeing nod.

"Now that you mention it, he did say 'lost' not 'stolen,'" Julia replied. "And he followed that up with, 'Now we'll never find the pirate treasure.'"

Carmen frowned. "Is there really any pirate treasure?"

"No!" Julia and Meredith declared in unison.

Then Meredith raised another interesting question. "How did Joe find out the ledger was lost—stolen, gone, whatever? When he called the day after the little Inquisition, asking to come to our office and see it, I told him we no longer had it in our possession, but I didn't mention that we'd returned it to Ed. I didn't say it was lost either."

"Surely that's not what he meant exactly," Julia proposed, leaning against Carmen's desk. "He must know it's stolen."

Julia's cell rang then. She rummaged in her tote bag. "It's Ed," she said, noting the caller ID. "I need to take this." Flipping her hair over her shoulder, she held the phone to her ear. "Hey, Ed."

"Julia?" There was a pause followed by a sigh. "I called Jubal Jones this morning regarding the break-in and the theft of the ledger. He wasn't as angry as I feared."

"Really?" She gave Meredith a glance. "What about Miss Dicey?"

"She was sleeping when I called. I told the nurse who answered the phone in her room that I would call again." Julia heard his sigh. It had been a stressful day for her pastor, she knew. She hoped most of his days were not so. At least they didn't begin with a break-in and a visit from the police. "Maybe I should go tell her in person," Ed pondered aloud.

"She'd enjoy the visit, I'm sure," Julia told him. "But you say Jubal wasn't that upset? I'm surprised. I thought he'd have an apoplexy."

"Well, he did bluster a bit. He wasn't pleased, of course, but concluded that it couldn't be helped and that maybe it would show up after all."

Julia declared, "That's not likely." After a pause, she added, "Frankly, I'm surprised that Jubal wasn't madder than a wet hen. He must have run into Joe McGibbons or called him and told him about the theft." Quickly, she related her encounter with Joe at the diner.

"Sorry about that, Julia," Ed apologized. "I'm sorry I even called you and Meredith to come look at the secret panel in Miss Dicey's music room. I had no idea at the time it would lead to such a hubbub." She could hear the sorrowful tone in his voice.

A bell tinkled as the front door of the agency opened, letting in a gush of wind and rain. Julia turned to look. So did Carmen and Meredith. Tamika Simms strode in through the door wearing a bright yellow rain slicker. "Ed, I'll talk with you later. Thanks for calling," Julia said and then disconnected the call.

Carmen made a show of turning her swivel chair to face the newcomer and greet her with a polite, professional smile. "Good afternoon. How may I help you?" she asked.

Meredith shot Julia a quick warning glance. Julia responded with a brief nod. She moved around the corner of Carmen's desk, saying, "Hi, Tamika." She stretched her arm forward to shake hands.

Shyly, Tamika took the proffered hand and gave it a hesitant shake. "Hi, Mrs. Foley." She flipped back the hood of her slicker, releasing a sprinkle of raindrops onto the carpet.

"I'll bet you've come to claim your lost earring," Julia said with a smile.

Tamika nodded. "Your secretary"—she acknowledged Carmen with a glance—"called my grandmother and said y'all had found it somewhere."

"Yes, we did," Julia replied as Carmen retrieved the earring from her middle desk drawer. After slipping it from the baggie she had put it in, Carmen passed it to Julia, who dropped it into Tamika's open palm.

"My folks gave me the earrings on my sixteenth birthday," Tamika said. "I wouldn't want to lose this—but the french hooks slip out of my ears sometimes. I noticed it was missing yesterday after y'all came out to River View when my grandmother and I were there."

Julia waited for Tamika to ask where they'd found it. When she didn't ask, Julia wondered if Tamika simply assumed they'd found it on the kitchen floor at River View or in one of the other rooms.

"Didn't I see you last night at the Atlantic over on Victory Drive?" Carmen leaned across her desk, giving Tamika one of her winning smiles. "I love their braised lamb, don't you? And you were with a tall, good-looking guy."

Tamika blinked twice. Closing her fingers around the earring, she said, "No, you must be mistaken. That wasn't me. I was at my grandmother's. Spent the night there. My sister and I sometimes take turns doing that." To Julia, she said, "Thanks again. I'm glad to get this back."

"You're welcome. Glad we found it," Julia told her, following her to the door. Tamika pulled her hood up over her head and stepped outside. The drizzle was a little steadier now but not quite a rain shower.

As the door closed behind her, Julia turned to Carmen. "What was that all about?"

"That's what I want to know," Meredith added, leaning toward their receptionist, who sat in her desk chair with a coy smile on her face.

"If you want to catch a girl in a lie, ask about a guy," Carmen quipped. "Now all you have to do is call the *abuela* to find out if Tamika really spent the night with her or not."

Julia and Meredith exchanged a glance. "I'll do it," Meredith volunteered. When she retreated to her office, Julia faced the front windows and stared out at the raindrops dotting the glass. There were no tourists ambling down the street this afternoon. But she bet there were a few in the Bonaventure Cemetery. It was an atmospheric place at any time, but especially on gloomy days.

"You like her," Carmen said, interrupting her reverie.

Turning, Julia gave her a half smile. "I do. I'll be quite disappointed if we discover she's the thief. But honestly, I can't imagine why Tamika would steal that old ledger."

"Maybe that Jubal Jones guy paid her a couple hundred bucks to steal it and give it to him," Carmen suggested.

Julia shrugged. "I suppose so." She and Carmen both turned to look at Meredith when she came out of her office, looking grim.

With a sigh, she announced, "Tamika lied. She didn't spend the night with Ruth. In fact, she told her grandmother she had basketball practice at the school."

There was a long silence, each woman lost in her own thoughts. Finally, Meredith asked, "Now what?"

Julia tucked a lock of silver hair behind her ear. "I don't know. Technically, tracking down the perp who broke into the church and stole the ledger isn't our business. It's a case for the police to investigate now. When Ed asked for the ledger back, it ceased being our concern—even though we're still curious about the cryptic message scribbled by Charles Wesley."

Meredith crossed her arms over her chest. She gave Julia a searching look. "So what are you suggesting? That we do nothing?"

"I'm not sure what I think we should do from this point on." She broke off to ask Carmen to brew a fresh pot of coffee. Carmen sprang to her feet, seemingly eager to have something to do. Julia could tell by Meredith's expression that she seemed quite disappointed. But interfering with a police investigation was a crime. So was withholding evidence. Julia wasn't even sure that Ed did the right thing by not reporting the missing ledger.

Releasing a sigh, she said, "I think we should have told Greta and Ed to turn the earring over to the police. That's my fault. If there are any repercussions because of it, I will take the blame...and the responsibility."

"I don't know if there will be any legal repercussions, but we will certainly have to deal with the fallout when Beatrice and the committee hear about the theft of the ledger," Meredith pointed out.

Julia gave a mild snort. "You can bet they already know all about it. Jubal knows. Joe McGibbons knows something or the other. But remember, the ledger is no longer our responsibility."

"What about the research you were going to do in regard to the Wesley brothers and General Oglethorpe?" Carmen asked over her shoulder. The coffeepot began to burble, and the smell of fresh coffee brewing began to permeate the office. "Have you had time to look up any of those resources the librarian recommended?"

"No," Julia admitted. She walked over to the sink to rinse out her favorite coffee mug. "Does it even matter anymore, now that the ledger is lost?"

Meredith declared, "Of course it matters! It's historically important. You have the digital photos of the pages—that's something. Perhaps we should turn those over to Beatrice. That might keep her and Jubal from creating more of a flap and bothering Miss Dicey."

"I'd be glad to do that." Julia gave her a half-hearted smile and said a silent prayer of gratitude that she'd had the foresight to photograph the pages—all that was left now of the old ledger. It might resurface, true. But somehow she doubted it. She supposed she should at least peruse the list of sites Rebecca recommended, if for no other reason than to learn a little about the Moravian settlers. Maggie Lu seemed to think there might be an important link between them and the Wesleys. Julia said as much to Meredith.

"Really?" Meredith shrugged a shoulder. "I wouldn't have thought there'd be a connection, but if Maggie Lu says it's worth looking into, then we should. Or somebody should."

"Coffee?" Carmen held up the pot. Julia thrust her cup forward while Meredith scrambled around for one of her own.

Julia took a sip. "I don't know what to do about Tamika either. I don't want to get her into trouble."

"But it must be connected, don't you see?" Meredith gave Julia's arm a squeeze. "We've got to figure out what happened to the ledger and what Wesley meant about the treasure. I'm certain that's why the ledger is missing in the first place."

"I don't want to waste agency time or money on this," Julia protested. "Remember, when this whole thing started, we didn't believe there was a treasure—at least not one that can be discovered now. So why should we pursue it any further?"

"Because God tossed this puzzle into our laps, and we need to solve it," Meredith replied with certainty.

Julia gave her a crooked grin. "You always did love puzzles."

Meredith's cheeks turned pink and her blue eyes snapped. "I feel it's important. We have to see this thing through."

Julia and Carmen exchanged a poignant glance. "Whatever you say," Julia quipped. She glanced at the clock on the wall. "Where has this day gone? I need to get to the nursing home to hunt down Tate. I can't let another day pass without speaking to him. Until I find out what he's up to, I won't be able to think clearly about anything else."

The office phone rang then. While Carmen answered it, Meredith motioned for Julia to follow her into her private office. "Are you going alone?" she asked in a worried tone. A frown creased her brow. "Do you want to take Carmen with you? I'd go along, but I'm behind on these background checks. School will be starting in a few short weeks and school administrators are still waiting on me to give the all clear on potential employees."

"Don't worry, Mere. I'll be fine," Julia reassured her. "It's a public place. He'll hardly do anything drastic at his place of employment. He might lose his job, and I'm certain he wouldn't want to do that. If all goes well, I'll be back in an hour and a half with answers to my long list of questions."

Meredith clutched Julia's hands. "Let's pray. I don't want anything to go wrong." Julia flashed her friend a smile of thanks and bowed her head as Meredith asked the Lord to watch over Julia and to bless them both with wisdom regarding what to do about Tamika.

"Amen," Julia concluded. "And thanks, Meredith. You're a good friend."

Blushing, Meredith asked, "Are you going home to change first?"

"No, not now. I'm clothed in the armor of God," Julia grinned, adding, "and am charging right in. I won't come back until I have answers."

"You go, girl!" They exchanged high fives.

On the drive to the nursing home, the windshield wipers seemed to flap out a warning. Julia felt slightly keyed up but more with anticipation than fear or dread. She was eager to confront Mr. What's-His-Name Tate, to demand what in the world he was doing following her around. She had a pile of questions that had accumulated like children's building blocks, heaped on top of one another. Something had to topple soon.

As she pulled into the parking lot, the rain had stopped—again. She stepped out of the car, pulling her tote bag across the front seat. That's when she saw Lovejoy Stewart hurrying down the sidewalk, away from the building. What was she doing here? Visiting Miss Dicey or a relation of her own? Slipping her tote over her shoulder, Julia raised a hand, calling out, "Hey, Lovejoy! Wait up!"

The young woman checked her stride for the briefest of moments. She cast Julia a wide-eyed stare before hurrying to her own vehicle without responding to the greeting in any way. She practically squealed out of the parking lot in her eagerness to get away—from Julia, presumably. Julia frowned. How odd. She knew Lovejoy had seen her. So why didn't she respond in some way? Julia felt a tingle of unease. Something wasn't right.

As she walked in through the front door, Julia paused at the receptionist's desk. "Y'all here to see Miss Oglethorpe, I'm betting," the smiling, dark-haired woman said. She wore a cheery yellow-and-black polka-dot tunic over slim black slacks, reminding Julia a little of a bumblebee in a children's book she'd had once. "I saw you come in the other day with Reverend Markham."

Julia returned her smile. "Actually, I'm here to speak with Mr. Tate. Is he working today?"

"He is. Shall I page him for you?"

"Yes, please do," Julia replied. She pointed to the guest lounge. "I'll wait for him over there. What's his first name?"

"Gus," the receptionist told her. "And your name?"

"Oh, let's surprise Mr. Tate, shall we?" Julia flashed her most winsome smile before dashing off to find a comfortable chair near the window and in view of the busy corridor where she could see who was coming in and going out of the building. Heart pounding, mouth dry, Julia plopped into the chair and waited. She felt slightly ridiculous. *Get a grip, Jules!* As a judge she'd met with many a tough customer in her courtroom and in chambers. Mr. Tate did not fall into that category, she felt sure.

He walked into the lounge then, wearing khakis and a blue polo shirt with the nursing home logo emblazoned on the pocket. Tate checked his steps at the threshold when he saw her. His sad little mustache appeared to twitch. His burly chest sank. He resembled a frightened rabbit ready to flee for its life.

Julia rose. "Just the man I want to see," she said, lurching toward him, her hand outstretched. If he tried to run, she intended to grab his arm. But he took her hand, rather reluctantly, she thought, and gave it a shake. She was taller than he was, Julia noted. That realization boosted her confidence. "Come have a seat." She indicated a well-padded chair next to her own, separated by a small end table. He walked forward hesitantly. "We can talk here or in your supervisor's office," Julia added, with a forced smile. "Sit."

Tate sat.

"Now, you have some explaining to do," Julia told him, resuming her own seat. She leaned forward. "Start at the beginning."

Heaving a sigh, Gus Tate gripped his knees with splayed fingers. "I suppose I do owe you an explanation."

Julia quipped, "You think?"

Slowly, a smile spread across his face. His eye gleamed in a friendly way. "I should have known you'd come track me down sooner or later. I'll bet you've even got the whole thing figured out."

Caught off guard, Julia asked, "Figured what out?"

"I followed you and the pastor after you came to see Miss Oglethorpe the other day. I know y'all spotted me," Tate told her. With a quick shake of his head, he added, "I felt like a failure, let me tell you." Then his face lit up once again. "But, y'all gotta admit, that reverend can drive like an Indy 500 driver."

"You *wanted* to be noticed?" Julia asked, still confused.

"No, I was hoping you wouldn't notice. I was tailing you on purpose, but I guess I didn't do it right. Are there classes to learn those sorts of things?" Tate leaned forward, giving her a questioning stare.

Julia flopped back in her chair. This just kept getting stranger by the minute. "You also followed me to the library."

Tate's face lit up. "You *are* good!"

"Gus, what's your game?" Julia didn't dare admit she wasn't that good. Good at what? She hadn't realized she was being followed. Wouldn't have known a thing if Rebecca hadn't told her that someone posing as an employee of the agency had come in asking for the list of informational sources she'd requested. "I suppose you're after the old ledger too?"

Frowning, Tate asked, "What ledger?"

"Don't play innocent with me," Julia snapped. "You were in Miss Dicey's room when Pastor Markham and I visited her and showed her the ledger. You pretended not to be listening, but you were. I know it."

With a shrug, Tate admitted, "Sure, I heard bits and pieces of the conversation, but it meant nothing to me. What's up with the ledger?"

More confused than ever, Julia said, "Let's start over. You admit you followed Pastor Markham and me from the nursing home. You admit that you followed me to the library and later told the librarian that you work for Magnolia Investigations. For all I know, you've been dogging my steps for days. Why?"

Tate's face turned a bright crimson. His mustache twitched. "I'll just come out and say it," he declared. "I want a job with your agency. I want to be a detective like you and Mrs. Bellefontaine."

Chapter Nineteen

FOR A MOMENT, JULIA WAS struck dumb. The man wanted a job? She'd hardly expected that to be the reason he'd been following her.

"Ever since I read about you and your partner in the newspaper in regard to the old Besset estate, I knew I wanted to work with you—for you. I've been taking a class in criminology at the community college. I sure don't want to spend the rest of my life working here." Gus glanced over his shoulder with mild disdain. "Do you think you could take me on as an intern—show me the ropes? Be my mentor?" He leaned forward, his face aglow with hope.

Julia felt as though someone had pulled a rug out from under her feet. Did she believe him? She wasn't quite sure. Fixing him with a slight frown, she asked, "So the day you tailed us in the car…" She left the statement unfinished.

"I hoped to follow you around and make note of everywhere you and Pastor Markham went," Gus explained. "And then I planned on showing up at your office with my notes neatly typed up. I hoped you'd be impressed." He shrugged in a dismissive manner.

"But instead we gave you the slip."

With a sheepish grin, Gus said, "You sure did. That Pastor Markham drove like a race car driver. I was too embarrassed to come see you after that. I'd flubbed up."

"So then you…" Julia extended a hand, inviting him to go on.

"So then I followed you from your office to the library. You left and I decided to pretend I worked for your agency, that I'd been sent to pick up whatever it was the librarian was putting together for you."

"You followed me into the library," Julia accused.

Gus flushed. "Yes, but it was for a good reason."

"No, it was for a selfish reason," she contradicted him.

His flush deepened. "You're right. I just wanted to have a good excuse to drop by the Magnolia Investigations office. I planned on presenting you with the list and hoped you'd be impressed by my sleuthing—impressed enough that you'd give me a part-time job."

Julia demanded, "Did you pay a teenager to try to steal my tote bag the other night?"

This time Gus looked stunned as he sank back in his chair. "No, I wouldn't do such a thing. It's criminal. I can't afford to break the law if I want to be a private investigator." He thrust his chin forward, almost daring her to not believe him.

But Julia did believe him. She hoped it wasn't a foolish thing to do.

"Do you think you could use me part-time in your agency?" Gus asked, squaring his shoulders and sitting up a little straighter.

Sighing, Julia shook her head. "I'm sorry, Gus. We can't afford any more employees at this time. The agency is just getting on its feet, and we've had to pay for extensive repairs and remodeling projects. It may be quite some time before we have enough paying clients to take on anyone else—even part-time."

He looked so crestfallen that Julia felt convinced the man was telling the truth. "I tell you what, in a couple of weeks, let's get together for lunch and I can suggest some courses you could take to better prepare you for the job. We're not the only agency in town, you know. Maybe I could ask around, find out if anyone would be willing to take you on part-time."

"Mrs. Foley, I would certainly appreciate that." He grinned. Rising, he offered to shake hands. "I have to get back to work. It's time for the afternoon meds run. You've made my day, let me tell you."

Julia gave him a half smile. "Let me have your cell number or your home phone where I can reach you when you're not working." She retrieved her cell phone from her tote.

"You bet." Gus gave her the number, which she added to her contacts list. "I'll be waiting to hear from you."

She gave him a nod and watched him retreat down the corridor. "If that don't beat all," she muttered. Then, glancing at her phone again, she saw that she had several texts and voice mail messages. One of them was from Beatrice Enterline. Julia groaned. She'd been dreading this. She wondered if the Queen Bea had pestered Meredith too. For a brief moment Julia considered visiting Miss Dicey before leaving, then she dismissed the idea. It had been another stressful day in a rather stressful week. She simply wanted to go home, have a shower, and an early supper.

Julia returned to her car. And after turning on the AC, for it was still sticky and humid despite the off-and-on drizzle, she called Beatrice and braced herself for a scolding, which is just what she got—but one that was as genteel and sugarcoated as that pseudo Southern belle could muster.

"Julia, dear, thank you for returning my call," Beatrice drawled. "I'm certain you can guess why I want to speak with you, hmm?

I'm disappointed, I must admit it, and if truth be told, I'm shocked. How could y'all lose that old historic ledger? Why, it's so…so…" She struggled for the right word. "So unprofessional. Y'all never should have had it in your possession in the first place, and so I told you."

Julia cleared her throat. "Beatrice, the ledger is not lost. It has been stolen from Pastor Markham's church office. There was a break-in. Cash from the Wednesday night offering was taken as well as the ledger. The police are investigating. I shudder to think what will happen if the perp proves to be an officer or a member of the historical society."

"What?"

Julia heard Beatrice's breathless gasp.

"Do you know something about this unfortunate affair that I should know?" Beatrice demanded.

"I do not know who broke into the church and stole the ledger," Julia admitted. "But what I do know is this: several society members—yourself included—called or came by the agency's office to ask to see the ledger. Meredith and I refused to allow you to do so. Shortly after that Pastor Markham requested that we return the ledger to his care, which we promptly did. You, Jubal, Joe McGibbons, Lovejoy Stewart, and I don't know who else learned that the pastor had the ledger again." Julia paused to catch her breath. Her pulse raced. She could feel the heat in her cheeks. She felt her temper beginning to flare. "The next thing we know there's a break-in at the church building—something that has never happened before. Is it a coincidence? I rather think not. I shouldn't wonder if you all get a visit from the police soon."

"Why, Julia Foley, whatever do you mean?" Beatrice fairly squeaked. "Surely you don't think I would steal from a church!"

"I don't think *you* are personally responsible," Julia replied. But was the historical society director shady enough to have paid some-one—Tamika Simms perhaps—to do the dirty deed for her? Julia hoped not.

"Who do you suspect?" Beatrice probed.

Julia threw out the first name that came to mind. "Lovejoy Stewart." The young woman had acted pretty squirrelly when Julia had hailed her in the parking lot. She'd darted away like a scared rabbit without even acknowledging Julia's greeting. Something was up, that was for sure.

"Lovejoy Stewart!" Beatrice echoed in disbelief. "Surely you jest."

"I'm quite serious," Julia replied. Although she didn't really believe Lovejoy had committed the crime, she had to admit, if only to herself, that the young archivist had a motive. Her rather fanati-cal passion for historical artifacts made her a likely suspect. She might do anything to get her hands on the ledger. Hadn't she brought an archival box to put it in—hoping no doubt to do the honors? She clearly believed no one but a professional had a right to take posses-sion of it. Hadn't she tried to convince Ed to allow her to take a look at it? So, perhaps in a fit of pique, she later broke into the church, stealing the thing.

"I don't believe it for a minute," Beatrice said, interjecting her opinion and interrupting Julia's train of thought.

Julia didn't really believe it either, but she wasn't going to admit that. She'd have to question Lovejoy to see if she had an alibi for the night of the break-in. She also wanted to ask her why she was visiting the nursing home today. Did she have a relative living there or had she come to speak to Miss Dicey? And if so, what about?

Beatrice tried again. "I don't believe Lovejoy stole the ledger, Julia. She comes from a good Savannah family. You must remember that."

"Of course," Julia replied vaguely as she rolled her eyes. In her days on the bench she'd met a lot of criminals who had been raised in good families. "I'll speak with her," she promised. "I'm sure she'll have an alibi." Julia *hoped* she had an alibi. The only thing she couldn't quite figure was if Lovejoy did commit the crime, how did Tamika's earring end up on the floor in the church office? And why would she steal the cash as well as the ledger? Such a paltry sum too. Was she hoping to throw the police off the scent, thinking they'd figure the money was the motive and the ledger simply an impulsive theft?

Increasing the AC's airflow, Julia decided it was time to wrap up this conversation. "Beatrice, I have to go. I'll keep you posted if I learn anything of interest."

Ignoring her, Beatrice interjected, "If anyone is suspect, it must surely be Joe McGibbons."

Julia suppressed a smile. So the Queen Bea was willing to throw her vice president under the bus. She could hardly wait to share that tidbit with Meredith. "Why do you think that?"

"Now, dear, I'm sure you've noticed that Joe carries this pirate thing just a wee bit too far sometimes," Beatrice replied. "He certainly has motive, and breaking and entering is just the sort of thing a modern-day pirate would do. If he used the contents of the ledger to locate a missing pirate treasure, it would boost his reputation, and he could charge big bucks for his performances. Why, he'd be cock of the walk at the Tybee Island Pirate Fest, don't you know?"

"That's true," Julia acknowledged. "I'll question him too. Talk with you later, Beatrice." She quickly disconnected the call before the woman had an opportunity to propose someone else as a likely suspect. As far as Julia was concerned, there were far too many possible suspects on the list already. Hot and irritable, she drove straight home. After a quick shower and some cantaloupe and cottage cheese, she called Meredith.

"Are you still at the office?" Julia asked, glancing at her watch. "It's suppertime. You've put in a long day. Surely you're not still checking references at this hour?"

"No, I'm not," Meredith admitted. "I've been going through that box of newspaper clippings and police reports that Ron saved—the one I showed you the other day. The more I think about it, the more I wonder why on earth he saved all this. It's weird. You know, he never mentioned this case to me ever. Not once. And yet it's obvious that the murder-suicide fascinated him. Why else would he have collected all this stuff?"

Julia pondered the problem for a moment. "I know you talked with Chase and Carter about it before, but why not ask them again? It's been a while since their dad died, and maybe they'll remember something now that the initial shock and grief is over."

"Maybe," Meredith said, uncertainly.

"Why not ask Chase to look into the incident?" Julia proposed. "He's a history professor. This sort of research is just his bailiwick. But on a different subject, did you get a call from Beatrice today?"

Meredith sighed. "Yes, I did. Once on my cell and again later on the office line. Carmen took the call and asked if she could take a message. She knew I didn't want to speak with the woman, and I'm certain she guessed Beatrice would call to badger me about the stolen ledger. I haven't called Beatrice back though."

"Don't bother," Julia told her. "I spoke with her earlier, and Carmen was right. The Queen Bea chastised me for losing the ledger."

"Losing it? Doesn't she realize it's been stolen?"

Julia gave a mild snort. "She knows now. And get this, she proposed Joe McGibbons as a likely suspect." Chuckling, she added, "I guess there's no love lost there, huh?" She went on to summarize the earlier conversation, remembering to mention how quickly Beatrice had come to Lovejoy's defense.

"Maybe there's a power struggle going on between Joe and Beatrice," Meredith suggested. "Since a great deal of society money has gone into the restoration of the Besset home, I'm sure there's less money for Joe's pirate exhibits and school visits and such. There's never enough money to fund everyone's pet projects. There never was, even when I was president." She sounded weary.

Julia had half a mind to call Chase herself and have him come take that box off Meredith's hands. It seemed to be worrying her so. Maybe Chase could make heads or tails of the contents and figure out why his father had collected all the clippings and photos and reports in the first place. Then he could enlighten his mother and that would be one less worry on Meredith's plate. Julia guessed that had the box and its contents belonged to anyone else but Ron, Meredith would have tossed it out by now. But because Ron had saved it, she must feel some sort of obligation to hang on to it.

"Call it a day, Mere," Julia advised. "I'll see you first thing in the morning, and I'll help out with those background checks so we can get those cleared off your desk."

Meredith began, "But—"

"No buts," Julia interrupted. "Go home and get some rest. As Scarlett O'Hara so wisely pointed out, tomorrow is another day."

Meredith reluctantly agreed. After saying goodbye, Julia disconnected the call and padded on bare feet into the kitchen for a glass of sweet tea. She wondered briefly what Beau and his boys were doing at that moment. Sitting around a campfire, she supposed, spinning exaggerated stories about their past fishing exploits. She thought about how lonely she would be without her husband and felt a pang of sympathy for Meredith, who still missed Ron sorely. Ron had been a great guy. Julia and Beau missed him too. She'd often pondered the similarities she and Ron experienced in their workaday world—crime and punishment for the most part. There were no new sins under the sun. Most were committed for the same old motives too—financial gain, passion, or power—or combinations thereof. Even looking back on the cases taken on by Magnolia Investigations in the past several months, Julia could see the same patterns, from the long ago disappearance of Harriet Besset to Meredith's recent kidnapping and now the theft of the ledger. The pursuit of treasure or any sort of financial gain provoked people to do all sorts of illegal things.

Putting all thoughts of crime and motives out of her mind, Julia determined to enjoy her evening curled up with a good book. Then the doorbell rang. Glancing through the clouded glass, she could make out a female form wearing an apricot-colored dress.

Julia opened the door, mildly astonished to see Lovejoy Stewart on her doorstep.

"Mrs. Foley, I have a bone to pick with you!" the young woman exclaimed, frowning fiercely.

"Then I guess you'd better come inside," Julia told her, taking a step back and opening the door wider.

Chapter Twenty

"I CAN'T BELIEVE YOU THINK I stole the Oglethorpe ledger!" Lovejoy sat stiffly on Julia's sofa, her shoulders tight with tension. Her face appeared flushed, and her hands were clasped tightly in her lap. She left the glass of sweet tea untouched on the end table at her elbow, but every now and then her gaze would flit to the small plate of Lorna Doone shortbread cookies that Julia had placed next to her glass.

"Who told you that I think you stole the ledger?" Julia asked, knowing full well it had to be Beatrice Enterline.

"Well, if you must know, it was Beatrice," Lovejoy admitted. "She called me this afternoon after she spoke with you on the phone."

Julia suppressed a smug smile. "Then you misunderstood her or she misunderstood me. I simply said that you were a suspect, as is everyone who knew that Pastor Markham took the old ledger from our agency's office."

Eyes snapping, lips pursed, Lovejoy gave her a glare. "That may well be, but Beatrice seemed to think I was at the top of your list. And I came here to see you face-to-face, to assure you that I would never do something so despicable. Besides, I have an alibi."

"You do?" Julia quirked an eyebrow.

"Indeed I do." Lovejoy gave a curt nod. "I took my two young nieces to the movies and then brought them back to my apartment to spend the night. We made hot fudge sundaes and played Parcheesi. They stayed up past their usual bedtime. It was an end-of-the summer treat, since they will be going back to school soon. Their mother—my older sister—can verify that I was with them all evening, and so can my neighbor who lives across the hall." She leaned over to retrieve her small handbag. From it she withdrew a piece of lined notebook paper, which she thrust toward Julia. "I've written down their phone numbers so you can call them, if you don't believe me."

Julia took the paper, glancing briefly at the names and numbers written there. "Thank you. This is helpful." She toyed with the idea of putting Lovejoy out of her misery by telling the young woman that she really wasn't a *serious* suspect. Then she decided against it. Why not keep Lovejoy on her toes? Nervous people made mistakes—especially if they were both nervous *and* guilty. It might be a good thing to get all the likely suspects riled up. Sooner or later someone would make a mistake or drop a hint without realizing they had done so. Julia wondered just how far she could provoke Lovejoy.

In her most serious tone, Julia said, "Of course, the police don't know what time the break-in occurred. We assume it was quite late at night or in the wee hours of the morning. I don't suppose you would have left your nieces unattended in the middle of the night."

Lovejoy stared at her, aghast. "Heavens, no! They are only six and eight years old. I would never do such a thing." She gave Julia another glare of righteous indignation.

"I felt certain you would not." That was true. Really, it was hard to imagine Lovejoy Stewart skulking along the corner of the New Beginnings church building, armed with a screwdriver or crowbar, hiding in the clumpy lilac bushes attempting to break in. On the other hand, she could easily imagine Joe McGibbons in baggy black pants and a dark hoodie darting from the parking lot around to the back door of the church and committing the crime. Yep, she could imagine it. Had he risked taking along someone to serve as a lookout? Or an actual accomplice? Did he know Tamika Simms?

Forcing these contemplations to the back of her mind for the time being, Julia calmly pushed the cookie plate a little bit closer to her fuming guest. Lovejoy finally helped herself to a cookie. She chewed slowly. Her face regained its normal color, and her heavy breathing seemed to slow down some.

After swallowing the last morsel, Lovejoy said, "Mrs. Foley, I warned you that something like this might happen, and if you recall, I warned you about Joe McGibbons."

"I do remember you mentioning how clever and sneaky he is," Julia agreed.

"Yesterday when I was working in the society archives, he came in to speak with Beatrice. Before he left, he got on the computer and did a search." With a challenging gleam in her eyes, Lovejoy asked, "Do you know what he was looking up?"

"No, what?" Julia asked, intrigued.

"The New Beginnings website." Lovejoy thrust her chin up as she sat back against the sofa cushions in a triumphant manner.

Julia felt her pulse quicken. Maybe Beatrice had been right— Joe McGibbons might indeed be the thief. Maybe her earlier contemplations hadn't been so far off base after all. Had Joe been looking up the address of New Beginnings? If so, why? She doubted he would be calling to find out what time services were held. Julia couldn't help feeling that Joe had something more sinister in mind. Had he called to make an appointment with Ed, Julia felt sure her pastor would have mentioned it. The two had met that evening at the so-called Inquisition. Ed certainly would have said something if Joe had called or stopped by since then.

"I will certainly have to have a word with Joe," Julia assured her.

Lovejoy agreed. "If he stole the ledger, he needs to return it pronto. As old as it is, it could crumble to dust if not handled with the utmost care." At the mention of the fragility of the ledger, her face paled.

Julia sighed. Yes, the ledger was in poor condition—worse than poor Lovejoy even knew. She could imagine Joe McGibbons stealing the old ledger because of some misguided notion that it would lead him to elusive pirate treasure. But snatching the offering too? That part of the crime was hard to swallow. Then again, he may have done it so the police would assume some kid needed the money to buy drugs.

"Mrs. Foley—Julia, I wonder if you would allow me to see the digital photos you took of the legible pages." Lovejoy fixed her with a wide-eyed, hopeful gaze.

"If Miss Dicey says it's okay, then I'll be happy to send you an electronic file," Julia told her.

Lovejoy leaned forward slightly. "I've spoken with Jubal Jones, and he told me it was all right with him if I see them."

"Really?" Julia frowned. Jubal was certainly free and easy with Miss Dicey's possessions. He might be the legitimate heir, but that didn't give him the right to dispose of Miss Dicey's property or share it with others without her permission first. "What were you doing at the nursing home earlier this afternoon, Lovejoy? Did you go to speak with Miss Dicey? Didn't you hear me call out to you or see me wave? You appeared to look right at me before you left. I know you saw me, but then you purposefully ignored me. Why?"

Lovejoy blushed and ducked her head, fixing her gaze on her hands. "I did see you. I thought you'd followed me there. Later, after speaking with Beatrice, I was convinced that you had been following me because you think I stole the Oglethorpe ledger." She took a deep breath. After expelling it, she added, "I'm here now because I just can't bear for you to think I would do such a thing. I couldn't bear it."

"I wasn't following you. I was at the nursing home on business— different business altogether," Julia told her. "But you were there to see Miss Dicey, weren't you?"

"Yes." Lovejoy helped herself to another cookie. "I thought as the ledger had been so recently found, maybe there were old journals, diaries, and other family papers lying around somewhere at River View that might be of historical interest."

"And what did Miss Dicey say?"

Lovejoy shrugged. "She recalled donating a couple of boxes of family memorabilia to the historical society several years back. She couldn't recall when or what was in the collection. She said she'd given the library some old books too—rare first editions that had been in the family for generations."

"If you'd like, I'll speak with Meredith about it," Julia offered. "Miss Dicey might have donated the items during the time Meredith served as president of the historical society. Were you hoping to find anything in particular?"

With a shake of her head, Lovejoy said, "Not really. And I don't give a flying fig about any old treasure—only about the historical significance of the treasure. Do you know what I mean?" She gave Julia a searching look.

"I understand."

"Beatrice has given me permission to do a little digging on my own, as long as I don't fall behind in my work," Lovejoy told her. "We're trying to get everything digitized, and I do mean everything. There's so much paper and all of it aging and deteriorating."

Lovejoy rose from the sofa, smoothing the front of her apricot-colored peasant dress as she did so. She cleared her throat. "I'll be going now. You can verify my whereabouts, if you must, and I hope that will be the end of any speculation on your part regarding my guilt or innocence." She fixed Julia with a rather anxious gaze.

Julia rose too. She felt slightly dismayed by Lovejoy's unease about the situation. She wanted to say something reassuring. "Please don't worry so. I'm sure everything will check out. If it matters at all, I believe you. But as President Ronald Reagan used to say, trust but verify. I appreciate your cooperation." Julia tipped her head toward the end table on which she'd placed the piece of paper with the names and phone numbers Lovejoy had given her.

As they walked to the door together, Lovejoy asked, "You will speak with Miss Dicey, won't you, regarding the copies of the ledger pages?"

"First thing in the morning," Julia told her, smiling. "Who knows? You may be the one who can read the illegible script. I'll even send you my rough transcription of the parts I could decipher."

Lovejoy's face lit up with pleasure. "Thank you. That would be great. It's so uncomfortable not knowing. I'll look forward to hearing from you then."

Julia flicked on the front porch light and watched the young woman swish elegantly down the sidewalk to her car. Something Lovejoy had said triggered a thought that had been sitting on the back burner of Julia's mind for a while. As soon as Lovejoy was on her way, Julia reached for her cell and called Chase Bellefontaine—Meredith's younger son, a handsome sandy-haired, blue-eyed history professor, who was popular with impressionable, romance-minded coeds. He taught at Emory University in Atlanta and usually came down once a month to spend a weekend with his mother. Julia decided Chase needed to visit soon.

Chase answered on the third ring. "Hey, Aunt Julia, how are you?"

"I'm as fine as frog hair and so is your mama," she assured him, before he could get anxious about her reason for calling. She carried Lovejoy's untouched iced tea glass into the kitchen. "I want to ask a favor of you."

"Okay, shoot."

Despite his quick agreement, Julia noted a touch of apprehension in his voice. "When you've got some time, I'd like you to come on down to Savannah to see your mom and take a box of old newspaper clippings off her hands." She went on to explain about the box and how his mother seemed consumed by worry over its contents.

"She doesn't know why your dad saved the box of clippings and case notes, so she's unsure what to do with them. It's been troubling her unnecessarily, Chase. She said she showed it to you and your brother. Do you remember seeing it?"

"Vaguely," Chase answered. "But why is she saving it? As I recall, it wasn't one of Dad's old cases."

"You're right. It was a sensational murder-suicide over in Pickens County that took place decades ago," Julia told him. "Ron would have been just a kid when the crime took place, so I can't imagine why he collected articles and case notes about it. Anyway, your mama can't seem to bring herself to throw them out. So I want you to come take the box. You know how it is: out of sight, out of mind."

Chase chuckled. "She'll wonder why I want them."

Julia paused. She didn't want her best friend to think she was doing anything sneaky behind her back. But Julia was concerned. She didn't like to see Meredith brooding over something she could do nothing about. It had been almost two years since Ron had passed away. If he'd been saving the box for a colleague, someone would have come to fetch it by now. Meredith needed to move on. Julia felt certain Quin Crowley, the handsome lawyer who occasionally called Meredith to take her out for lunch or dinner, would feel the same.

"Why not tell her the old case came to mind, and you'd like to go through the box?" Julia suggested. "After all, you're a history professor. The crime may have some sort of historical significance."

"Like what?" Chase queried, a touch of humor in his tone.

"How should I know? You're the history buff. Think of something."

After a pause, Chase said, "I'm really surprised Mom has held on to it all this time."

"Me too," Julia said. "So come get it. I know your new semester will start soon, but surely you can squeeze in a weekend to come down. I'll even take you out to dinner—any restaurant you choose. Just don't tell your mama that I've called you about this, okay?"

"Okay," Chase agreed.

Julia added, "I'm sorry to put you to all this trouble, but I don't like to see her fretting over this. She's distracted by it. You'd be doing her—and me—a favor."

"It's no trouble," Chase assured her. "At least she's not been abducted again," he added. "Besides, you've aroused my curiosity. Now I'm wondering what my dad was up to. That crime took place so long ago it couldn't possibly involve him in any way. Or could it?"

Julia answered truthfully, "I have no idea." But she felt a wave of relief that Meredith would soon have that meddlesome box out of her office and could concentrate on the new cases at hand. If the agency was going to grow, they'd both have to focus on bringing in new clients—cases that paid. "Remember, don't tell your mama I called, okay?"

Chase agreed. On Friday morning Julia went into the office early, determined to help Meredith with some of the background checks. The faster they could turn those around, the better pleased the clients would be. Happy clients would share their positive experiences. Everyone knew that word of mouth was the best form of advertisement. In the privacy of her own office, Julia verified

Lovejoy's alibi. Everything checked out, as she knew it would. At around two o'clock, when she and Meredith divided up the last of the employee references that needed to be done, Carmen tapped lightly on the door, announcing with a happy grin on her face, "Meredith, you have a visitor."

Chase stood in the front office, blue eyes shining, looking handsome in crisp jeans and a faded blue denim shirt with the sleeves rolled up. His eyes seemed to dance with humor. Julia was as surprised as Meredith, who rushed forward to embrace her younger son with affectionate enthusiasm. "Chase, what on earth are you doing here? Why didn't you call to let me know you were coming?"

Grinning, Chase replied, "Can't I surprise my favorite mother once in a while?" He kissed Meredith's cheek and cast a guileless glance at Julia over his mother's shoulder. He acknowledged Carmen with a shy smile.

Meredith bombarded him with questions. "How long can you stay? Have you eaten lunch? Will you be here long enough for me to bake you a sweet potato pie?"

"Yes, I had a quick lunch in Dudley," Chase told her. Dudley was halfway between Atlanta and Savannah.

"Well, come into my office and have a seat," Meredith said. "We've been rather swamped with employee background checks the past couple of weeks."

"That's a good thing, isn't it?" Chase asked.

While Chase and his mother chatted a bit about the agency's current workload, the office phone rang. Carmen answered it in her most professional tone. Julia's eyes roamed from Meredith's happy face to Carmen's more serious one. The young woman glanced up at her, arching a dark eyebrow. "Yes, ma'am, I will give Mrs. Foley the message," she said and then hung up.

Julia became immediately alert. "Who was that?"

With a toss of her head that set her lush, dark curls dancing, Carmen said, "That was the church secretary at New Beginnings. She said to tell you that the stolen money from the offering was returned sometime today in an unmarked padded envelope. She found it in the church's mailbox out front."

"And the ledger?" Julia asked, heart racing. "Was that returned too?"

Carmen shook her head. "She didn't mention it."

"Stolen money? What's this about?" Chase asked, pausing in the doorway of Meredith's office.

"Nothing like this ever happened when your dad ran the business," Meredith said with a sigh. "It's a long story."

"And an interesting one," Carmen added with a wag of one finger. "Very interesting."

"Let's hear it," Chase said.

Julia leaned against the edge of Carmen's desk and folded her arms across her chest. "It all began when my pastor discovered a secret panel at the River View mansion. Inside, he found an old ledger which may or may not have been kept by Charles Wesley, the hymn writer."

"And that old ledger was stolen because it mentioned treasure of some sort," Carmen threw in.

Chase gave his mother a sympathetic eye roll. "Not long-lost treasure again?"

Meredith shrugged in a helpless manner. Carmen sprang to her feet. "I'll make coffee."

"Somebody start at the beginning," Chase prompted, sitting down in the chair across from Carmen's desk.

So while the fresh aroma of hazelnut coffee filled the office, Julia began at the beginning. Every once in a while, Meredith would toss in a detail or two. When they were done, Chase—his blue eyes wide with astonishment—stared at each woman in turn. "Good night in the morning!" he exclaimed. "What mess have you ladies gotten yourselves into this time?"

Chapter Twenty-One

Johanna Hus
Georgia Colony, June 1737

The barest hint of a breeze kissed her cheeks as Johanna watched the youngsters running to and fro, playing a game of chase. She stood in the doorway of the small cabin that served as the school for the Yamacraw children. Some wore little more than breechcloths and beads. Others donned simple garments made of hide or burlap sacks, their brown feet bare or clad in simple shoes made of deer hide. The three children from the community seemed cruelly overdressed in their heavy, stifling clothes with shoes and stockings.

Restless and squirmy, the youngsters had been inattentive all morning, so rather than punishing them, Johanna had called for an early recess, and was glad now she'd made this decision. Their laughter and high-pitched squealing lifted her spirits, distracting her from the dark thoughts she'd been nursing in secret. As she leaned against the doorframe, she allowed herself to revel in their laughter, hugging close this brief moment of happiness.

Since the elders had made up their minds to obey the lottery—to go out from among them—*the days had become difficult and anxious, the nights restless and often without sleep.* How can we leave? When should we go? *Everyone had questions. Brother Reidel assured them in Sunday's sermon that if leaving was the Lord's will—and all believed it must be so—then God would make a way. But how they would repay the trustees, they did not know. It was the subject of many a prayer of petition. They were ever mindful of the unpaid debt. They still owed for their passage and the goods they purchased for the voyage on credit. It stood to reason that the community could not pay for a second passage to sail north. There was no money to relocate.*

Johanna knew her days of teaching the children were numbered, and she intended to make the most of them. When two of the young men from the tribe asked if they could come learn the letters too, she had readily agreed. As they did not wish to join the children's classes—considering it beneath their status as warriors—they usually showed up most early afternoons when the younger students had been dismissed. It was too hot to teach in the afternoons.

Although irregular in attendance, the two young men seemed eager and applied themselves to the lessons. Johanna felt a surge of excitement at their progress. She was never alone with them—or with the children for that matter. One of the elders from the community was always present during the lessons, just for safety. Sometimes, one of the other women accompanied her to the school. Always two by two. It was the Lord's way.

Johanna leaned against the doorframe, listening to the trill of birds in the pines and the screeching children. The tangy smell of the salt marsh seemed strong today. She would miss this place but not the gnats or the summer's heat. She tried not to think how her heart was breaking at the thought of leaving the children and the school. Sister Reidel assured her there were many children in Pennsylvania she could teach. The elders had already written the community there to inquire about joining them. They had also asked for financial assistance in paying off their debt to the trustees. The northern brethren had shared generously, but it was not enough.

Go out from among them.

The words made Johanna shudder. The lot had been drawn. The decision made. Her darker thoughts focused upon the men and women of Savannah—so merciless in their insistence that the men of the community serve in the militia. If only they would let them live in peace and follow their own consciences.

Not everyone in the community seemed happy about the idea of moving north. It showed in the way they performed their everyday tasks. The vegetable gardens were overrun with weeds at times and necessary repairs to the cabins and wagons ignored. One Sunday, Brother Konrad had taken them to task for it too. He then went on to encourage them with a sermon comparing their upcoming journey to that of Moses leading the Hebrews out of Egypt into the Promised

Land. But as Johanna recalled, he'd preached the same message back in Bohemia before they departed for England and then on to Georgia.

But not everyone found it difficult to uproot from Georgia's sandy soil mixed with clay. John Wesley's brother had already departed, returning to England. And he'd been eager to do so.

Johanna's pleas for the elders to consider leaving her behind had been ignored. She knew they would be. The community was her only family now. She could not return as Charles Wesley did to his home abroad. She had no one but these people, and she thanked God for them. Still, there was much here she had come to appreciate. The towering pines, the wildflowers, the way the sun sparkled upon the greenish-brown water of the river. And the birds—so many lovely birds like jewels with wings. She didn't recall so many at home in Bohemia. And certainly none of the deep red color that brightened her mood every time she glimpsed one flitting in the tree branches. She likened it to a king's ruby.

Sister Rachel Dober stepped up behind her then, interrupting her reverie. Rachel held her knitting basket propped on one hip. She'd been making stockings in a serviceable gray color, for the winters in Pennsylvania were colder than what passed for winter here in the Georgia Colony. Her doe eyes were heavily lashed. Smiling, she watched the children at their play. "I shall sit outside now in the shade, if you don't mind," she said. "My cheeks are hot." She placed the back of her long-fingered hand upon one of her flushed cheeks.

Johanna chuckled. *"Everything I have is hot."*

Giggling, Rachel blushed. *"It is said that Pennsylvania has a more comfortable climate."*

"Don't you have an uncle there among the brethren?"

Rachel nodded. *"And an aunt and several cousins."*

"So you are eager to move north, I suspect." Johanna looked at her questioningly.

With a shrug, Rachel shifted the reed basket higher. *"I want to settle and put down roots. I dread another long journey—especially by ship."* She shuddered. *"But we shall never be comfortable or safe here. The other colonists are..."* She paused as if looking for just the right word. *"They are not neighborly."*

"Sister Reidel says they are afraid," Johanna told her.

Rachel cast her a perplexed look. *"Afraid of us? Why?"*

"She says the Savannah colonists are so afraid of the Spaniards that they cannot forgive our men for not helping to build the fort and for not training in the militia. They do not trust us."

"My husband rode out to see the construction of the fort," Rachel said then, tucking a stray strand of brown hair behind her ear. *"It is large enough for all in the settlement to seek shelter within—should the need arise."*

Johanna gave her a sidelong glance and crossed her arms over her chest. *"Even those of us in the community? I think not. They will not let us in, should we come seeking shelter."*

"But would we do so?" Rachel asked, frowning. *"Surely we have nothing to fear from the Spanish. We are not English."*

With a mild guffaw, Johanna said, "And you think the Spaniards can tell the difference between the German and the English?"

The children's squealing grew louder then as young Elias tumbled in the dirt with one of the Yamacraw boys. Straightening, Johanna looked to see if the boys were fighting and if she should interfere. It happened sometimes. But not on this occasion. Soon the laughing children tumbled in a pile—intent on their game. No ill feelings were evident, simply high spirits.

"Sometimes I wish I were a child again," Johanna said wistfully. "Life was so simple then. I would strip down to my shift, kick off my shoes and stockings, and join their game."

Rachel giggled again.

Suddenly, tears stung Johanna's eyes. She felt a sense of loss so strong she feared she'd break into sobs. She mourned the loss of her parents all over again. She missed her homeland. And soon she would be wrenched away from this school—this beloved school. It was unbearable. Sensing Rachel's scrutiny, Johanna brushed away the tears that threatened to spill down her cheeks. She cleared her throat and said, "When the children come back inside, why not teach them a song?"

Rachel stared in astonishment. Her large brown eyes appeared even larger and so achingly beautiful. "I am not a teacher," she stammered.

"But you have a lovely voice," Johanna told her. "Everyone says so. Surely you can think of something short and melodious. The children love to sing."

Blushing with pleasure, Rachel shrugged. "Perhaps a simple nursery song."

"Yes, they would enjoy that," Johanna assured her. She then made her way to the water bucket on the bench up against the front of the cabin to make sure it was filled with fresh water. The children would be thirsty after their morning romp. Johanna lowered the ladle into the bucket and took a gulp of the lukewarm water, letting it dribble down her chin. Drops fell upon the bodice of her simple gray gown. The dampness felt cool against her skin. Just as she contemplated clanging the bell to bring an end to the morning recess, Rachel pointed, calling out, "Rider coming."

Squinting against the sun's glare, Johanna raised her hand to shade her eyes. She recognized the horse before its rider—John Wesley's dun-colored mare. He came riding toward them at a brisk gallop. Her heart thundered in her chest. It could only mean bad or urgent news for him to travel at such a pace. She felt her shoulders and neck grow stiff with tension. Beside her, Rachel began to breathe heavily—no doubt from fear. A few of the children paused in their rowdy game to watch his approach. Recognizing the minister in his usual black coat and white collar—attire he insisted upon wearing no matter the weather—they quickly dismissed him as no one of importance, and they returned to their game.

The closer he came, Johanna took comfort in the fact that his expression did not appear as grim as she feared it might be. Something about his countenance seemed eager, hopeful, and even excited. As she stepped forward to meet him, she held out a hand to Rachel, saying, "Sister Dober, watch the children, if you please."

John reined in his horse at her approach and swung out of the saddle with a jerk. "What brings you out this way, Herr Wesley?" Johanna greeted him.

In an unexplained emotional state, he forgot all propriety. "Johanna, I must speak with you," he said, using her first name. He tossed the leather reins over the rickety hitching post. "I do not wish to be overheard. May we speak privately?"

John's words, his flushed countenance, confused Johanna. His errand seemed an urgent one, but he did not appear dismayed. "Is this a matter of concern? Is someone ill or injured?" Her ribs felt the pressure of her pounding heart so she could scarcely breathe. Perhaps the Spaniards had attacked after all.

Her gaze shifted quickly over his shoulder in the direction of the small settlement she called home. No smoke, no screams of terror. Had someone collapsed, perhaps, or suffered an accident?

John grasped her arm to lead her around to the back of the school cabin. She glanced over her shoulder at Rachel, who stared after her with a knowing smile. Johanna released a short sigh. She knew what her friend was thinking, and Rachel was wrong. Could not a godly man and woman share a friendship without romantic ties? Apparently not, for none of the women in the community believed her protestations that she and John Wesley were not forming an attachment to one another.

"Johanna"—John took a deep breath—"your prayers and those of the elders have been answered. The Lord indeed provides. You will be able to leave this place sooner than you imagined."

"That is not my prayer," Johanna contradicted him. "I am resigned to it, but I long to stay to keep the school going. However, that is not to be."

"But the elders believe it is God's will that you all go from this place. They wait only to be delivered of the debt to the trustees." With a tremulous tone, he added, "The Lord has answered their prayer." His face glowed with excitement and perspiration. He removed his hat and swiped his coat sleeve across his forehead before replacing the hat upon his tangle of damp hair.

"And so?" she prompted impatiently as she gripped the heavy skirt of her garment.

In his eagerness, John clasped her hands. His were moist and hot. Did she only imagine the slightest tremble? Johanna could not hide her astonishment. She had a sixth sense that whatever he had come to say, her life would be forever changed from that moment. For good or ill she could not say. "What is it, Herr Wesley? You frighten me."

He dropped her hands as though he'd been scorched. "Our God provides!" he declared with fervor.

"I do not doubt it," Johanna assured him.

"Today He has provided the necessary resources for all of you to pay your debt to the trustees and to join the brethren in Pennsylvania." He beamed at her.

Johanna still felt perplexed. "How so?"

Sighing, John continued, "You know that I have joined my prayers with yours and the elders that some way could be found to pay the debt that you might leave this place—as you feel it is God's will."

Johanna remained silent. What could she say? Still puzzled, she wondered if some unknown benefactor in England had paid their debt. If so, how had John Wesley come to know of it? It seemed most unlikely. And it would be even more unlikely that the trustees would forgive the debt all altogether. But her friend's excitement was now obvious. It was also contagious, for she could feel her own heart lift with hope.

"Thank you for your prayers on our behalf," she told him. "The Good Book says the prayers of a righteous man availeth much."

John blushed deeply. "I found something on the beach today—something wonderful and most unexpected. I was on my way to visit a sick parishioner. As I did so, I prayed for your plight, and it was while I prayed that I made my discovery."

"What did you find?"

John ignored her question. "Such was my excitement at the discovery in the sand that I could hardly execute my ministerial duties," he babbled on. "I've already shown it to the general, and I told him what I intend to do. He thinks my plan is a good and generous one."

Johanna felt a surge of frustration. "What plan? I know not what you speak of."

Again grasping Johanna's hands between his own, he declared, "Johanna, if the elders refuse to accept this gift, together you and I must persuade them to do so. It is God's gift, not my own. I have no doubt this is God's providence for all of you, and I am glad of it. You will be able to pay the debt. When you do, the trustees must release you. I want to be assured of this as I am leaving Savannah and will not be able to have peace of mind wondering what is to become of your community."

"Leaving?" Johanna exclaimed, startled. "When? Why? Where will you go?"

John shrugged. "I have not worked out the details yet, but soon. My work here—it is not what I expected. I am returning to England. I will seek a new position there."

"But what have you found that can possibly convince the trustees to allow us to leave as well?" she demanded. "That is all that keeps us here—the debt. Already the brethren in Pennsylvania make ready for us. They urge us to come in all haste, but it is not yet possible."

Heaving a contented sigh, John's stern face softened with something resembling a boyish grin. "Your debt will surely be paid and then some." He reached deep into his coat pocket and pulled forth something wrapped in a large, rather dingy cambric handkerchief.

"Johanna, close your eyes and hold out your hands."

Chapter Twenty-Two

"I'LL SAY ONE THING, THE agency certainly has tackled some odd cases lately," Chase said, shaking his head. Julia wasn't sure if he meant this in an admiring way or an exasperated one. "And speaking of odd, do you still have that box of old clippings Dad saved about the weird murder-suicide case that took place over in Pickens County a few decades ago?" He fixed his eyes innocently upon Meredith.

"Why, yes, as a matter of fact, I do." Meredith regarded her youngest son with mild surprise. "Why do you ask?"

Julia made a Herculean effort not to give Chase a warning glance. Instead, she fixed her gaze upon Carmen's paisley pencil cup. He'd have to pull this one off on his own.

"It came up in a conversation the other day," Chase answered truthfully. "I'm wondering if the incident has any historical significance. That sort of thing was not on my mind immediately following Dad's death, but now I think I'd like to have another look."

"Actually, I have the box here in my office," Meredith told him. "Julia and I were just looking through those files the other day, weren't we, Jules?"

"Indeed we were. I can't believe your mama has held on to them all this time."

"I'd like to take them off your hands, Mom, for the time being," Chase said.

Meredith readily agreed—to Julia's great relief. While Julia silently congratulated herself for the success of her plan, Chase offered to take them all out to dinner after they quit work for the day. "Not on your life," Meredith protested. "I insist on giving you a home-cooked meal. You eat out far too often as it is. Carmen, you and Julia can join us at my place at six thirty."

Carmen's face lit up with pleasure. Julia politely declined. "I hate to be a party pooper, but I have some things I need to follow up on. Besides, Beau is coming home tomorrow, and I have several things around the house to tidy up." Even though Meredith tried to convince her to change her mind, Julia remained resolute. She retreated to her own office and shut the door. She'd started a list of things to do before leaving the office for the weekend, and she intended to get them all done.

The first task was to call Miss Dicey to ask permission to share the digital photos of the ledger and the rough transcription she'd made of its legible contents. "You surely may," Miss Dicey told her when the call went through. "But why anyone would want to read a list of household accounts, I can't imagine. I guess the old general put the ledger away and completely forgot about it. I can't believe he held on to it on purpose, can you?" she asked in a wavering voice.

"I don't know, Miss Dicey," Julia answered truthfully. "It was stashed in that secret panel downstairs. Out of sight, out of mind, maybe?"

As Miss Dicey didn't mention the fact that the ledger had been stolen, Julia decided not to bring it up either. With permission received, Julia made a note of the phone call in her call log, noting the date and time that she'd spoken with Miss Dicey—just in case Jubal or somebody else should question the fact that she had indeed received permission to share the ledger's contents. This done, Julia logged into her email account and sent Lovejoy Stewart a PDF copy. The young archivist would be thrilled. Of course, had Lovejoy been given possession of the actual ledger, she would have been even more thrilled, but Julia couldn't help that now.

Not wanting to ruffle feathers, Julia then promptly sent the same document to Beatrice Enterline's email address, along with the digital photos she'd taken of each page in the ledger. Checking that item off her to-do list, she called Jubal Jones to inform him that Miss Dicey had given her permission to share the contents of the ledger with anyone who was interested.

"And if you'd like a copy, Jubal, I'd be happy to send you the PDF," she told him.

"Don't bother, sugar. I'll take your word for it that there was nothing important I should know about."

Julia paused. What had come over the man? Earlier in the week, he'd hauled them in before a tribunal of sorts to demand that the ledger be turned over to him. Now he couldn't care less?

"Well, Jubal, you've certainly changed your tune." She rubbed the furrows in her forehead, feeling a headache coming on. "I wish you had been this easygoing at the beginning of the week."

Jubal chuckled. "What can I say? I guess I did get up on my high horse. I humbly apologize, Julia. You'll extend that apology to Meredith too, won't you?"

Julia responded with a thoughtful, "Hmm."

"And if you see Pastor Markham at services on Sunday, you can assure him there are no hard feelings about his losing that old ledger. As Miss Dicey said, it contained nothing but household accounts. We got hot around the collar for nothing."

We? Julia felt another thread coming loose from the already frayed edges of her temper. "Jubal, the pastor didn't lose the ledger. It was stolen."

"Yes, sugar, I understand," he insisted, his tone jovial and patient as though speaking to a slow-witted child. "Lost or stolen, it's gone all the same. Might as well put that whole treasure business to rest. All a tempest in a teapot, according to Miss Dicey, and I believe her. Gotta go, sugar." And he disconnected the call.

Julia sat motionless for a moment, staring blankly at her iPhone. Perplexed and irritated, she also felt mildly relieved. Jubal felt no ill will toward Ed. She was thankful for that. The pastor couldn't be blamed for the theft and shouldn't be. But what had Miss Dicey said to Jubal to convince him to forget about the cryptic remark regarding the mysterious treasure? Julia couldn't imagine.

Next, she pondered whether or not she should call Joe McGibbons to see if he'd like to have a copy of the ledger's contents too. On the one hand, if Beatrice wanted her vice president to be in the know, she'd surely share. But on the other hand, there didn't seem to be any love lost between the two. Julia guessed Beatrice wouldn't send along a copy of the PDF to him. Should she? Even if Jubal had calmed down, Joe probably hadn't. She could still see the vein standing out on his neck as he'd confronted her and Maggie Lu in the diner the other day.

With a short shudder, Julia decided that Joe should have a copy. Why not? Nearly everyone else on the committee did. She didn't have his email address, but she did have a phone number. Carmen had thoughtfully included that on the pink WHILE YOU WERE OUT slip when she took the man's irate call earlier in the week. She tapped in his number. Joe answered with a blunt, "What do you want?"

Momentarily taken aback, Julia swallowed her annoyance. "Hi, Joe. Miss Dicey has given me permission to share the transcription notes I made from the Oglethorpe ledger. If you give me your email address, I'll be happy to send you an electronic copy."

There was a brief pause on the other end of the line before the loud click. The insufferable man! He had disconnected her call! Julia placed her phone on her desk and waited to see if Joe would call back. Perhaps he hadn't hung up after all. Maybe the call had simply dropped and was lost in cyberspace somewhere. Drumming her fingers on her desk, Julia waited. When five minutes had passed, she knew he wasn't going to call back. Well! It was obvious that he had his knickers in a twist. As angry as he'd been the other day, Julia felt certain he would jump at the chance to get his hands on a copy of the ledger's contents. It seemed everyone was behaving oddly all of a sudden. What was wrong with everyone? Gloomy weather sometimes had that effect on folks, she knew. Still, it seemed remarkable that everyone seemed to be behaving out of character. Maybe he would call back when he simmered down. She couldn't imagine that he wouldn't want to get his hands on the ledger's contents—the next best thing to possessing the ledger itself, surely.

Julia made another checkmark on her to-do list. Her gaze settled on Gus Tate's name. She had forgotten about him. She'd promised him a list of other Savannah PI agencies, and she intended to keep her promise. There were over five hundred, she knew, but not all in Savannah. She'd also made a note to herself to peruse the online course offerings at the community college to see if she could recommend any particular classes he might find useful. And of course, she should provide him with a link to where he could find the certification and training requirements for the job.

But that would all have to wait. The next piece of business on her list was a face-to-face meeting with Tamika Simms. She wouldn't go into the weekend with the nagging uncertainty hanging over her head. Beau was coming home, and she wanted to enjoy his return. She wouldn't be able to do so if she kept fretting about Tamika's lie and the girl's reason for telling it. Surely Tamika realized how easy it would be to double-check with Ruth concerning whether or not Tamika had spent the night? Well, maybe not. If there was one thing Julia had become aware of in her many years on the bench it was that many young people had no critical thinking skills. Many teens held two conflicting points of view or took two different stances on any given issue and couldn't see the obvious contradiction.

Sighing, she did a quick online search which revealed that the Lady Warriors at Jenkins High School had basketball practice this afternoon. Tapping her pen on her desk blotter, Julia glanced at the wall clock. She had time to get to the school and confront Tamika face-to-face. Should she come right out and tell the girl she knew she'd been lying? Or should she surprise her with the news that her earring had been found at the church following a break-in?

Julia dropped the pen on her desk and reached for her tote bag. She'd work out her approach on the way over to the high school. It was best to meet Tamika in a neutral place. The agency office would be too intimidating. And to arrange to meet her at home or at her grandmother's seemed risky. She didn't want to get the girl in trouble—especially if she'd already done something she was now regretting.

After grabbing her phone, Julia closed her office door behind her, telling Carmen, "I'm leaving and won't be back until Monday. Enjoy your weekend."

"You too," the smiling receptionist replied.

"I will. Beau's coming home." It gave Julia a lift just thinking about her husband's return.

Friday afternoon traffic was heavy as usual. Julia found herself waiting at one light after another. She absently drummed her fingers on the steering wheel as she contemplated the best way to approach Tamika. She prayed for the Lord's guidance too. No one liked conflict. No one enjoyed being caught in a lie either. But sometimes one had to care enough to confront. This was one of those times. Julia wanted to be careful in her approach, speaking the truth in love. That was something Ed always admonished his flock to keep in mind.

She thought too about Chase's unexpected visit to the agency office. She'd asked him to come, sure, but she hadn't expected him to do so immediately. It said a lot about the love Chase had for his mother, that he would make the four-hour journey on such short notice. Julia felt sure he'd had to change his weekend plans, and she was thankful he had done so. If he could take that box of worrisome clippings out of Meredith's reach, it would be a good thing. Meredith fretted too much about it. Julia felt sure Ron wouldn't have wanted Meredith to do so.

She smiled recalling the happy surprise on Meredith's face when she walked through the door and saw Chase standing beside

Carmen's desk. She'd glowed. Come to think of it, Carmen had had a certain glow on her face too. Julia couldn't help wondering where that relationship might be going.

Shortly after passing Forrest Hills Park, Julia turned onto East Derenne Avenue. It was easy to find a parking space. School wasn't in session. There were few cars in the parking lot and no busses. A man on a riding mower manicured the grassy lawn at the front of the school property. Sprucing up for the new school year. She'd never been to this particular high school before but guessed finding the gym would not be a problem. It wasn't.

She signed in as a visitor at the front office. After going through the intricate security protocol, she made her way to the gym and took a seat on the bleachers to watch the team practice. There were a few teens not in uniform watching from higher up in the stands. The players and two coaches were on the floor. A younger girl with a cornrowed hairstyle watched from the sidelines. She seemed to be in charge of a cooler filled with iced sports drinks and bottled water.

Tamika was easy to spot. Tall and athletic in her black and red uniform, she raced up and down the court with the grace of a young gazelle. It was evident, as Ruth had said, that the girl played with heart. Once Tamika cast a glance at the bleachers as she paused during a play to catch her breath. She did a double take when she noticed Julia. The action appeared almost comical, like in a cartoon. Julia wiggled the fingers of one hand at her. Tamika lifted her chin in recognition.

She made her way over to the bleachers when Coach blew the whistle, calling for a ten-minute break. Julia rose as Tamika came toward her in long strides, her expression cautious and perplexed.

"Hey, Mrs. Foley," she said, wiping the back of her hand across her perspiring forehead.

"Hi, Tamika, you're looking good out there." Julia gave her a bright smile, hoping to disarm the girl a little.

Tamika gave her a shy rather lopsided smile. "Thanks." Then on a more serious note, she asked, "Is everything okay? My grandma all right? Why are you here?"

"As far as I know, your grandmother is fine. I'm here to talk to you about your earring—the one you lost."

Tamika lifted her eyebrows in surprise. "Okay."

Julia regarded her thoughtfully. "You see, you never asked us where we found it."

"I didn't?" Tamika placed her hands on her hips and shifted her weight to one side. She looked more perplexed than ever. "I figured you found it at the big house—at River View the day you and Mrs. Bellefontaine were there."

Julia decided to plunge right in. "Actually, we found it in the church office at New Beginnings. There'd been a break-in the night before. Someone stole the offering—and other things. Did you hear about that?"

Shaking her head, Tamika said, "I don't listen to the news unless we have to for a class assignment."

Julia accepted this admission with a nod. "So do you have any idea how the earring could have ended up on the floor in the church secretary's office?"

"No, I do not." The girl's tone was emphatic and tinged with confusion. If she was acting, she was darn good at it. Julia believed her.

"I'm also wondering why you lied to us about spending the night at your grandmother's house," Julia told her. "That's the night the church break-in happened. I know you weren't at your grandmother's and there was no practice that night either. So you can see why I am suspicious."

Tamika's expression became stony. Her deep brown eyes grew wide with cautious uncertainty. "Does my grandma know about this? Or my parents? Have you talked with them?"

Julia shook her head. "I thought I'd come speak with you first, to see if you would explain things to me. You see, a crime has been committed, and I need to get to the bottom of things."

The girl's shoulders slumped with relief, and she blew out a sigh. Wrapping her arms across her chest, she admitted, "Yeah, I lied, but I didn't break into a church. I wouldn't do that. I was helping out a friend."

Julia could guess where this was going. It wouldn't be the first time a girl lied about meeting a boy. "A boyfriend?"

Tamika shook her head. "My friend Sylvia. She got drunk and lost her car keys. She needed a ride home from a party and didn't know who else to call." With a heavy sigh, she added, "My folks won't let me hang with Sylvia anymore. She's been in trouble for drugs and stuff, but I had to do something. I've known her since first grade. I picked her up and took her to the Waffle House for coffee and something to eat. Tried to sober her up some, and then I took her home."

Julia considered this for a moment. It would be easy enough to find someone at the Waffle House who would remember the two teens, and if necessary, Julia could always track down Sylvia to verify Tamika's claim. "I believe you." And she did.

Tamika looked tremendously relieved. "Thank you," she murmured softly. "I'm sorry about lying, but…" She shrugged, leaving the sentence unfinished.

"But there's still the problem about your earring being at the church," Julia pointed out.

"Mrs. Foley, I have no idea how that happened. Honest, I don't. I've never even been to that church before."

Julia believed her, but the puzzle still had to be solved. How did Tamika's earring end up at the church? The teen seemed to be contemplating the puzzle too as she stared down toward her athletic shoes and chewed her bottom lip.

"Mrs. Foley, do you think somebody is trying to set me up?" Tamika's brown eyes flashed with worry. "I could get kicked off the team if I'm even suspected of a crime. The coach is tough like that." She reached out a long, well-defined arm and grabbed Julia by the wrist. "Please, Mrs. Foley, you've got to help me."

Chapter Twenty-Three

DURING THE SUNDAY MORNING SERVICE at New Beginnings, Julia stood next to Beau singing a lively rendition of "O for a Thousand Tongues to Sing." A Charles Wesley hymn, she noticed in the hymnbook. Although the words had been projected on a large screen overhead, Julia always sang from the hymnal when possible. She liked to feel the weight of the book in her hands, to hear the flutter of pages. Charles Wesley—the gentleman who'd sparked the week's hullabaloo with a cryptic message in an old journal. It seemed appropriate they should be singing one of his hymns this morning. Or perhaps ironic. Of course, it hadn't even been proven that the ledger was written in Charles Wesley's hand. If they didn't recover the ledger, they might never know for certain.

Julia wore a lightweight cardigan over her pink cotton sheath because—as usual—the air conditioning had been cranked up. Smelling delightfully of Old Spice, Beau stood next to her, looking spiffy in navy slacks, a blue shirt, and an off-white linen sports coat. It was a far cry from what he'd looked like when he'd returned home the day before—rumpled, unshaven, and smelling of wood smoke and old fish. She tried to concentrate on Ed's sermon, to keep her mind focused on worship, but bits and pieces of the puzzling ledger case kept intruding upon her thoughts. Clues began to fall into place like missing puzzle pieces.

By the time they stood for the closing song, she'd had an epiphany, in a manner of speaking. When Ed ended the service with a closing prayer, Julia turned to Beau, touching him on the arm. "I know who stole the ledger."

He regarded her with a raised eyebrow. "You do?"

"Yes. We're going to wrap this up today. I hate loose ends. I need to speak with Ed." She hurried away to find the pastor, who stood at the back greeting members of the congregation as they filed out the door. Julia waited patiently, exchanging greetings with a few friends and giving Ed's wife Naomi a big hug, asking about the couple's youngsters who had recently attended church camp.

At the first opportunity, Julia dashed over to Ed. "I'm pretty sure I know who stole the ledger from your office, and I need to ask a favor." She briefly explained her plan.

Ed chuckled. "This reminds me of those scenes in the Hercule Poirot mysteries when the detective gets all the likely suspects together, explains the crime, and reveals the killer."

"I'm thankful no one got killed in the course of this adventure," Julia declared with heartfelt sincerity.

"Amen, sister!" Ed gave an emphatic nod.

"So, is it okay to meet in the kitchen this evening, say six thirty? There are no evening services in the summer, I know. But I want to make sure there's not a youth activity or baby shower or something else going on in the fellowship hall."

"It's fine. I'll come a bit early and open the doors," Ed promised. "I would love to see this matter resolved. I've been praying about the situation. The deacons and I agree we don't wish to press charges. The money has been returned, as you know. And the ledger..." He left his statement unfinished.

While enjoying lunch with Beau at their favorite Chinese buffet, Julia explained her plan. Her husband had listened with rapt attention the night before when she'd told him about the crazy week—starting with the discovery of the old ledger in the secret panel to being followed by Gus Tate. Now, over sweet-and-sour pork, Beau insisted, "I'm coming with you to the church. I want to see how this thing is going to play out." He reached over to squeeze her hand. "I sense you're feeling a bit guilty about the loss of the ledger. It's not your fault, you know."

Julia shrugged. "Intellectually, I know that. But sometimes my emotions and my intellect don't line up exactly. I guess I do feel rather responsible, so it's important for me to wrap this up, if I can."

After lunch, they returned home, and while Beau caught up on his email and other tasks, Julia called Meredith, explaining what she planned to do. "Can you come to the church at six thirty? Bring Chase if you'd like. The more witnesses the merrier."

"I wouldn't miss it for the world," Meredith assured her. "But Chase won't be coming with me. He already left for Atlanta after lunch. Oh, and guess what? Last night he went through every single one of those files in the box and guess what he discovered?"

"I have no idea," Julia admitted truthfully.

"Ron saved all the clippings and case notes because he had considered writing a book about the incident—you know, one of those true crime books. Chase found some notes scribbled in Ron's handwriting and even a list of possible book titles."

"Really? Well that's one mystery solved. What did Chase do with the box?"

"He took it with him back to Atlanta," Meredith told her.

Julia called down a silent blessing upon Chase Bellefontaine's sandy-haired head, thankful the box was out of Meredith's office. She hoped it would soon be off her friend's mind also.

"Who knows?" Meredith went on. "He might decide to write the book himself. He's got enough research to get started anyway. By the way, may I bring Maggie Lu? She got us into this predicament in the first place."

Julia frowned. "She did?"

"Yes, she did. When your pastor discovered the ledger inside the secret panel, he called Maggie Lu first. She recommended that he call us. Don't you remember?"

"Now I do," Julia admitted. "Yes, bring Maggie Lu."

"And you're sure you know who stole the ledger?" Meredith pressed.

"I'm pretty sure. The clues all add up."

"Can you give me a hint?" Meredith teased. "All the likely suspects have motive, means, and opportunity, so it could be anyone of them. Well, except Lovejoy. Her alibi checked out."

"Wait and see," Julia replied with hint of laughter in her voice. "You're a detective. You'll probably figure it out before we meet at the church. You're good at puzzles."

With Meredith on board, Julia set about implementing the next part of her plan. She texted everyone who had been at the rather hostile meeting last Tuesday night. Beatrice, Jubal, Lovejoy, Joe McGibbons, and even Jeannie Bell Hansen. She sent them all the same message:

I HAVE DISCOVERED SOMETHING!

She asked them all to meet at New Beginnings at six thirty sharp. Julia didn't explain why or what she'd discovered. This affair had begun with a cryptic message. It might as well end with one. She ignored the text replies she received in turn and concentrated on what she planned to say and do once everyone had assembled at the church. She prayed too. If ever she needed the Lord's help, this was one of those times.

The afternoon seemed to creep by. When it came time to leave, she asked Beau to stop by the Magnolia Investigations office first. "I need to pick something up. I'll make it quick," Julia promised. While Beau waited in the car, Julia skipped nimbly up the steps and unlocked the door. How she hoped everything would turn out all right. At the church, they found Joe McGibbons sitting in his pickup truck in the parking lot, the window on the driver's side rolled down.

"What's all this about?" he called out as Julia and Beau prepared to enter the church. He appeared scruffy and grumpy as he slouched behind the steering wheel of the truck.

"Come in and find out," Julia called back.

"Who is that?" Beau asked in a quiet voice, casting a suspicious glance in Joe's direction.

"Joe McGibbons," Julia said. "He's Beatrice Enterline's vice president."

Beau responded with a disapproving snort.

They noted the aroma of fresh coffee as soon as they entered the front door of the church and followed it to the fellowship hall off the kitchen. They found Naomi Markham arranging slices of her famous marble pound cake neatly onto a platter. She'd changed from her Sunday ensemble into a comfortable wrap skirt and a red boatneck tee that looked particularly attractive with her dark hair.

"Oh, Naomi, you shouldn't have," Julia said, indicating the cake and coffee.

Naomi shrugged. "I've found over the years that it's hard to say mean things to one another when your mouth is full of cake."

"And she's a bit worried mean things might be said here this evening," Ed added, retrieving coffee mugs from an open cabinet.

"I'll try to keep things as civil as possible," Julia promised.

Lovejoy came in then looking fresh and crisp as usual in a long striped T-shirt dress that reached to her ankles. She carried a large canvas tote that matched her wedge sandals. Eyes bright, she looked young and eager to please. Obviously, she was willing to let bygones be bygones.

Julia asked her, "Do you know if Beatrice is coming?"

"No, she has family visiting from out of town. She sent me a text requesting that I report to her as soon as we're done here. Is that okay?"

"Yes. That's fine," Julia replied with a nod. "I'm glad you could make it." She already knew Jeannie Bell would not be coming. She hadn't expected she would.

Meredith and Maggie Lu arrived next. Seeing them, Naomi gave a cry of delight and hurried over to give Maggie Lu a hug. While the two old friends caught up with one another briefly, Jubal strode in looking more than a little perplexed. He was followed by a sulky Joe McGibbons, who muttered to no one in particular, "If you ask me, the reverend stole the ledger himself. It would be easy to do, and no one would suspect him."

Naomi fixed him with a hard stare as she served him a slice of cake on a small plate. "My husband wouldn't steal a thing," she said. "Why should he? As you said, he had the ledger in his possession and access to it any time he wanted."

Slightly flustered, Joe explained. "What I mean is he's told everyone it's stolen, but he's still got it. He just doesn't want anyone else to see the contents."

Meredith, standing next to Julia, leaned over to whisper, "I don't believe your pastor actually stole the ledger, but didn't you tell me Ed didn't list it on the police report as being stolen? Don't you find that odd?"

Julia whispered back, "I'm sure he had a reason for doing that. You'll see."

"Your text said you found something," Joe said to Julia. "So, what is it? I haven't got all night." Joe seemed impatient to get on with things. That was fine with Julia. She didn't want to drag this on any longer than necessary. She feared matters would become embarrassing for all concerned.

"Yes, I found something and it proves who stole the old ledger. It's someone in this room."

Her unexpected announcement brought a stunned silence. Maggie Lu and Meredith exchanged knowing glances. A few of the others appeared stone-faced.

"Who is it?" Lovejoy asked, sitting down at the nearest table. "Don't keep us in suspense. We should demand that the thief turn over the ledger ASAP."

Jubal turned to Ed. In a harsh voice, he snapped, "You're responsible for stirring up all this trouble—you and Julia. You should never have taken the ledger from Aunt Dicey's home."

"Then you wouldn't have known anything about it," Julia pointed out. "Even your aunt had no idea there was a secret panel in the music room at River View."

Jubal frowned, perplexed. "There's a secret panel in the music room?"

"That's where we found the ledger," Julia told him. "And I know you have it now. Out of respect for our longtime friendship, I have not told the police."

All eyes swiveled in Jubal's direction.

"We don't intend to press charges," Ed spoke up. "I told the police the money had been returned and asked them to close the investigation."

Julia added, "I know it's you, Jubal. Just admit it, and let's be done with the matter."

"How?" he demanded with pain-filled eyes.

Glancing around the table, Julia noted everyone staring at her in expectation. "The broken Wedgwood vase in the secretary's office. That puzzled me. You see, it wasn't just broken, it was shattered beyond repair," she explained. "Pastor Ed"—she nodded at him—"thought it had been damaged when the burglar broke into the office. But it wasn't located anywhere near the door. Even if the burglar had come charging in like a bull in a china shop, the vase wouldn't have even wobbled on the shelf. It had been deliberately picked up and smashed on the floor. Someone did that in a fit of anger, and that's you, Jubal. You've been angry from the beginning. You were angry that Miss Dicey let us keep the ledger for a while. When you saw the vase, you knew Miss Dicey had donated it to the church. That made you angry too. You broke that vase, Jubal. You broke it in a fit of pique. You have made a selfish assumption that everything that belongs to Miss Dicey should belong to you as well."

"You can't prove a thing!" Jubal declared.

Julia sighed. "That's not all." She reached into the pocket of her stylish tunic and pulled out a small, snack-sized plastic baggie. "I found this outside in the dirt near the back door where it had been jimmied." She held it up so others could see it.

"What is it?" Lovejoy asked. "Bits of a broken necklace?"

"No, parts of a medical bracelet," Julia told her. Turning to Jubal, she asked, "Where's your medical bracelet, Jubal? Show us."

He answered gruffly, "What makes you think I have one?"

"I saw it on your wrist last week when we ran into each other at the nursing home. I noticed it particularly because Meredith used to wear one following her heart attack. I wondered what your medical condition might be. Hold up your wrist, Jubal."

Jubal lowered his head. His broad shoulders slumped. "I don't have it. It's broken. I haven't had time to order another."

"Just admit what you've done, Jubal," Meredith urged. "You know it's the right thing to do. You heard what Pastor Markham said earlier. He's not going to press charges."

"Man up," Joe McGibbons said, punching Jubal lightly on the arm.

"But what about Tamika Simms's earring?" Meredith wanted to know, glancing from Jubal to Julia. "Did you deliberately drop that on the floor in the secretary's office?" When Jubal hung his head and set his jaw, Meredith exclaimed, "How could you? What a horrible thing to do! That girl could have gotten into serious trouble."

Julia leaned toward him. "Why did you do it? Jubal?"

His eyes sparked with anger. "I found out from dear old Aunt Dicey that I won't be inheriting River View." This caused a ripple of surprised murmurs. "Oh, she's not cutting me out altogether. I'm getting some money and the contents of the house—all except the sheet music and the items in the music room, such as the Wedgwood collection. That along with the house has been bequeathed to some musical arts organization to be used for music retreats, performances, office space, whatever." He gave a disgusted snort. "It's the property that's valuable, not the contents of the old house."

Maggie Lu fixed him with a frown. "You're greedy, Mr. Jubal Jones, that's what you are. You should be ashamed of yourself. Why does Miss Dicey need to leave you anything at all? Isn't she entitled to do with her own property as she sees fit? You wouldn't like your own children or grandchildren telling you what to do with your property, now would you? And they are even closer kin to you than you are to Miss Dicey."

"Maybe he's the sort of man who has made a habit of taking what doesn't belong to him," Naomi added, fixing Jubal with a frown of her own.

"I returned the offering money," Jubal protested.

"You shouldn't have taken it in the first place," Beau spoke up. Julia gave him a surprised smile.

Jubal shrugged. "I thought it would throw y'all off the scent, that you'd think some fool kid with a drug habit had broken in to steal the money and just picked up the archive box as an afterthought."

Lovejoy spoke then. "So you really did take the ledger? Where is it now? Will you hand it over to me or Julia or Meredith? It's still in the archival box, right?" She looked to Jubal for confirmation. "If it's as fragile as you say, we need to begin to preserve the pages as soon as possible."

Jubal flushed, turning such a deep beet-red color that Julia feared for his blood pressure. He cleared his throat. "I can't give you the ledger."

Lovejoy gave a soft exclamation of frustrated disgust.

Meredith tipped her head to one side. "Why not?"

"It was old, really old, as you know." Jubal heaved a sigh. Julia held her breath. She dreaded what he might say next. "I wanted to take a good look at it—see for myself if there were other mentions of treasure, other than the one Julia and Meredith shared with us." He paused. His face turned redder. "I accidentally dropped it. The old leather binding cracked, and the pages inside—most of them—crumbled to dust, literally."

Lovejoy gave a cry of dismay. Julia felt sick to her stomach and silently thanked the Lord that she'd had the foresight to take photos of the legible pages and try to transcribe what had been written on them. "Does Miss Dicey know?"

"No," Jubal replied vaguely.

Helping himself to another slice of marble cake, Joe said, "Well, that's that. You've made a fool of yourself, Jubal. You're lucky the padre here isn't going to press charges." He gave Ed a nod of approval.

"You need to tell Miss Dicey what happened," Ed urged. "As soon as possible. I'll go with you if you'd like."

"I will tell her," Jubal promised. Julia noticed he'd not touched his cake or coffee. She felt sorry for him in a way. Greed was one of the seven deadly sins. She feared his relationship with Miss Dicey might be forever altered.

And then she remembered. "Jubal, did you pay a teenager to try to steal my tote bag from me earlier this week?"

Jubal's mouth fell open. "Me?" he said incredulously. "No, I did not, Julia. I broke into an empty office to get the ledger, yes, but I would never be party to actually robbing a person."

"Well, that's that, then," Julia said. "I'm just going to mark that incident up to coincidence." She looked at Meredith. "Even private investigators have to let some things go."

Maggie Lu rose then. Turning to Naomi, she thanked her for the cake and coffee. "Meredith, you can take me home now, if you'd be so kind." To Jubal, she said, "And you can thank the good Lord that these kind people will not give you the justice you deserve, but instead have served up mercy."

"No, don't go yet," Lovejoy exclaimed when Meredith rose. "I have something to tell y'all. Now is as good a time as any." She took a breath and eagerly explained, "I spoke with Miss Dicey earlier in the week. She told me she'd donated a box of Oglethorpe family papers to the historical society some years ago, back in the 1980s. So I checked our archives and found that many of the documents had already been preserved and entered into our online database. Some of the letters were *very* interesting." Then she rummaged in her canvas bag to retrieve a file folder. Her blue eyes glowed, and her cheeks turned pink with pleasure. Holding up the folder, she said, "I think I found an important clue regarding the treasure!"

Chapter Twenty-Four

EVERYONE REGARDED LOVEJOY WITH ASTONISHMENT. Following a moment of stunned silence, Julia said, "Let me see what you have." Lovejoy passed her the sheet of paper. Julia scanned the copy of the old letter—not an easy task considering the faded ink and old-fashioned handwriting. The writer's nib had not been well sharpened either. She recalled they used quills to write in those days—from ducks, geese, and turkeys. The signature was clear enough though. Johanna Hus.

"Is it a treasure map?" Joe asked, leaning forward with eagerness.

"No!" Julia snapped. Would the man ever give up on the treasure idea? "It appears to be an old letter."

"An old, old letter," Lovejoy added, her voice vibrating with emotion. "It is dated 1737."

Jubal held out his hand. "Pass it to me." He glanced at it and then asked Lovejoy, "Who is this 'Sir' it is addressed to?"

Smiling, Lovejoy said, "I think perhaps General Oglethorpe, Miss Dicey's notable ancestor."

"But we can't be certain," Meredith pointed out.

Lovejoy shrugged. "Perhaps not."

"But what does it say about the treasure?" Joe persisted.

"Read it to us, child," Maggie Lu said.

Lovejoy stood up, holding out her hand. Jubal passed her the sheet of paper. She cleared her throat and began to read:

Dear Sir,

As we prepare to leave Irene, I am tasked with thanking you for your past kindness to our community. You have been a friend indeed and a true advocate when we most needed one. Please give our best regards to our esteemed Brother in Christ. We have heard of his departure for England. Should you write, let him know we still thank God for every remembrance of him and his generosity to us. I still marvel that God provided gold coins upon the beach, just as Peter's fish revealed a gold coin for the temple tax.

Indeed, we look to God for everything. He has been proven faithful and steadfast. We put ourselves and our work in His almighty hands. The Lord has been most gracious to me, unworthy as I am, allowing me to teach the dear Yamacraw children the Good News of our Lord Jesus—our most Precious Treasure. Although I leave this place most reluctantly, I trust Him fully and will follow Him down this untrod path to Bethlehem. I put my work and myself in His hands. My eyes fill with tears, and my heart overflows with joy, for I hear the whisper of heaven's bells ringing out across this land.

Johanna Hus
Irene, Georgia Colony
September 12, 1737

When Lovejoy finished reading, Meredith sighed. "I love that line about the whisper of heaven's bells ringing out across this land."

"I suppose that if the letter is indeed addressed to General Oglethorpe, the esteemed brother in Christ could refer to John Wesley," Julia suggested. A few of them nodded in agreement. "And now we know more about what 'February 17, 1736 J to Irene' means," she said. "We don't know who the 'J' is, but we can assume we know when whoever it is arrived at the colony."

"But who is Johanna Hus?" Beau asked.

"I'm still looking into that," Lovejoy said. "The name is a German one, so perhaps she was one of the Moravians who settled in Savannah before moving on to Bethlehem, Pennsylvania."

With a bright smile, Maggie Lu declared, "I knew the Moravians might be involved in the mystery somehow. Didn't I say so, Julia?"

"You sure did," Julia agreed, grinning back at her.

"But this is all speculation on our part," Meredith reminded them.

Joe McGibbons scooted his chair away from the table and crossed his arms against his chest. "The letter doesn't shed any light on the treasure at all. And what's all this about gold coins and fish mouths?" He looked from Julia to Meredith and then to Lovejoy.

"It's an account of one of Jesus's miracles as recorded in the Gospel of Matthew," Naomi spoke up. She quickly related the incident and how Peter had been told to catch a fish. When he did, there was a coin in its mouth sufficient to pay the temple tax.

Joe still looked perplexed until Maggie Lu said, "Gold coins washed up on the shore, don't you see? John Wesley found them and gave them to the Moravians. I'm guessing old Spanish coins."

Joe's frown eased as light began to dawn. "Sure, gold doubloons. Spanish coins. I get it. A lot of sunken treasure has been washed ashore over the years. But why would this Wesley fellow give it to the Moravians?"

Meredith answered with a shrug. "We can't be certain, but based on this letter, Johanna Hus and members of her religious community used the money to relocate to Pennsylvania."

"They started a school for the Yamacraw Indians when they first arrived in Savannah," Maggie Lu added. "But the other colonists didn't take to them."

"That's right," Lovejoy interjected. "The Moravians were pacifists. They wouldn't participate in militia drills and such."

Ed, who had been quietly attentive during this discussion, recited the cryptic message that had started the whole hullaballoo. "'J found treasure. O intrigued. Fear trouble ahead.'"

"Was there trouble, I wonder?" Julia asked.

"I'll keep researching," Lovejoy promised. "Here's my theory: I think Reverend Wesley showed what he'd found on the beach to his brother Charles and the general. Naturally, the men would be intrigued. They probably wondered how many more coins might wash up onshore."

Ed picked up the story. "Then Charles, knowing human frailty all too well, feared there would be mass treasure hunts on the beach. The settlers might neglect their day-to-day work to pursue treasure seeking instead."

"But John Wesley didn't broadcast his discovery," Julia added. "Instead, he quietly turned over the gold to Johanna Hus and her companions. They used it to leave Savannah."

"They would have needed the funds to pay for travel expenses and to pay off their debt—their passage expenses to come to Savannah," Maggie Lu added. Lovejoy and Meredith nodded.

Joe was the first to rise from the table. "This was all a waste of time," he declared. Turning to Naomi, he added in an uncharacteristically polite voice, "Thank you, Mrs. Markham, for the coffee and cake."

"You are welcome, Mr. McGibbons. You should join us some Sunday for worship service. Stay after when we have a potluck." Naomi gave him a warm smile. "We have some mighty fine cooks in our church family. You won't go away hungry."

Joe muttered something unintelligible before exiting the fellowship hall as quickly as he could. Julia's lips twitched. She and Beau exchanged amused glances. While the women cleared up the cups and saucers, Julia noticed Jubal sheepishly approaching the pastor. The big man, towering over Ed, appeared contrite and embarrassed. He held out a large hand. "I hope you'll accept my apology," Jubal said. "I'm sorrier than I can say."

Ed took the other man's proffered hand between two of his own. He said something to him in a low voice before patting Jubal on the shoulder, saying, "Go and sin no more. That's what the good Lord would say to you."

Julia paused to watch but didn't step closer, allowing the men their private moment together. It was more than gracious of Ed to forgive Jubal for what he'd done. Her heart soared with gratitude for the real treasures in life: grace and mercy, friends and family, faith and moral integrity. These were treasures one should cherish. With one eye on the two men, she also noted Maggie Lu and Lovejoy enjoying an animated conversation about something historical. That would be a good friendship to foster, she decided. The young archivist was smart and diligent and as tenacious as a bulldog. One day she might even take Beatrice's place as president of the historical society.

Noticing Julia watching them, Lovejoy turned, saying, "I'll be taking off now but wanted to thank you for inviting me here this evening. Maggie Lu and I are going to meet up and learn more about the Moravians together. The society should host a special exhibit about them, don't you think?"

"Sounds like a good idea to me," Julia agreed.

"I'll let Beatrice know what happened this evening. She's going to be shocked, I imagine." Lovejoy wiggled her eyebrows. "I'll show her the letter too. Do you think Miss Dicey might like to have a copy?"

"That would be very thoughtful," Meredith said, joining them. "I know the old dear must be curious."

Out of the corner of her eye, Julia noticed Jubal retreating from the fellowship hall. She hurried after him. "Jubal, wait up. I need to speak with you."

Turning, he held up a beefy hand. "I know, sugar. I've been a despicable villain. You don't have to remind me."

"It's about Tamika Simms." Julia fixed him with a penetrating stare. His shoulders slumped as he lowered his gaze. "She's worried to death that she's going to get into trouble with the police because her earring was found at the crime scene."

"But the police know nothing about the earring, right?" He looked at her then, deep wrinkles creasing his forehead. "You picked it up and gave it back to her, didn't you?"

"I did, but she is concerned about how it ended up at the church in the first place. You owe her an explanation and apology."

Jubal sighed. "I sure have been eating a lot of crow lately." Straightening, he said, "All right. I'll call her before I go see Miss Dicey in the morning."

Julia pulled out her cell. "Call her this evening. I have her cell number." She pulled up her list of contacts and showed it to him. He tapped the teen's number into his phone and promised to call. "Good. The poor girl is worried."

Jubal thrust his hands into the pockets of his trousers. "I understand. Be seeing you, sugar." With a wave, he was gone.

Julia turned around and saw Ed and Beau sharing a laugh. "What's so funny?" she asked, joining them.

"I was just telling your husband about our wild ride the other day." Ed chuckled.

Julia choked back a giggle. "You would have thought we were in a NASCAR race." To Ed, she added, "The orderly Gus Tate says you drive like a racer—but I think he meant it as a compliment."

"So you tracked down the man after all?" Ed asked.

"I did. Turns out he simply wanted a job with the agency." Julia grinned. She quickly filled him in on her conversation with Gus Tate.

Shaking his head, Beau declared, "This has been quite a week, I can see that now. I'm rather sorry I missed all the excitement."

Maggie Lu, Meredith, and Naomi emerged from the kitchen to join them in the foyer. "Yes, it has been a rather exciting week—too exciting to my way of thinking," Meredith insisted. "I'm hoping the coming week will be a quiet, routine one."

"I'd like to have seen those secret hidey holes," Maggie Lu spoke up. Turning to Ed, she asked, "Do you think Miss Dicey would mind if you took us out there to show them to us?"

"That's a great idea," Beau agreed. "I would like to see them myself."

Ed shrugged. "I don't see why not. I'll ask her when I drop in to see her this week."

Folding her arms across her chest, Julia said, "All right, you take Beau and Maggie Lu out to River View. But if you find another secret panel or something hidden inside, don't call us." She tipped her head in Meredith's direction. "Right?"

Meredith smiled. "Right. Call Jubal or Beatrice. I don't want to hear that troublesome word *treasure* for a long, long time."

Dear Reader,

Writing this novel has been such a delight. When I was a young girl, I loved Nancy Drew mysteries. From the moment I read *The Secret of the Old Clock*, I was hooked. I've carried that love of mysteries and hidden artifacts into my adult years. I briefly visited Savannah a few years ago and found it to be vibrant yet charmingly quaint too. And the food—oh my! Fried green tomatoes, shrimp and grits, peach cobbler—I could go on and on. You haven't lived until you've eaten a grilled pimento cheese sandwich on sourdough bread! Believe me, I enjoyed every mouthful. The city is worth a visit for the food alone.

But like Julia and Meredith, I am fascinated by old historic homes too. If they have hidden panels and secret gardens, all the better. Although River View is a fictional mansion, Savannah is blessed with many fine historic homes and buildings. Even the cemeteries are picturesque. Visitors can actually take a Bonaventure Cemetery tour.

So, get settled in your favorite chair, pour yourself a glass of sweet tea, and enjoy the further adventures of Meredith and Julia.

—Shirley Raye Redmond

About the Author

SHIRLEY RAYE REDMOND IS AN award-winning author of both women's and children's books. She grew up on the island of Okinawa, a proud graduate of Kubasaki High School. She has been married to her college sweetheart for forty-five years. They have two children and several grandchildren. Shirley Raye (yes, it's one of those Southern double first names!) lives in the mountains of northern New Mexico, where she takes long walks, feeds the birds, and keeps an eye out for black bears. She loves Jesus and is privileged to serve as prayer chairwoman for her community Bible study class. She's also rather fond of green chiles and fine chocolates.

You can visit with her on Facebook or at her website: shirleyrayeredmond.com. She occasionally blogs on serendipitous topics at stitchesthrutime.blogspot.com. Please stop by and say hi! She'd love to meet you.

The Truth Behind the Fiction

Brothers John and Charles Wesley

SUSANNA WESLEY (1669–1742) HAS ALWAYS impressed me. The well-organized and seemingly tireless woman raised nineteen bright children, survived two devastating house fires, and somehow managed her household and fed her brood of children even when her pastor husband was sent to debtor's prison. But until I began working on this novel, I had no idea that her two famous sons, John and Charles Wesley, lived in Savannah for a brief period of time. General James Oglethorpe warned the clergymen that most of the colonists were "ignorant and licentious." The brothers discovered, to their dismay, he had not exaggerated. The one bright note was meeting the German-speaking Moravians on board the ship to America. Witnessing firsthand their unwavering faith when faced with possible shipwreck, John never forgot their influence on his spiritual growth. When the Wesleys returned to England, they established the Methodist Church, and Charles penned some of our best-loved Christian hymns.

SOMETHING DELICIOUS FROM A
Downhome Southern Kitchen

SWEET POTATO PIE

Ingredients:

¼ pound of butter (do not substitute margarine)

1 cup sugar

3 eggs

2 tablespoons lemon juice

½ teaspoon nutmeg

2 cups cooked and mashed sweet potatoes

2 tablespoons maple syrup (or dark Karo or King syrup)

½ cup milk

1 unbaked pie shell in deep-dish pie pan

Instructions:

Cream the butter, sugar, and eggs. Add lemon juice and nutmeg. Add mashed potatoes, syrup, and milk. Mix well. Pour into pie shell.

Bake for 10 minutes at 425 degrees.

Lower heat to 300 degrees and bake for approximately an hour.

Read on for a sneak peek of another exciting book
in the Savannah Secrets series!

Where Time Stood Still

BY BETH ADAMS

MEREDITH BELLEFONTAINE FINISHED SCANNING THE stack of claims and closed the folder on her desk. Investigating insurance fraud was exactly as boring as it sounded, as it turned out. It paid the bills, but if she had to scan one more line of medical code right now, her eyes would give out. She needed a break.

Meredith pushed herself up, stretched her arms over her head, and then walked out into the hallway and took a mug from the table outside her office.

"More coffee?" Julia Foley called from inside her own office.

"Just one more." Meredith lifted the carafe and poured herself a cup of rich, dark coffee then wandered over to the doorway of Julia's office. The old wooden floorboards creaked under her feet. "Are you having any more fun than I am?"

"For sure. I'm working on our favorite cheating spouse." A map of Savannah was spread out on Julia's desk, and she had highlighted several spots scattered throughout the city.

"You don't *know* that Isabella's cheating," Meredith clarified.

"I don't know for sure," Julia said. "But I have a pretty good idea."

Julia was working on a case that had come their way a few weeks prior. A lawyer she had worked with many years before was handling a divorce for one of the city's wealthiest businessmen, Dennis Healding, and he was hoping to prove that his wife was having an affair. This would mean that the wife, Isabella, wouldn't be entitled to his money, according to the terms of their prenuptial agreement. It was the kind of sordid business that made Meredith even more grateful for the long, happy marriage she and Ron had enjoyed. But, well, like investigating insurance fraud, it paid the bills.

"What are you doing?" Meredith nodded at the map. She heard the front door open, but she knew Carmen was at the front desk, so she focused on Julia.

"Marking off the places she used her credit card," Julia said, pointing at the highlighted areas on the map. "Since Isabella disabled location services on her phone, I'm stuck trying to trace her path by looking at her credit card bills."

It was the kind of tedious work that made up much of the day-to-day running of a private investigation business, and normally Meredith didn't mind. But today she was antsy. Sun streamed in through the large windows, and the oppressive muggy heat of summer had finally given way to cooler temperatures and a bright, sunny late-September day.

"I don't know whether to say I hope you find what you're looking for or not," Meredith said. She always hoped investigations like this came up empty. She wanted to find that a spouse hadn't been cheating, that it was all a big misunderstanding, and that the marriage might be saved after all.

Julia, a former lawyer and Chatham County judge, was more pragmatic. "I hope I do. I know she's cheating. I can feel it. I just need to find proof."

Meredith took a sip of her coffee and turned when she heard footsteps coming down the hall. It was Carmen, her lush black hair pulled into a ponytail.

"Meredith?" Carmen said. "*¿Tienes un momento?* There's someone here asking for you. She says she's the daughter of a friend of yours."

"Who is it?"

"Her name is Rachel Martin."

It took Meredith a moment to place the name, but then it popped into her head. "Lindy's daughter!"

Meredith had been in a Bible study with Lindy Martin a few years back, and she had enjoyed her wry humor and insightful take on the scriptures. Lindy had talked about her daughter Rachel many times and had asked for prayer for her while she'd gone through a rough patch in college.

"She says she has something she's hoping you can investigate for her."

"As long as it's not insurance fraud or another cheating spouse, send her on back."

"*Sí.*" Carmen turned to go, but then turned back and cocked her eyebrow. "The businessman's wife is totally cheating."

"Told you!" Julia shouted from her office.

Meredith shook her head and waited while Carmen walked back down the hallway and then returned a few minutes later with a tall woman in skinny jeans and boots following behind her. The woman had the same aquiline nose and brown hair as her mom. She was probably in her late twenties or early thirties, Meredith guessed.

"Rachel." Meredith smiled.

"Hi there. You must be Mrs. Bellefontaine." Rachel had pale skin and a light sprinkling of freckles over her cheeks.

"Please, call me Meredith." She held out her hand, and Rachel shook it gently. "How is your mother?"

"She's doing fine. The Garden Club has its annual fundraiser this weekend, so she's all in a tizzy, but other than that she's pretty much the same as ever."

"All in a tizzy" was a pretty accurate description of Lindy on a normal day, but Rachel seemed to have a calmer demeanor.

"Please give her my best," Meredith said, and led Rachel into her office. She gestured toward the two olive-green chairs opposite her desk, and Rachel took a seat in the one closest to the wall. Meredith sat down on the flowered couch.

"This place is beautiful," Rachel said, setting her purse down on the floor. "I love that fireplace, and that old trumpet is gorgeous."

"Thank you." Meredith had worked hard to make the office feel homey and welcoming when Ron had been alive, and now that she and Julia ran the agency, she'd added a few more feminine touches, including an antique trumpet on the mantel. "This was the music room when this was a house, so I put that there to honor the past."

"My mom is the same way." Rachel smiled. "Thank you for seeing me. I wasn't sure if I should call and make an appointment, but Mom said I should just come in and talk to you, so…"

"I'm glad you're here." Meredith was growing curious about what this was all about. "So what can we help you with?"

"Well… I have kind of a strange thing to ask. I'm not really sure you all do this, but…"

"Don't worry about that. We've heard it all." Meredith heard quiet footsteps in the hall. "Actually, would it be all right if I ask my business partner to come in and hear this too?"

"Of course." Rachel nodded.

"You couldn't keep me away if you tried." Julia was already coming through the doorway. "Not after I heard that intriguing opening."

Rachel laughed while Julia settled into the other wingback chair.

"So, I just bought a property out by Ebenezer Creek," Rachel said.

"Oh wow." Meredith was familiar with the area, about twenty-five miles north of Savannah. It was a rural area, swampy—and notable mostly for an incident in which hundreds of enslaved black people had escaped but were drowned in the creek during the Civil War.

"I want to build a small hotel and run ecotours of the swamp from it. Kayaks, mostly, paddling tours, that kind of thing."

"Ooh. That sounds really intriguing," Julia said.

It sounded like a good way to get eaten alive by mosquitos to Meredith.

"I found a beautiful piece of land adjacent to the creek, and my lawyer has checked it out. It's owned by Effingham County, and they were anxious to get rid of it, so I was able to get it for a song," Rachel said. "It's beautiful too. It's pretty much exactly what I was looking for."

"What's the catch?" There had to be one, Meredith knew, or Rachel wouldn't be sitting here now.

"Well…" Rachel let out a sigh. "There's a house on the property now. It's stood empty for the last thirty years or so."

Meredith didn't even want to imagine the state of that building. The humid summers had probably turned it almost entirely to rot.

"It's a tear-down at this point," Rachel said. "That's not the issue. The problem is that…well, don't laugh when I say this. I know it sounds crazy. But apparently there are rumors that the place is haunted, which is probably why the county wasn't able to unload it all those years."

"A haunted house?" She didn't believe in such things. But the idea was interesting.

A Note from the Editors

WE HOPE YOU ENJOY THE Savannah Secrets series, created by the Books and Inspirational Media Division of Guideposts, a nonprofit organization that touches millions of lives every day through products and services that inspire, encourage, help you grow in your faith, and celebrate God's love in every aspect of your daily life.

Thank you for making a difference with your purchase of this book, which helps fund our many outreach programs to military personnel, prisons, hospitals, nursing homes, and educational institutions. To learn more, visit GuidepostsFoundation.org.

We also maintain many useful and uplifting online resources. Visit Guideposts.org to read true stories of hope and inspiration, access OurPrayer network, sign up for free newsletters, download free e-books, join our Facebook community, and follow our stimulating blogs.

To learn about other Guideposts publications, including the bestselling devotional *Daily Guideposts*, go to ShopGuideposts.org, call (800) 932-2145, or write to Guideposts, PO Box 5815, Harlan, Iowa 51593.

Sign up for the
Guideposts Fiction Newsletter
and stay up-to-date on the books you love!

You'll get sneak peeks of new releases, recommendations from other Guideposts readers, and special offers just for you . . .
and it's FREE!

Just go to Guideposts.org/Newsletters today to sign up.

Guideposts®

**Visit Guideposts.org/Shop
or call (800) 932-2145**

Find more inspiring stories in these best-loved Guideposts fiction series!

Mysteries of Lancaster County

Follow the Classen sisters as they unravel clues and uncover hidden secrets in Mysteries of Lancaster County. As you get to know these women and their friends, you'll see how God brings each of them together for a fresh start in life.

Secrets of Wayfarers Inn

Retired schoolteachers find themselves owners of an old warehouse-turned-inn that is filled with hidden passages, buried secrets, and stunning surprises that will set them on a course to puzzling mysteries from the Underground Railroad.

Tearoom Mysteries Series

Mix one stately Victorian home, a charming lakeside town in Maine, and two adventurous cousins with a passion for tea and hospitality. Add a large scoop of intriguing mystery, and sprinkle generously with faith, family, and friends, and you have the recipe for *Tearoom Mysteries*.

Ordinary Women of the Bible

Richly imagined stories—based on facts from the Bible—have all the plot twists and suspense of a great mystery, while bringing you fascinating insights on what it was like to be a woman living in the ancient world.

To learn more about these books, visit Guideposts.org/Shop